IF, THEN

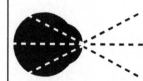
This Large Print Book carries the
Seal of Approval of N.A.V.H.

IF, THEN

KATE HOPE DAY

THORNDIKE PRESS
A part of Gale, a Cengage Company

Farmington Hills, Mich • San Francisco • New York • Waterville, Maine
Meriden, Conn • Mason, Ohio • Chicago

Copyright © 2019 by Kate Hope Day.
Thorndike Press, a part of Gale, a Cengage Company.

Thorndike Press® Large Print Core.
The text of this Large Print edition is unabridged.
Other aspects of the book may vary from the original edition.
Set in 16 pt. Plantin.

LIBRARY OF CONGRESS CIP DATA ON FILE.
CATALOGUING IN PUBLICATION FOR THIS BOOK
IS AVAILABLE FROM THE LIBRARY OF CONGRESS

ISBN-13: 978-1-4328-6453-8 (hardcover alk. paper)

Published in 2019 by arrangement with Random House, a division of Penguin Random House LLC

Printed in Mexico
1 2 3 4 5 6 7 23 22 21 20 19

For my parents

I believe, and so do you, that things could have been different in countless ways.

— DAVID LEWIS, *COUNTERFACTUALS*

■ ■ ■ ■

I
THE MAN IN THE
WOODS

■ ■ ■ ■

ONE

The earth trembles. She tastes metal. That's how it starts on a moonless Sunday in Clearing, Oregon, in the shadow of the dormant volcano locals call Broken Mountain.

Just after 10:00 P.M. Ginny stands at the bathroom sink, a toothbrush in one hand and a paperback in the other. She always reads like this, in minutes parceled out from her packed days — in the bathroom after everyone has gone to bed, or parked in her car when she gets to the hospital a little early. The heat whirs in the vent. She considers staying up to read another chapter. Her husband, Mark, is already asleep in the next room.

Her pager buzzes from the bedroom and she retrieves it from her bedside table. A series of familiar numbers scrolls across the tiny backlit screen. The emergency room. "Damn."

She dials the number. "ER," the nurse answers.

"This is Dr. McDonnell. I was paged?"

"Let me get Dr. Pierce."

Classical music plays energetically in her ear. She sits down on the edge of the bed. Suddenly she's tired.

One of the cats jumps down from the comforter and stalks out the door toward Noah's bedroom. But Mark doesn't stir. He's learned how to sleep through her nighttime pages. His face is naked without his glasses, his curly hair black against the white sheets.

She turns down the volume on the phone and switches on her lamp. Mark rolls over on his side but doesn't wake. The music is tinny and faraway in her ear. The floor shakes; there's a metallic taste in her mouth. Her vision abruptly alters —

Where Mark was sleeping a woman appears. Her face is so familiar . . . Edith. Her friend's hair is always pulled back in a bun at the hospital. Now it fans out in crinkly waves across the pillow. Freckles stipple her shoulders and the tops of her breasts.

Ginny smells warm skin and damp sheets; she hears her own quickened breath. A swell of desire, uncomfortably strong, rises inside her abdomen. The woman reaches out, as if

12

to stroke Ginny's hair.

Then, in an instant, she's gone. Mark's back in the bed.

Ginny rubs her eyes, blinking furiously.

"Dr. McDonnell —" Brian Pierce's strident voice comes through the phone. "We've got a seventy-five-year-old man with a rigid abdomen, white blood count of 24,000, fever of 101.2, peritoneal signs, and free air on abdominal films. Came into the ER about an hour ago. His name is Robert Kells. Can you come in and take a look?"

She's silent for a beat, her mind still anchored to Edith's lovely face. "Any major medical issues?" she finally musters.

"A history of liver disease —" There's the rustle of paperwork. "We've admitted him a couple of times for pancreatitis. That's it."

"We need to set up for an ex-lap." Her brain has come back to life, has switched into the proper gear.

"I'll tell the charge nurse. Just get on the road. This guy isn't going to last long."

Ginny follows her usual routine: pulls on scrubs, scrapes her hair into a short ponytail, and rubs lip balm on her lips. She climbs into her Acura SUV and backs out into the deserted cul-de-sac. Her neighbors' porch lights are off. Behind her house the forest is a dark blank. Rain mists her windshield.

She drives down the hill and across town, and the mountain recedes in her rearview mirror. She usually likes the ride to the hospital at night — the empty streets, the sealed-in quiet of her car, the gentle *tack tack tack* of her turn signal as she idles at stoplights. But tonight these things don't bring her peace.

She's disturbed by what she saw. She must have fallen asleep for a second. Or she has a brain tumor. She recalls a list of symptoms from her neurosurgery rotation in residency:

headaches
problems with balance
blurred or double vision
seeing things that aren't there . . .

She turns into the staff parking lot. The scrubs, the ponytail, the car ride — they haven't done their job. There's an irritating flutter in her chest.

Inside, the fluorescent lights of the ER are a welcome slap in the face. Her clogs squeak against the polished floors. Her patient waits, supine, behind a green curtain in the freezing pre-op holding room. As soon as she pulls the thin cloth closed behind her she feels better.

"Mr. Kells, I'm Dr. McDonnell, the surgeon who will be taking care of you." She enunciates each word, speaking over the beeping racket that surrounds them, and looks steadily into the man's broad, ashen face. He says nothing but holds her gaze firmly.

She picks up his chart. "My apologies. Professor Kells."

"Robby," he says in a hoarse whisper. He has thick eyebrows and a full head of gray hair, and she can easily imagine him at the front of a lecture hall.

"I'm going to examine you now. Is that all right?"

He nods.

She rubs her hands together to warm them, lifts his hospital gown, and feels along his pale stomach. "I'm going to press down on your abdomen. Can you tell me if it hurts more or less when I release the pressure?"

She presses, lets go, and watches his face twist into an ugly grimace. He makes no sound. She's impressed with his stoicism. His silent scowl makes her think of her father, when he first got sick. Professor Kells is about the same age her father would be if he were still alive.

She puts her stethoscope in her ears and

listens carefully to the four quadrants of his belly.

"Do you teach at the university?" she asks.

He nods.

"What subject?"

"Philosophy."

"Impressive." She picks up his chart again. "Just want to double check. No history of heart disease or arrhythmia? Any cardiac events at all?"

He shakes his head.

"Good. We want to get you back to your books and your students. But to do that I need to find out what's causing the discomfort in your abdomen. There's a good chance you have a perforation in your intestine. If you do, and it isn't repaired soon, you could die. We're ready to take you to the OR now. Do you give your consent?"

"Yes."

"We'll do the very best we can for you."

He grips her hand with surprising strength. "How about better than your best?" he asks, with a hint of a smile.

"All right." She laughs. "You got it."

Ginny pushes through the heavy swinging doors marked OR 3, SURGICAL ATTIRE ONLY BEYOND THIS POINT, AUTHORIZED PERSONNEL ONLY. She pulls paper booties over her shoes, tucks her ponytail into a surgical cap, and loops a mask over her mouth. She hopes she can keep Professor Kells alive. She doesn't know him, but from what she's seen, she likes him. When she told him she was his surgeon, he didn't flinch. A lot of men his age do when they learn the person about to cut them open is a woman who stands barely five foot three inches tall.

At the scrub sink, she twists her wedding band from her finger and threads it onto the drawstring of her scrub pants. She knots it once, twice, three times, and thinks briefly of her husband, asleep in bed at home. He used to tell her it bothered him, waking up and her not being there, but after fifteen years of marriage he doesn't mention it anymore. She takes a scrub sponge, bright orange from Betadine antiseptic, and starts in, fingernails first.

Tricia, the circulating nurse, joins her at the sink. Her glasses swing on a metal chain as she leans to turn on her faucet.

"Who's the scrub nurse on this case?" Ginny asks.

"Edith. Why?"

Ginny feels the warmth of a blush. "No reason." The agitating flutter in her chest returns in full force.

"How's that little athlete of yours?"

"Noah's great. Asleep right now."

"What season is he in?"

"Soccer. And swimming." Even on a normal night Ginny doesn't like to chat right before a case. Tricia knows that, but always tries to get her talking anyway. Tonight, of all nights, she wants to keep her head down and do her job.

"Busy kid." Tricia gives her a big smile. "We're ready when you are."

In the operating room Professor Kells is already intubated, and the anesthesiologist has taken up position at the top of the operating table to watch his vital signs. A mask obscures his face, but she can tell it's Jeff Lee by his dark eyebrows. Edith stands to his right, bent over a tray of gleaming surgical tools. "Hey," she says, with a soft Southern accent. "Called in again?"

"Yeah." Ginny presses her mask to her burning face. "Again," she adds, too loudly.

Edith pushes a crinkle of red hair into her cap. "You okay?"

Ginny pulls the surgical task light closer to Professor Kells's midsection and the sharp smell of antiseptic solution fills her nose. "I'm fine. Just tired."

Edith turns her attention to a neat pile of sponges, gauze, and sutures on another tray,

18

double-checking the counts, and Tricia ducks in with the final paperwork, calling out, "Incision time 11:57 P.M.," before disappearing again through the swinging doors.

"Ten blade," Ginny says. She makes her first cut, from xiphoid to pubis. Then two more cuts, opening the whole belly wide. She holds out her hand and Edith gives her a Bookwalter retractor. The patient's insides are a sticky mess. He has a perforation somewhere, that's for sure, and there's a good chance he'll go into septic shock before she can find it. Jeff knows it too. His concentration is fixed on the patient's blood pressure.

"Shit," Ginny says.

"Literally," Jeff says, grimly attempting a joke.

She gives a halfhearted snort.

Across the table Edith repositions the retractor. A thin necklace glints at her freckled throat. "Saline?" she asks.

"We need to be quick," Ginny says, unnecessarily. Edith is already irrigating saline through the patient's abdominal cavity.

Ginny sweeps her fingers between loops of bowel and along the mesentery, clearing wisps of scar tissue. She calls for suction, and then slowly runs her hands along the

19

length of the GI tract, starting at the stomach and working her way down the small intestine, feeling for a tear. She remembers the last time she and Edith had a case together. It was a long one, five or six hours. When it was done in the early hours of the morning, they had gone for breakfast, despite the fact that they both had trouble keeping their eyes open. Over the years Edith has become a friend. Ginny always looks forward to seeing her at work. But she's never considered —

"His blood pressure's not where I'd like it." Jeff's voice snaps Ginny to attention.

She concentrates on the ropes of pink intestine, gingerly pushing them this way and that until she spies a tiny perforation in a fold of the colon. "Two bowel clamps," she says, "and get a 3–0 Vicryl suture ready." She clamps either side of the tear, excises the segment of perforated intestine, and begins sewing the bowel back together, layer by layer. Focused on the stitches, she doesn't raise her eyes from the operating table until she completes the repair, and Professor Kells's blood pressure has stabilized.

TWO

Mark pulls out of the driveway in his fourteen-year-old Jeep, the mountain hazy at his back, and swerves to avoid his new neighbor Cass and her large black dog. It's quiet in the car, except for the sound of his restless thumb on the steering wheel. His son Noah is in the backseat, looking out the window. Mark checks his watch. He's giving a talk this morning to his colleagues in the Department of Fisheries and Wildlife — a presentation of his research on the northwestern spotted frog he hopes will change the course of his career.

Out from under the wooded canopy of their neighborhood, past a community garden grown wild with sunflowers and sage, Mark makes room for the bicycle traffic on the main road. His left knee jiggles. In the rearview mirror Noah retrieves a football the color of a yellow warbler from his backpack and tosses it in his hands. His

21

backpack looks a little light. Does he have all the books he needs today? Mark doesn't want to nag. This isn't easy when all he wants is to go back to when Noah was three or four and everything that went on in his little head was open to Mark. He only needed to ask, and Noah would tell him.

It's his son's last year in elementary school. Next fall he'll attend Linus Pauling Middle School, a fact never far from Mark's thoughts. His son will be a teenager soon. Very soon. And Mark isn't ready. For Noah to be grown up, for him to move out. It will just be Mark and Ginny then. He doesn't want to think about how empty the house will feel when Noah's gone.

Mark turns onto Cedar Lane. On people's front porches, squat pumpkins and gourds crowd ceramic pots of asters and chrysanthemums and black-eyed Susans. In front yards, signs stick out of the bright, wet grass:

LOCAL CHOICE YES, FLUORIDE NO!

KEEP OUR URBAN GROWTH BOUNDARIES:
VOTE YES ON 133

LOVE MAKES A FAMILY

They pull up to Noah's friend Peter's

house, a split-level with a lichen-covered roof. A girl wearing bright pink jeans stands on the porch. She holds a black instrument case the size of a brown bear cub or an overgrown badger. She's in Noah's class — Lydi or Livi? Mark has met her and her mother once or twice. She lives nearby.

They wait for a minute, but no one comes out of the house. The girl stares at them.

"Go get Peter will you?" Mark says.

Noah opens the car door and leaps out in one smooth motion, the football tucked under one arm. He waves at the girl as he cuts across the grass. Then he flips the football high into the air and jumps to catch it, his body making a shallow arc like an undrawn bow.

Mark's whole department will be at his talk this morning, and also the dean . . . maybe. Hopefully. His research project needs just a small percentage of the fifty million dollars recently donated to the university to fund natural disaster research. Everyone was getting a piece of it: the geophysicists, the people at the wave research institute, and of course the seismologists. But they were all focusing on the Cascadia subduction zone off the coast of Oregon, when the more immediate danger — Broken Mountain — was right under

23

their feet. His research, which centered on the connection between geothermal activity and animal behavior, revealed strong evidence that the mountain could erupt sooner than anyone thought. Possibly in the next twenty years. But his project had been awarded exactly zero dollars.

Noah kicks the ball with a *tump* and it soars into some azalea bushes. The effortless physicality of his son always astounds him. Where did this kid come from? Then he remembers — from Ginny. Noah digs the ball out from the bushes and talks to Livi, who balances on some decorative rocks that border the lawn. She's left her instrument case on the covered porch. Noah passes the football from one hand to the other with a relaxed, confident stance. Livi says something to him, her face close to his. She makes a dramatic gesture with her arms outstretched, and he laughs. Then she threads her arm around his waist.

Mark balks, and fights the urge to duck behind the dashboard. It feels like he shouldn't be watching and yet he can't look away.

Peter appears, finally, wearing green track pants and a sleepy expression. His right shoe is only half on and he stomps the ground to wedge his foot in. He holds up his hands. Noah disengages himself from Livi so he can toss Peter the ball.

Livi stands on tiptoe to whisper something in Noah's ear. Without the ball in his hands, Noah's less assured, less agile. He looks more like Mark. Not in his face, but in his bearing. Seeing it, Mark feels a mixture of pleasure and pain.

Inside her parents' kitchen Samara opens a cabinet full of her mother's too-bright Fiestaware dishes and pulls out a mug the color of pool water. She turns on the electric kettle and stares out the kitchen window at the wet pavement and shifting pine trees. Her parents' new neighbor Cass walks by with her furry black dog, and her oversized raincoat flaps in the wind.

The kettle clicks off. Outside Mark reverses his dirty Jeep into the cul-de-sac, his son Noah in the backseat. Samara tugs the blinds closed. She can't watch Dr. McDonnell's family going about their day, like everything's normal. Everything's not normal. Her mother, Ashmina, is dead. She went into the hospital a month ago and never came out.

She opens the fridge, still packed with gifted casseroles and platters, including an uneaten loaf of marionberry bread from

Mark and Ginny, and closes it. She hears her mother's voice in her head, urging her to get going. She has a listing appointment in a few minutes, a meeting scheduled by her mother six weeks ago, with the expectation she'd be able to go herself. She wants to cancel, but her mother's voice says no. She says, Go on, Sammy, it's better to stay busy.

Samara opens a cabinet and a mountain of tea boxes and tins falls onto the counter. Green tea with jasmine, green tea with lemon, raspberry leaf, garden mint, Moroccan mint, Ceylon, three tins of Assam, two of gunpowder, and chamomile with valerian. She chooses the Ceylon, pours the hot water, and puts the containers back, one by one.

She takes her mug to her bedroom and nudges Shawn, who's still asleep under her old dahlia-flowered duvet. "You need to get out of here before my dad gets up."

He raises his head from the pillow and squints. "Really?" His voice is gruff with sleep. "He knows I'm here."

It's true. She and Shawn have been seeing each other, off and on, since she moved back home ten months ago when her mom got sick.

"I know. But still . . ." She opens the closet

26

and tries to pull a skirt and shirt from a tangle of her mother's clothes, overflow from the master bedroom closet: dresses and pants and skirts in every color of the rainbow, scarves with twisting nautical knots or jaunty-looking parrots with flashing black beads for eyes, and saris in coral and aubergine and cadmium yellow, triangles of glass twinkling at their hems.

"So are you going to give me an answer?"

"About what?" Samara says into the folds of a dress printed with pink orchids that smells of sandalwood and orange peel. In her head, her mother's voice says, I always liked that dress.

He puts his elbows on his knees. His bare chest has just one patch of blondish hair, right in the center. "About when you're going back to Seattle?"

She turns and hugs her simple pink shirt and gray skirt against her body. She doesn't tell him she has nothing to go back to. That she gave up her job — an entry-level position she never liked much anyway — when her mom got sick. That her apartment in Seattle was a sublet she couldn't afford. Instead she appraises his broad forehead, short-cropped hair, and small, clear blue eyes. He looks nothing like he did when they were growing up. Back then he was tall and skinny, and always wore the same baggy athletic shorts. His family had a Ping-Pong table in their basement, and he used to try to talk to her while she and his sister played. If he had a friend over too, they'd play doubles. In her mind she hears the snap of the little white ball against the tabletop; she smells damp carpet and potato chips and strawberry gum.

"I haven't decided," she says finally.

"I think you should stay."

"In Clearing? It's where we grew up."

"I live here."

"That's different."

"How?"

Out the window Samara hears the industrious taps of a woodpecker. Get a move on, her mother's voice says. You're going to be late. "I don't know. It just is."

The extendable ladder rattles from the front yard, and her father yells, "Shoo bird —"

She sighs. "My dad's awake."

"What's he doing?"

"He's fighting with a woodpecker." She pulls on a fresh pair of underwear. "Where are you today?"

"The remodel on Woodland Avenue. What about you?"

"I have a listing appointment."

28

"You should come over later."

"I don't get having that big house all to yourself —"

"It's not just me. I've got my dogs."

"Maybe." She buttons up her shirt and pulls on her boots. "But go out the back door when you leave, okay?"

She has to hurry to reach the address on Arden Street on time, but when she gets there no one answers the door. She remembers the house; it's where her piano teacher used to live, Mrs. Kells. The exact inverse of her parents' 1959 ranch, the front door stands to the right of the garage instead of the left. The mountain, rising a few streets away, is a wall of green that cuts the bright gray sky in half.

She peers into the front windows, but can't see past the heavy curtains. When she took piano lessons she only saw the blue-wallpapered living room where the shiny piano stood. She recalls the tinkling sound of the high notes and the feeling of the hard pedal under her small foot. Mrs. Kells died when Samara was still in high school. She wonders if the piano is still inside.

Finally her phone buzzes inside her jacket pocket. It's Ben Kells, saying he can't make their appointment. He had to take his dad to the hospital in the middle of the night. Can she let herself in and evaluate the property alone? There's a key hidden in the side yard.

"Of course, no problem at all." She borrows her mother's sharply cheery phone voice. "I hope your father improves."

She follows a mossy concrete path around the house, finds the ceramic pot Ben mentioned, and tips it over far enough to slide a key out from its damp underside. She teeters in her boots for a minute, rights herself, and then makes her way back to the front porch. She tries the key in the unfamiliar lock, this way and that. Finally the dead bolt slides loose. The air in the entryway is close and warm. She tries to identify the smell: not mold or rot, but damp fabric, like an upholstered couch left in a basement too long.

She's surprised to see the house is empty — her mother had said it was wall-to-wall books. She crosses the living room, past a deep indentation in the carpet where the piano used to stand, on the lookout for anything unexpected. "Sammy," her mother told her once, "Watch your ankles. You never know what's hiding in an empty house." They were visiting a prospective listing on the other side of town, about five months ago. "One time a raccoon scurried across my feet." Ashmina laughed and the beads at the ends of the scarf wrapped around her bald head clicked together. "I went into the kitchen, and there he was. I remember his wild, furry face. And his eyes —" She circled her hands over her eyes in pantomime. "You don't want a face like that jumping out at you in the dark."

But nothing scurries from any corner of the Kells house, not yet anyway. Samara slides the door to the back porch wide open and lets in the cool breeze, and with it, the backyard smells of pinesap, bark mulch, wet grass.

The layout and square footage of the house is almost exactly the same as her parents' home, but it's amazing how much space there is when you take away all the furniture and lamps and pillows and potted plants and framed Audubon Society prints and stacks of hardback thrillers and bags of knitting yarn. She makes a circuit of both floors, pausing for a few minutes in each room. Everything's original, the limestone fireplaces, the steel kitchen cabinets, the gold-flecked linoleum floors. Her mother would have hated it. A tough sell, Sammy, she would have complained. No updates. But Samara likes it. The pink tiles in the upstairs bathroom are cool lozenges under her fingers. The mesh fireplace screen makes a sound like *wshhh, wshhh* when she pulls the cord. The drawers of the built-in banquette smell like cinnamon and cloves.

She stoops down to the baseboard in the living room and pokes at the corner of the carpet. She gives it an experimental tug, and it comes free with a sound like tearing out the stitches of a dress. She sneezes and runs her hand over the unmarked hardwood floors.

She hears her mother's voice, telling her to stop wasting time, to get on with the task at hand. Ashmina had a way of doing things, developed over thirty years in the business. She always walked through a house chatting about unrelated topics — what Samara was going to do with her life, how to attract more hummingbirds to her garden, a recipe she planned to make for dinner. All the while she was deciding which parts of the house added value, which parts detracted. Her internal calculator clicked as fast as her eyes could move, adding, subtracting.

In the past Samara has tried to imitate her. But as she walks through the Kells house she doesn't add and subtract in her mind. She doesn't jot down phrases to use in the MLS description — *well-maintained appliances, a patio perfect for entertaining, minutes from everything.* She doesn't do anything except visit each room, and when she's done, she starts again.

She imagines the people who lived here. She's never met Mrs. Kells's husband, although she knows he teaches philosophy at the university and used to sometimes appear on the PBS show *Great Minds in History.* All she can distinctly recall of Mrs. Kells herself is her voice, clear and firm over the sound of Samara's scales. But she finds little clues here and there in the house. Bobby pins inside a drawer in the master bathroom. The dusty outline of thick books in the built-in bookcases. A newspaper clipping inside the pantry:

ROAST A TURKEY, BY WEIGHT:

Weight	Cook Time (Unstuffed)	Cook Time (Stuffed)
4½–7 lbs.	2–2½ hrs.	2¼–2¾ hrs.
7–9 lbs.	2½–3 hrs.	2¾–3¾ hrs.
9–18 lbs.	3–3½ hrs.	3¾–4½ hrs.
18–22 lbs.	3½–4 hrs.	4½–5 hrs.
22–24 lbs.	4–4½ hrs.	5–5½ hrs.

She pictures a middle-aged man standing, tongs in hand, at a charcoal grill out on the square stone patio. In the air the char of steaks cooking. Long-limbed teenage boys loitering around the weather-beaten basketball hoop in the driveway. Their whooping voices and the smack of the ball against the hoop's backboard. She imagines a newly married Mrs. Kells, dressed for bed in a long pink nightgown, lying crosswise on a wide living room couch, her husband's lap cradling her feet. They both hold books, and the stillness of the room is punctuated only by the occasional turn of a page. Then the picture transforms, and it's her in the pink nightgown, and Shawn holding her feet. She shakes her head. What made her think of that?

Her mother's voice tells her to stop daydreaming. She's not here to appreciate the house, to imagine herself in it. She turns off the lights, closes the sliding door, and retrieves the keys from the kitchen counter. She's spent nearly an hour and has accomplished next to nothing. She pulls her hood up and runs to her car.

THREE

Cass listens at her daughter's nursery door, the dog's breath hot against the backs of her knees. A minute goes by, then two. The whimper she heard through the baby monitor has ceased. The only sound is the swish of Bear's tail.

She lets her shoulders relax a little and soft-steps back to the spare bedroom she's using as her study, past the moving boxes that line the hallway. Leah woke before five, and Cass has nursed her three times since then. *The Incredible First Year* says the baby's fierce hunger is normal for an eight-week-old. But nothing about it feels normal: Cass's eyes are gritty with lack of sleep; her breasts are chafed and tender.

In her study, she sits down at her desk, presses the baby monitor to her ear, and holds her breath.

Sweet silence.

She tucks her feet under the chair, the

wooden rungs cool against her toes, and gulps her lukewarm coffee. Bear settles with a low grunt on the carpet, and she taps out an email to her husband on her phone. He won't be able to read it or respond, not for at least a week, because he's on a five-week research trip to collect marine bacteriophage samples for his new lab at Oregon University, and there's no Internet on the ship. But she sends it anyway.

Dear Amar,
    I made a mistake. Turn the boat around, so you can come home and make me toast with cheese. Making toast with cheese requires two hands. Then you can walk the baby around the block, and I can take a long shower during which I'll hear no sound but the rush of the water past my ears.

Love,
Cass

Outside the window it's raining, or rather misting, and the mountain is a deep green. A *dormant volcano* her real estate agent, Mrs. Mehta, was careful to call it. She's now Cass's next-door neighbor; she keeps bringing her things for the baby, little toys her daughter used to love. When she showed them the house, Cass wasn't sure about the towering pines behind it. Or the way the mountain seemed to loom over the neighborhood, its jagged peak just visible above the dense forest. But Mrs. Mehta said they would wake up to the *birds singing,* and their baby would benefit from *healthful air.* She didn't point out the placards Cass found, later, at a nearby trailhead: BEWARE OF YOUR SURROUNDINGS. COUGAR, BOB-CAT, AND BLACK BEAR ARE PRESENT IN THIS REGION. KEEP CLOSE EYE ON CHIL-DREN AND PETS. She also didn't mention the slight vibrations that occasionally rise up from deep underground. Still, Cass likes the mountain. It smells good — like pine-sap and crushed leaves.

She stands up and surveys the stacks of boxes that fill the room. Amar sliced the tops open for her before he left. They contain books from her unfinished Ph.D. in metaphysics at Oregon University, where she was writing a dissertation on the philosophy of counterfactuals, "if . . . then" statements like:

If I hadn't been assigned a cubical in the sciences library, I would never have met Amar.

Or *If I'd remembered to pack my birth control pills on our camping trip to the redwoods, Leah wouldn't exist.*

37

She takes Quine's *Theories and Things* out of a box and opens its marked-up pages. She recognizes her own small, sinuous handwriting in the margins, but it feels like someone else wrote these words. Not her. She's a person who can't manage to put two words together when she goes out to buy diapers, whose thoughts move through her mind like wisps of fog.

She chooses a page at random. She forces herself to read one line. Just one, and to understand it. She scrutinizes the first sentence on page 34, once, twice, and then something catches. Something familiar, something strange, and the air seems to tighten around her head. She reads the sentence again. She scratches her scalp. She reads the note that hovers above it in the margin's white space. It reminds her of something. No, not that. Another thing. Not something she's thought before, or read before. Something new. Something —

An electronic whimper erupts from the monitor. Only one. But when she turns back to the page, the thought's gone. The idea that seemed like something solid, that made her feel like herself for a minute, has evaporated so completely she questions it was ever there.

She puts the Quine back and flips through

the stack of unopened mail on her desk, forwarded from their old apartment across town: their last electric bill, a notice that she can't access her school transcripts until she pays $10.75 in library fines, and a thin padded folder. She starts at its return address: "From the Office of Professor Robert Kells, Department of Philosophy, Humanities Hall, Oregon University."

Robert Kells — Robby — is her graduate advisor, mentor, and friend, a man whose mind is better than any book, dense and deep, full of surprises. Whose everyday observations pierce your brain like tiny fishhooks, towing your thoughts somewhere terrifying, or wondrous, or surreal. By the time Cass met Robby he hadn't published anything substantial in years, since his wife died. But scholars are still grappling with his book *Counterfactuals* more than twenty years after its publication. Cass has been grappling with it since she met him as an undergraduate in Philosophy 305. But after years of talking to him nearly every day, she hasn't spoken to him in months.

The last time they met they argued. She was seven months pregnant and wavering in her resolve to stay in school after her daughter was born. The bigger her belly got, the more unsure she became. She tried to picture what her life was going to be like, how it would be different. What particular details would change. Already it was different; spaces of her day that used to be for reading and writing and thinking were now taken up with napping and eating and doctor's appointments. Walking across the grassy quad to Robby's office, her swollen feet tight inside her shoes, she needed him to quell her doubts. She was in the midst of unraveling something vital in the field of metaphysics, building on his book *Counterfactuals*, but also developing an argument she hoped would be distinctly hers.

When she stepped from the elevator onto the seventh floor, she expected to find him in his office, as usual, smoking out the window, drinking cans of Coke, holding court with whoever was around, and if no one was around, leaning in his doorway so he could read emails over the shoulder of his secretary, Mrs. Trevy. But she found him alone at his desk, his large head listing to one side and his eyes half-closed. His feet were propped precariously on the edge of the desk. When she knocked, he opened his eyes and swung his long legs to the floor, toppling a pile of blue exam books. "Cass, my dear —"

She picked up the exams. She'd seen him

drunk at work, but never before noon. His gray hair was wild, sticking up on one side and flat on the other. He needed a shave. He pulled himself up from his chair and waved a finger in the air. "I've got something to show you." He was wide awake now and cheerful. His wool tie swung loosely from his neck as he crossed the room. He opened a drawer in his filing cabinet and peered inside.

She tried to find a place to put the exams on his desk, gave up, and sat down on the couch by the window, her T-shirt tight across her belly. She set the exams beside her, on top of volume 4 of *The Collected Works of John Stuart Mill.*

"Let me find it . . ." His blue shirt was rumpled and missing a button at the top.

"I need to talk to you about my proposal. You've had the draft for weeks." She ran her hands over her stomach and felt the pressure of a tiny foot or hand near her rib cage.

"Here it is." Robby held up a red file folder with her name on it. With his elbow he pushed the filing cabinet drawer closed.

"Are those your comments?"

He opened the folder and began reading. He rocked back and forth in his loafers. "This? No, this is —"

41

"Because I need to finalize my topic before the baby comes." A burning sensation was building in her chest, heartburn from the baby pressing on her diaphragm.

Robby closed the folder and sat back down at his desk. His face was suddenly sober. "About the proposal —" He laid his large hands on top of the desk. "It's not ambitious enough."

"It's limited in scope but —"

"You're playing it safe."

"I'm being realistic about what I can accomplish given the circumstances." She gestured to her stomach.

He waved his hand in the air dismissively.

"My due date's in August. And Amar has an interview for a tenure track job next week. They're talking about giving him his own lab."

"Excellent. Well done, Amar." He opened the red file folder and began reading.

"My husband Amar," she prompted.

"I know who Amar is." Robby tapped the folder with his finger. "Now, let's get down to business —"

"If he gets the job, we'll be able to move out of student housing. Buy a real house for when the baby comes."

Robby leaned back in his chair and began talking about when he was a graduate student. About his dissertation, which eventually became the book *Counterfactuals.* She'd heard all this before. Out the window she could see the tops of cedar trees, their red trunks bright against the green lawn. The smell of freshly cut grass and cedar sap and gasoline drifted into the room and turned her stomach.

Robby waxed on. "When you have a once in a generation mind," he was saying, "you have to make sacrifices. You owe it to —"

"The other committee members thought the idea was solid. They were excited about it."

"Who cares what they think." He made a face like he'd caught a whiff of something rank. "They're idiots." He was trying to get her to laugh, but she didn't want to play along.

"I'm going to be caring for a newborn and trying to write a dissertation at the same time." She struggled to keep her voice even. "Even with the topic I chose, I'm not sure I can do both."

Robby reached for his Coke. "What are you trying to say, Cassandra? Are you planning to have a bunch of kids, knit sweaters, and make jam?" One of his overgrown eyebrows hung suspended on his forehead.

She thought of Robby's house, its quiet

rooms and dusty stacks of books and papers. The photographs hanging on the walls, of his late wife and his grown sons. "Not everyone wants to spend their life holed up alone with their books and their computer —"

"That's true. But you do. At least you did when I met you."

He was right. When she was twenty years old she wanted to be just like him, to devote her life to big ideas, to write an important, groundbreaking book. But that was before she met Amar. Before she got pregnant.

"A lot's changed since then. I have a family now."

"This is bigger than that. I'm talking about creating work that will outlive us all."

"Let me start with the topic I chose —"

"It's not good enough. Not for you."

Her heartburn was worse now. "Do you hear yourself? You want me to write the book you can't write yourself." He'd been working on the follow-up to *Counterfactuals* for close to twenty years.

"That's not true." He pressed his thumb to the red file folder. "The very opposite actually —"

"Why can't you finish it yourself?" Her chest was on fire now. She pressed her breastbone with the heel of her hand. "What are you so afraid of?"

There was a pause. Out the window the cedar trees swayed. "I'm afraid of failing," he said, finally. "Just like you."

She blinked. "I'm not afraid of failing." She thought, again, of the stillness of his house, its silent rooms. "I'm afraid of ending up like you."

A flush sprang to his cheeks. Then his eyes skittered away from hers, and all the parts of his face she knew so well — the heavy-lidded, intelligent eyes, the prominent chin — rearranged themselves into something more ordinary and sad.

He swiveled his chair to throw his Coke can into the recycling, and when he turned back he smiled stiffly. "I hoped to work together for many more years. But if that's not what you want, I respect your choice." He reached for a book from one of the stacks on his desk and opened it. "I wish you the best, Cass."

She's had a lot of time to think about that morning, but she's mostly spent it trying not to think about it. That's been easy enough since Leah's birth, when her quick and agile brain turned into something entirely different, something soggy and slack. Except every so often, in the middle of the night when she's nursing Leah, her head will clear and she'll resolve to call

Robby, as soon as possible, as soon as the sun comes up. But she never does.

She opens the padded envelope and smells tobacco and printer ink and old window casings, the scents of Robby's office, and finds a single red file folder with her name typed across its label. Inside is an old term paper she wrote in the first class she ever took with him: "The Problem of Possibility in Leibnitz's Metaphysics."

She runs her thumb over Robby's familiar scrawl in the margins. His comments were often academic, *Have you considered the inverse argument? See page 24,* other times emphatic, *Yes, just so. Don't stop now — follow this line of thinking to its conclusion,* and occasionally cranky, *I'm bored.* On page 8 there's a wrinkled watermark where he set his Coke can.

Although she's forgotten the details of the paper, she remembers what Robby scribbled on the last page under the grade. *I expect great things from you, Cassandra.* In a way that comment changed her life. She switched her major to philosophy, became Robby's research assistant, and in her senior year, applied to graduate school.

Then she notices something: on page 14 Robby wrote something on the bottom of the page she doesn't remember. The color

46

of the ink is blue, not black, and the hand-writing's even more illegible.

Cassandra, I was a fool to lose my temper with you today. But you weren't listening. Will you listen now?

The rest of what he wrote must continue on page 15. But there is no page 15. She riffles through the whole paper, tips over the envelope, but finds nothing.

Bear stands up to shake himself and the air momentarily fills with tufts of black hair. He looks at Cass expectantly.

She could call Robby and ask him about the note. She should call him. She will.

She picks up her phone and dials his office number. After ten rings she hangs up and calls the department office. One of the secretaries picks up right away, and Cass asks if Robby has come in for the day yet.

In the background she hears voices and the thumping whine of a photocopier.

"Did you say Robby?"

"Professor Kells. Is he around?"

"May I ask who's calling?"

"Cass Stuart. He's my dissertation chair. Or, he was my dissertation chair . . ."

"He's taken a leave of absence. I'm sorry — that's all I know."

"Since when?"

"The end of spring term, I believe. Can I connect you to someone else?"

Cass tells her no, and hangs up.

She's not sure what to think. She picks up her old paper, puts it back down. The day she and Robby argued was at the end of spring term. She should have called before now. She's ashamed. He wasn't in good shape the last time she saw him. He'd probably gotten worse.

The baby monitor comes alive. She stands up, her breasts full of pins and needles, and moves toward Leah, ready to pick her up and feel the weight of her in her arms, to press her nose to her warm head and smell her soapy scent. She's eager, now, to settle herself in the rocker, offer up her sore breasts, and let her mind grow fuzzy and numb.

FOUR

Ginny raises her head from her desk and rubs her cheek where it pressed against some papers. Her pager rattles against her metal in-box. Gray light shines from the window.

She grabs the pager and reads the number; she stands up and her Dictaphone, forgotten in her lap, clatters to the floor. The room sways for a minute, and she holds on to the sides of her desk until it stops. She takes a drink from a half-empty can of Mountain Dew, warm and flat. She rubs her face with her palms, vigorously, three times, clips her pager to her waistband, and plunges into the fluorescent-lit hallway.

She blinks, coughs, and propels herself toward the elevator, and then to the coffee kiosk on the fourth floor. When she gets there she stands in line and inhales the coffee bean fumes. She closes her eyes for a minute. It feels like she could fall asleep, right here in line, standing up. She thinks of Edith. The freckles across the bridge of her nose.

"Next," the man behind the counter calls.

She holds out her ID badge to pay. Her intern, Seth Harper, is coming around the corner, waving his arms. She ignores him. She watches the woman behind the counter fill a paper cup with her Stumptown house blend. And then Dr. Harper's in front of her, talking fast about a patient who's "flipping out" on the surgical floor. His square, clean-shaven face is pink and animated. His hands gesticulate.

She takes her coffee and picks up a container of milk. She pours some into her cup. "Have her labs changed?"

"No . . ."

"So call for a psych consult."

"She says she won't talk to anyone but you. She's throwing stuff." His eyes blink rapidly. "Her food, her bedpan even. It was empty, but still —"

"Dr. Harper, are you a psychiatrist?" She shakes four Splendas into her coffee cup.

"No —"

"Am I a psychiatrist?"

He puts his hands in his pockets. "No."

"You're a surgeon. You cut people open and fix their insides. You're not in charge of people's emotions. Neither am I."

She takes a sip of the too-hot coffee. Her phone beeps and she squints at it. Damn, the OR moved up her gallbladder. "What's Professor Kells's white count and lactate level?"

"I haven't checked yet. I was dealing with Mrs. —"

"This is what's going to happen. I'm going this way." She points down the hallway. "And you're going that way." She points in the other direction. "I'm going to my meeting, where I have to explain to risk management why Ashmina Mehta died on the operating table, and you're going to call a psych consult. Then you're going to get Professor Kells's labs." She checks her watch — her meeting was supposed to have started five minutes ago. She takes a big gulp of coffee, and it scalds her throat. She hurries down the hall.

Mark calls out the window of the Jeep, "We're going to be late," and Peter and Noah hurry over.

"Livi needs a ride too," Peter says, and Mark waves her into the car.

The two boys get into the backseat and put their seatbelts on while Livi lifts her instrument case into the trunk. But instead of getting in the front seat with Mark, she climbs over Peter to sit between the two boys.

Dots of rain mist the windshield as Mark starts the car.

"Livi's my neighbor," Peter says. "Her mom couldn't drive her today." Livi doesn't add anything to this introduction. The zipper on her sweatshirt is pulled up to the very top in a way that looks uncomfortable. She whispers something to Noah, and he smiles.

They rattle past the Human Bean coffee drive-through, the Local Roasters café, and the Creative Cup coffee shop and gallery. The Natural Grains food co-op and the Flower Pot nursery. They're running about two or three minutes late. If they get to the school later than 8:10, he'll have to walk the kids into the office to sign them in, instead of just dropping them off, which means he'll get to work with only a few minutes to spare before his talk.

The Jeep is forced to a crawl when they reach the SCHOOL ZONE, 20 MILES PER HOUR sign. Mark takes his place behind a queue of Priuses and Subarus. They inch forward. Flanking the school's double front doors is a gaggle of bicycles: Strider bikes, pedal bikes, and low-slung recumbent bikes;

Burley trailers and Thule tagalongs. Above the doors a banner reads PEANUT-FREE ZONE; another says LEARN TO LOVE TO LEARN. Just beyond the school the mountain rises up, misty green; its snowy split peak prods the gray sky.

The kids unclick their seatbelts and pull their book bags onto their laps. There's a knock on the passenger-side window. Seneca's mom hovers behind the glass. She wears a sweatshirt that says, KNOW YOUR FOOD = GROW YOUR FOOD. Mark rolls down the window.

Her face is exasperated. "You didn't get it either."

"Get what?"

"The text message saying there's no school. Apparently we weren't the only ones." She gestures behind her, where her son stands on the sidewalk with some other fifth-grade boys, their backpacks a heap of brown and black on the sidewalk.

"What do you mean no school?"

"They've found mold or something." She pulls out her phone and reads out loud. "Dear parents, Classes at Niels Bohr Elementary are canceled today, Monday, October third, due to the discovery of toxic mold in the reading resource room. The school will remain closed until proper mold remediation procedures have been completed. We regret any inconvenience this may cause. As always, your children's health and safety is our number one priority. Sincerely, Jennifer T. Sloan, Principal."

"School's canceled?" Noah says from the backseat. He and Peter hiss the word *yes* simultaneously, and Noah flips the football to Peter across Livi.

Mark frowns. Peter's mother works an hour away and his father travels during the week. He has no idea how to contact Livi's parents. What is he going to do with these kids?

Ginny unclips her phone and pager from her waistband and sets them on the conference table. She sits down across from two administrators and a member of the hospital's in-house counsel. The fluorescent lights buzz overhead.

"If it's okay with you we'll jump right in." The lawyer turns on an audio recorder. "We're here today to discuss the death of Ashmina Mehta on September first, 2016." He reads from a file in front of him and summarizes, in a monotone, the circumstances that brought Mrs. Mehta into the ER, the details of her case, and the specifics of the complications that led to her death.

"We just need to hear, in your own words, what occurred during the surgery."

"Mrs. Mehta was in my care for ten months. I successfully removed a tumor from her colon in December, and when she presented in the ER with a suspected recurrence in August, we weighed the pros and cons of a second surgery. Her heart was a concern. After discussing the risks, she decided to go forward. I ordered a cardiac workup, and the results showed only minor evidence of an old myocardial infarction. Everything else was within acceptable limits —"

"Did you order a cardiac cath?" one of the administrators asks.

"The workup wasn't strong enough to warrant it. She was in the ER with an apparent bowel obstruction, with bleeding, and time was of the essence."

Ginny's phone buzzes. She turns it over, sees her husband Mark's name on the screen, and silences it.

"At what point in the surgery did her heart stop?" the lawyer asks.

"I had completed the resection and felt confident about the margins. It was going well, all things considered. I was nearly ready to close the fascia. Then her sats and pressure began to drop. Dr. Lee started pressors and a fluid bolus, but she was already going into v-fib." Ginny pauses, and in her mind she hears the shrill ventilator alarm, and feels the jolt of Ashmina's body under the defibrillator paddles. "Despite proper ACLS protocol and resuscitation efforts, we were unable to revive her."

The other administrator chimes in: "Do you think emergency surgery was an overly aggressive choice given her heart condition?"

Her phone buzzes again. Another call from Mark; she silences it and sets the phone in her lap. "If she wasn't bleeding we could have waited to do a more extensive cardiac workup. But given all the variables, getting her into surgery was the only viable option."

"Did your personal relationship with the patient cloud your judgment? I understand she was your neighbor."

She's surprised by this question. "I would have made the same choice with a stranger."

The lawyer nods at the two administrators. "I think that's all we need." He turns off the audio recorder.

"That's it?"

"Unless there's something else you want to add." His finger hovers over the button on the recorder.

She wants to say, I wish it had gone a different way. Ashmina was opinionated and demanding, and she often didn't follow Ginny's medical instructions. But she liked her. They'd known each other for years as neighbors, but had grown closer when Ginny became her doctor. She wants to say she tried to save her friend and failed. But instead she says, "I did the best I could. But my best wasn't good enough that night." She clips her phone and pager to her waist and stands up. "If that's all you need, I've got a gallbladder starting right now."

Ten minutes into her case, a circulating nurse pokes her head inside the OR. "Dr. McDonnell, your phone keeps ringing."

"If it's my infectious diseases consult, tell her I'll call her at lunchtime." Ginny sweeps her pinky finger into the incision she's just made below her patient's belly button. Her chief resident, Dr. Dawson, places the Hasson port and begins suturing it into place.

The nurse comes back with Ginny's phone. "It's your husband. Do you want me to answer it?"

"Damn." She never called Mark back. "Tell him I'm in the middle of a case." She holds out her hand to Dr. Dawson. "Laparoscope."

The nurse answers the phone and listens for a few minutes. She looks uncomfortable.

"Here, hold up the phone," Ginny says, and the nurse reaches the phone a few inches from her ear. "Mark, it's me. I'm scrubbed in. What's going on?"

Mark talks quickly. "School's canceled — today of all days."

"Okay . . ."

"My presentation is today. This is my big chance —"

"Right. I remember."

"And I've got a car full of kids who have nowhere to go."

"Kids?" She positions the laparoscope and checks the angles. "We have one kid."

"I've got Peter. And Peter's neighbor is —"

"Mark," she interrupts. "Tell me what you need."

"I need someone to watch these kids."

"Don't we have a babysitter you can call? What about Mrs. Bloom next door?"

"Mrs. Bloom moved to California four months ago. You know that."

"Right. Well . . ."

"Can you meet me at campus?" His voice has a desperate edge to it, and it's clear he already knows her answer.

"I'm in the middle of a gallbladder. I won't be done for at least another hour."

Mark is silent on the other end of the line.

"I'm sorry, Mark." Dr. Dawson waits to position the trocar ports. "I have to hang up. I'll call you when I'm done." She waves the phone away and inserts the forceps into the lateral port, grasps the apex of the gallbladder, and lifts its underside.

Mark tosses his phone onto the passenger seat and maneuvers the Jeep around two minivans. It was pointless to call Ginny. He feels a surge of irritation for all the times he's had to deal with these kinds of situations alone.

"Livi, who's at home right now?" he asks.

"At my house?"

"Yes, at your house." He taps his thumb on the steering wheel.

"Nobody."

"Your mother's not there?"

Peter interjects, "What's wrong with mold?"

"It's not like the mold in your fridge," Mark answers. "Livi? Your mother?"

"She's in Portland."

Mark takes a deep breath.

"What kind of mold is it then?"

"Peter, I don't know. The kind that can

make you sick I guess."

"What about your dad, Livi?"

"He doesn't live there."

"Where're we going?" Noah asks. Mark has taken the turn toward campus automatically.

"He doesn't live in town?" Mark asks Livi. These questions are hopeless.

"I don't know where he lives."

"I never saw any mold in the reading resource room," Peter offers.

"I guess I'm taking you three to work with me." Mark thinks for a minute, his thumb setting a manic pace on the steering wheel. "You'll have to sit in my office and wait for me."

"Your office?" Livi scrunches her face into a pout.

Noah has the football again. "Can't we go to the food court in the campus center instead?"

Mark recalls Livi's arm around Noah's waist. He weighs the awkwardness of showing up at work with three eleven-year-olds against his desire to keep an eye on those two. "You need to be where I can keep track of you. Besides," he adds brightly. "I'm giving a talk you'll find interesting. You can sit in the back."

"What kind of talk?" Livi is skeptical.

"It's about —" He stops himself from saying The Predictive Power of the Non-Migratory Movements of the Northwestern Spotted Frog. "It's about how animals react to geothermal changes in the earth, and could predict a natural disaster like a volcanic eruption . . ."

In the rearview mirror, only Noah is listening. Livi has pulled a library book out of her backpack. Peter kicks the back of the passenger seat despondently.

Rain speckles the windshield and Mark turns on the wipers. His annoyance with Ginny has drained away. He doesn't feel angry anymore, just small and alone. This feeling isn't new; it's as familiar as his Jeep's worn steering wheel in his hands.

FIVE

The conference room on the fifth floor of Hurley Hall smells of dust and burnt coffee. Mark stands at the front of the room with his laptop, and the large-paned windows behind him rattle in the wind. His colleagues and a few students mill about in the back of the room near a folding table with a stack of dented pastries and two large stainless steel carafes, one for coffee, one for tea. Slowly, everyone moves toward the rows of folding chairs, paper cups in hand.

The kids are already settled in the last row. Noah and Peter try to stuff whole muffins in their mouths; Livi reads her library book. Mark scans each face in the crowd for the dean and doesn't find him. There are a lot of empty seats.

At five after nine, he begins. He projects a picture of Mount Etna on the screen behind him. "On January fifth, 2012, hot ash erupted from the top of Mount Etna. But the mountain goats that roam its cliffs didn't have to run from the lava that began pouring down the sides of the mountain . . . because they had disappeared from their native habitat the day before. In 2009, in Italy's Abruzzo region, residents noted that toads had mysteriously disappeared in the middle of their spawning season. Then, three days later, an earthquake killed more than three hundred people in the city of L'Aquila. What did these goats and frogs know that humans didn't?"

His bald-headed department chair, Fred Hellerman, sits in the front row. Mary Clarke, still wearing her rain slicker, takes up two seats a few rows back, her head bent over her phone. When she looks up flecks of rain obscure her glasses. She offers Mark a distracted smile. There's Randal Stepp; his snub nose always reminds Mark of a musk-rat. And one of his upper-level undergradu-ate students, Claire something, scribbles energetically on a notepad in the back row. There's still no sign of the dean.

"They knew danger was coming. But how?" He summarizes the many docu-mented instances of animal behavior pre-dicting earthquakes, volcanic eruptions, and tsunamis. Fruit bats in Ghana, highland cattle in the Himalayas. At his back the *spat*

spat of rain hits the windows. His graduate student Katie now stands in the doorway to the conference room. She wears jeans and a gray fisherman's sweater, her hair wild from the wind outside. She gives him an apologetic shrug that says, "Sorry I'm late."

He projects a picture of a northwestern spotted frog with a tracking collar fastened to its leg. "It's clear animal behavior holds the key to predicting a wide range of natural phenomena. And Oregon, with its unique geological properties, is one of the best places in the world to study the predictive power of animal behavior in earnest." He opens the real-time data from his research ponds, and points out the bright green dots, each representing a single frog, as they move across a gray screen.

"My research on Broken Mountain has shown a predictive correlation between the movements of the frogs that mate in ponds B, E, and F and the geothermal activity in hot springs and steam vents located less than a mile from the ponds." He clicks to the live video feed from Pond F, although there's not much to see at this time of day, just horsetails and murky water, the glint of a water bug, the ripple of a frog moving under the surface of the water.

He allows that his study of the northwestern spotted frog is a small one. "But I believe my data points to a disturbing trend —" He clicks to a bar graph showing how the movements of his frogs have changed over the last four years, the way their behavior has become increasingly erratic. "A trend that suggests Broken Mountain is not actually dormant."

At that his department chair, Fred, sits up in his chair, sets his coffee on his knee. "Now, Mark," he interrupts. "We've all experienced the mountain's seismological blips. But there's just no data coming out of volcanology or seismology to support such a large claim. You're getting ahead of yourself again —"

Mary and Randal are nodding.

"This is our town. The place we've made our homes," Mark says. Mary holds up her hand, but he ignores her. "Where we're raising our kids." He looks at Noah sitting with his friends. "And as a community we are woefully unprepared for an eruption."

"The thing is, Mark" — Mary gestures at the bar graph — "your sample is statistically tiny."

This is like his last talk all over again. They're not listening. How can he get them to listen?

Randal chimes in. "Has anyone been able

to repeat your findings? There are a lot of possible explanations for what you've recorded. Ground water pollution, climate change —"

"How many of us know the protocol for sheltering in place if Broken Mountain blows," Mark says, "and covers the entire valley in volcanic ash? How many of us have the proper supplies —"

"You're making it sound as if it's imminent," Mary says. "Even you don't think that's true."

"We're all competing over the same money," Randal says to Mary, loud enough for Mark to hear. "I think it's leading some people to inflate their results —"

"I don't know if there will be an eruption in our lifetime." Mark talks over Randal. "But what about our children's lifetime?" He looks at the kids again, and Noah gives him a concerned smile. "We owe it to them to take these findings seriously. To investigate further, in a comprehensive way."

He hurries to click to his next slide, a picture of the globe, with clusters of little yellow triangles representing animal populations in seismic hot spots. "Imagine a network of sensors, attached to the sea lions that populate the Oregon coast, with the power to predict the next tsunami, or to the

66

mountain goats that roam the side of Mount Jefferson, with the ability to warn us of an impending eruption.

"Picture a global observation system that would allow us to use animals as sentinels for our own well-being." In the audience Mary wipes her glasses and shakes her head. Katie still hovers in the doorway. "I call this method Disaster Alert Management using Nature, or DAMN for short." A few people snort at the acronym, but he presses on. "DAMN could save countless lives. But to make it a reality we need to implement large-scale tracking of animal behavior across the state of Oregon, and eventually across the globe. And that requires a commitment to significant long-term funding." He directs this statement at his department chair, but Fred is frowning into his coffee cup.

The video feed from Pond F is still open on his computer screen, visible to him but not the audience. A dark figure has walked into the video frame. A man. It must be a hiker who's lost his way, or a ranger. Mark frowns. There are signs posted all around his ponds. They warn people of his ongoing research; they ask them to steer clear so they don't corrupt his data.

"We appreciate your enthusiasm, Mark,"

Fred says. "And maybe with a larger data sample . . ."

But Mark is only half listening. It's hard to get a good look at the man on the screen because the hood of his jacket obscures his face. The man raises his arm and . . .

The video screen shudders and goes black.

Mark drives fast up the mountain through the pelting rain, and the kids bump against each other in the backseat. He's told them where they're headed, that his equipment was damaged and he's got to go retrieve it, but Noah's face is skeptical in the backseat.

"Why are we driving so fast?" he asks. "Is something wrong?"

"I just want to get up there as quick as possible. Maybe I can still salvage the camera." The road climbs, and the forest grows thick. He parks the Jeep at a trailhead. Pond F is half a mile up the mountain, so there's no way around it — they're going to have to walk. When he tells the kids they'll have to hike to get to the camera they groan in unison.

He thinks about his wife in the bright white of the operating room, telling other people what to do. "Come on. I can't leave you here," he says, and they straggle out of the car.

Livi and Peter don't have proper shoes, but Mark has a couple of ponchos in the back of the Jeep. "It won't take long," Mark says. "Let's go."

They trudge up the trail, the earth slick under their feet. Mark goes first, then Noah, followed by Livi and Peter. Livi refuses to put the hood of her poncho up, and the rain plasters her hair to her face. Peter's sneakers squish with each step.

Mark knows this trail so well he could walk it in his sleep. His legs know its turns and hollows; his nose knows its sodden earth and decomposing leaves. His mind is on his talk and his colleagues' interrogations. On his expensive camera that some asshole decided to destroy. They pass the turnoff for Pond L, and Pond E; in five more minutes they'll reach Pond F. Behind him the kids struggle up the rocky and increasingly steep path.

Pond F is a glint of light through the dripping trees. It looks like it always does. There's no sign of the figure he saw on the video feed. The camera is attached to a western white pine tree. He pulls it down and inspects it. He shakes his head. There's nothing wrong with it. No damage at all.

He tells the kids, "Wait here. I'll be right back," and they huddle under a large hemlock. He looks for footprints, for crushed vegetation. Any sign of a recent human presence, but he finds nothing.

The rain agitates the surface of the pond. He walks a little ways into the shallows. His boots sink into the mud and make a sucking sound with each step; a weedy funk fills his nose. A dark green streak moves through the murky water. There's the pop of a bulbous eye, the spring of a green leg — his frogs diving under pondweed and through slough grass.

He squints through the rain, into the forest. He knows these woods as well as his own living room. He's spent half his adult life here, observing, recording. He sees nothing that strikes him. Nothing at all.

He shakes the mud from his boots, chooses a direction at random, and pushes his way into the brush. He steps over disintegrating logs, the air heavy and sweet with decay. Blackberry brambles catch at his elbows and knees, and he waves them away. He pauses at an old logging road, overgrown with cedar saplings, listens to the *tiptiptiptip* of the rain against wet leaves and the mewing call of a green-tailed towhee. The wind picks up and the rain turns sideways. There's a metallic taste in his mouth. He ought to go back; he's left the kids alone too long. The ground shudders —

A man emerges from a thicket of brambles. He steps into the overgrown road, and wet leaves blow against his legs. It's amazing how much the man looks like . . . Mark blinks. The man looks exactly like . . . him. Only he's filthy. His clothes are torn and ragged. He moves across the road at a diagonal, shoulders slumped. Dirt streaks his face. His eyes are tight with pain, or fright.

Mark backs away. He stumbles, reaches for a tree trunk, and holds on hard with a shuddering hand. But the man appears oblivious to his presence. He's crossed the road now, limping slightly; he moves slowly toward the trees.

Feet crash through the brush behind Mark. "Dad!" Noah yells. The kids tumble onto the road, red-faced and scared. "Was there an earthquake?"

Mark holds up his hand. "Stop." He turns back to the man.

But he's gone.

Mark scans the forest. "There was someone there," he says. "Did you see him? A man —"

"What was that?" Noah's voice breaks. "That shaking?"

71

"You shouldn't have left us there." Livi hugs her poncho.

"Everything's okay." Mark moves to the spot where the man stood just a moment ago. "The mountain does that sometimes. They're called microseismic events . . ." He can't see anything. The man has left no trace. Even the wet earth — there should be footprints — appears untouched.

He turns back to the kids. "Everything's okay," he repeats. "I would know if there was any real danger. My frogs would tell me."

But their faces aren't convinced.

On the hike back to the car Mark's alert to every twig snap, every rustle of an animal in the brush. The trees and rocks and logs have taken on a sinister cast. When they reach the Jeep, he hurries the kids into their seats. He locks the doors, blasts the heat, and puts the car in gear. A creeping doubt has come over him. He told the kids the microseismic event meant nothing. It happened all the time. And that was true. But the two things have become ominously linked in his mind — the shaking and the man. The shaking, the man. He pulls away from the trailhead and speeds down the mountain, his tires hissing on the wet road.

SIX

When Samara gets home she finds her father in the kitchen, kneeling in front of a low drawer, Tupperware piled on the floor beside him. She perches in a chair at the kitchen table and watches him try to match clear Tupperware bottoms to blue or green or red tops. She turns the lazy Susan in the center of the table and her mother's pill containers go round and round with an uneven squeak. "What are you doing?"

"Cleaning. How was your listing appointment?"

"It was Mrs. Kells's house. Remember her?"

"I remember how beautifully you used to play her piano." He gives up matching tops and bottoms, gathers the Tupperware, and drops it into an empty cardboard box. "Does her husband still live there?"

"Nobody lives there. What are you doing with those?"

"Just sorting through some things. What's the condition of the house?"

"Dated." She chooses a word her mother would use. "Almost like no one ever lived there . . ." She thinks of the sunburst doorbell, the pastel bathroom tiles.

"Tough sell?"

She draws herself up. "I'll be able to sell it, no problem." She affects a confidence she doesn't feel.

"Sammy, you don't have to carry on with it. She didn't expect you to."

She turns the whining lazy Susan again.

"You'll be wanting to get back to your life in Seattle." He opens another drawer, this one full of napkin rings. Metal, wood, glass, ceramic; little beads dangle from some, miniature silver squirrels adorn others. He takes them out, one by one, and sets them on the counter.

"If I leave who's going to stop you?" She grabs one of the squirrel napkin rings and holds it protectively.

"Stop me from what?"

"From pitching it all out."

"That's not what I'm doing."

"You are."

"I'm organizing."

"You always hated the clutter, and now you're thrilled to get rid of it."

His face sags. "I'd carry every object in this house on my back if it meant I could have one more day with your mother."

"She cared about this stuff."

He takes the squirrel napkin ring from her and frowns at it. "Did she?"

"Why can't they stay in that drawer?" She points at the open cabinet. "It's not like we need to use it for anything else."

He picks up the box of mismatched Tupperware. "They're just things, Sammy. They're not her."

After her father leaves the house, Samara turns on the kettle. She doesn't understand him. How he can be so calm, so methodical, so practical. He's not angry at all. Out the kitchen window Ginny and Mark's driveway shines with rain. Ginny's probably at the hospital right now, going about her day, like she's done nothing wrong. Samara imagines her striding down the hallway in her white coat followed by three or four residents. She pictures her face, with no makeup and an arrogant expression.

The kettle clicks off. She opens the cabinet where they keep the tea, and where this morning there were at least twenty containers. Now there are three. She starts to open another cabinet, and the mountain rumbles. She has a bad taste in her mouth.

She hears the tapping of a woodpecker from outside. But it's too loud to be a woodpecker. Out the window, in the front yard —

A woman hammers a FOR SALE sign into the bright grass with a large mallet. A pink and orange scarf drapes her shoulders; a long brown braid swishes down her back. Her mother. Her mother is out in the yard. She looks . . . like herself. Before she got sick. *Tamp, tamp, tamp.* She drives the sign into the ground with gusto.

Samara presses her hands to one pane of glass and then another, her eyes fixed on the figure outside. When she reaches the front door, she grasps the handle and swings it wide. She lunges into the front yard before she realizes . . . she's gone. The yard's empty. There's no Ashmina. No FOR SALE sign. No mallet. Just a stretch of bright green lawn littered with big yellow leaves.

Samara stands in the yard and stares at the spot where her mother appeared until her bare feet turn numb in the wet grass. Until her new neighbor, Cass, comes out of her house with her dog. She waves at Samara as she passes. Samara doesn't wave back. She hurries into the house and locks herself inside.

Mark lingers in Noah's room at bedtime. He asks him about the book he's reading, and he changes the bulb in the lizard-shaped night-light he no longer needs. All the while, the man he saw, the Other Mark, haunts him, harasses him. Demands his attention.

The Other Mark keeps asking and asking and asking the same question. What's going to happen, Mark, what?

What?

What?

His evening routines — feeding the cats, checking the doors are locked and the garage shut — provide no relief. He tries to drown out the questions with the television, switching between *Nova* on PBS and CNN. But nothing holds his attention. The news is tame tonight, the world quiet.

He goes into his study, sits down at his computer, and curses the fact that he has no recording of this morning's Pond F video feed. He's certain the man he saw was the same man from the feed.

He opens the real-time data from his frog ponds, E, F, L, and P, little green dots flickering against a gray screen. They're all there, within a few yards of the ponds. He watches the green specks creep, a quarter of an inch this way, a quarter of an inch that way, for a long time.

When he goes upstairs just after eleven, Ginny's in bed reading. He lies down on the bed with his clothes still on, and props himself up on his elbow. He stares at his wife's unpolished fingernails, their perfect pink half-moons. He thinks about all the pale skin under her fuzzy robe, warm and smooth, covered in tiny hairs. He feels possessive of that skin. It's always too covered up. If he could just run his hands across her shoulders, inside her elbows and her knees, over the shallow dimple at the top of her rump, he's certain that would quiet the Other Mark, would silence the constant *what what what*'s?

"Are you coming to bed?" She rests her hand on his shoulder for a too-brief moment.

"In a minute." He reaches under the covers and tugs at the tie of her robe. "Mark." She nudges his hand away. "This is the first time I've sat down all day."

The skin under her eyes appears bruised. She never gets enough sleep.

"Did you eat any dinner?" he asks.

"I had a bowl of soup in the doctors'

lounge."

"That's not a real dinner."

She shrugs. "I'd rather sleep than eat."

"You're not sleeping now."

On the cover of her book two figures stand together on a snowy street, their coats drawn around them.

"Did you have the meeting about Ashmina?" he asks. "What did they say?"

"It was —" She runs her hand over her face. "It's nothing you need to worry about."

One of the cats scratches at the door and he stands up to let him in. "Tell me."

"You haven't said anything about your talk."

Mark hesitates. "It was all right."

She turns off her light. "Was the dean there?"

Mark doesn't answer. The Other Mark's dirty face surfaces in his mind.

"And what's the story with the mold?" Ginny's eyes are closing. "It's just one room, right?"

"That they've found." He thinks of Livi's arm around Noah's waist. "It makes you wonder what else is slipping through the cracks at that school."

"If you're that concerned we can tour the private school again," she says.

He sighs. "They don't have football, and you know what Noah will say about that."

Ginny rolls over and her breathing slows. "I'm sure they'll figure it out," she murmurs.

"Yeah," he says flatly. He gets up and goes into the bathroom, closes the door without switching on the light.

In the dark bathroom, away from Ginny's skin, he feels tired and dull. Shaves of light sneak through the window blinds — his new neighbors, Cass and Amar, have left their porch light on again. Rain patters softly on the roof. He turns on the shower.

In the half-light the tiled shower is a pearly gray cave. He undresses. There's a funny feeling, down at the base of his spine. He stands, naked, leaning forward against the shower door. As he waits for the water to warm, the floor shakes; he tastes metal. Headlights sweep the window blinds, and there's the sound of an idling engine —

Outside his Jeep is running. He approaches the window. Someone sits inside the Jeep, the man. The Other Mark. His mouth is a thin dark line behind the rain-speckled windshield. His head twitches nervously back and forth. Mark backs away, nausea rising in his throat. He crouches down and grips the toilet's cold porcelain.

He tells himself to turn around. He needs to see everything there is to see.

He gets up, his hand clamped over his mouth. He moves to the window again. But the Jeep's headlights are off. Its engine is quiet, still. He stares hard at the front seat. There's no one there.

Ginny's phone buzzes and she grabs for it without opening her eyes. She blinks in its blue glow. It's not work, but a text from Edith.

I waited for you after our case last night. Where did you go?

Ginny's thumb hovers over the screen. The sound of the shower comes from the bathroom. She starts to type, stops, and then deletes. There's a flutter in her chest. She turns to Mark's empty side of the bed, and remembers how Edith appeared in that exact spot last night. What she looked like with her hair down, how she reached for Ginny. The shower switches off in the bathroom. Ginny sets her phone aside.

She wonders where Edith is right now. Her house is a yellow bungalow near the university. She's been there a few times. It's small, just a living room, kitchen, two bedrooms. It has old-fashioned radiators that click when the heat comes on. Ginny pictures Edith by the kitchen sink, wearing patterned pajama pants and a tank top; she wipes the counters with a dishcloth. Then she puts the cloth down and picks up her phone, expecting Ginny's reply.

Ginny presses her cheek into her pillow. She feels it beside her — her phone, the unanswered text. She feels Edith in her kitchen, her phone in her hand, waiting.

Mark opens the bathroom door a crack. He should wake Ginny. But instead he turns off the water, gets dressed, and walks unsteadily through the bedroom, past her sleeping form. In the hall he pauses at Noah's room, watches the rise and fall of his breathing under the covers, and shuts his door tight. Downstairs he pulls on a pair of hiking boots and a raincoat and goes outside. His Jeep sits in the driveway. He shakes his head and walks around it. He touches the hood. Cold. He peers in the front seat, the back-seat. Empty.

His neighbors' light is off now. The three houses in the cul-de-sac are in shadow. Above them the mountain rises up, dark and dense, menacing. The Other Mark is up there somewhere. He might even be watching him, right now, from the trees. Mark backs away from the forest; he goes into the house and locks himself inside.

SEVEN

Just after midnight an angry electronic wail wakes Cass from a deep, thirsty sleep. The dog noses open the door and sits, waiting, at her side of the bed. "Hi, Boo-Bear," she croaks. She swings her legs to the floor, and as she feels her way down the dark hallway her breasts grow taut with a tingling ache.

The baby's room smells like Burt's Bees diaper cream and spit-up. In her crib, Leah's face is a furious scrunch. Scooping her up, Cass settles into the rocking chair and props the baby to her breast. At the first pulling suck, a delicious relief spreads across her chest. Leah's tiny face is determined now.

"You're a hungry little teacup," Cass murmurs. "Yes you are, yes you are."

She rocks, Leah sucks. The sound machine goes *washhha washhha washhha* from the corner of the room, a simulacrum of a mother's heartbeat in the womb. The dog circles three times and settles himself on the floor.

Soon the rhythm of Leah's sucking slows. Then, as if sensing Cass's fingers hovering close, ready to unlatch her lips, she starts up again. Cass pushes the rocker back with her heels, stretches her bare toes long. She strokes Leah's patchy hair with one hand and draws the curtain open with the other.

A single humming streetlamp lights the circle of wet pavement outside. To the left is Mrs. Mehta's blue ranch with shrubs that crowd its small windows and a FOR SALE sign stuck in the front lawn. To the right, Mark and Ginny's split-level with new cedar shingles and a satiny black garage door. A couple of tennis balls glow from the grass out front, spots of neon in the darkness.

Most nights, when Cass is up with Leah, it feels like she's the only person awake in the world. There's something clandestine about it, as if the nighttime is an exotic locale only she's been granted access to. But tonight it just feels lonely. The note Robby wrote on her old paper tugs at her.

She remembers what it felt like to write that paper — when she was twenty and reading Plato and Aristotle and Longinus, Descartes and Kant and Hume in Philosophy 305. Robby was thinner, then, with hair more brown than gray. Surrounded by twenty copies of *Critique of Pure Reason,* splayed open on the table like orange tepees, he held his glasses aloft in his hand and danced them through the air to punctuate his sentences. Nothing in that impossibly dense book scared him. Sitting at the wooden seminar table, with Robby at its head, it felt possible to solve the biggest philosophical problems — the existence of the soul, the nature of beauty, the concept of free will — in the span of a ninety-minute class. Like they could be the ones to accomplish what every other philosopher had tried and failed to do — to discover the theory that would explain all theories, what Robby called a TOE, a Theory of Everything.

Leah's eyelashes flutter; she stops sucking, and then starts again. Cass pulls the curtain farther and she's startled to see that tonight she's not the only one awake. Her neighbor Mark sits inside his muddy Jeep.

When they first moved in, she saw Mark all the time. He loaned them things: a ladder, a rake. He brought over sacks of tomatoes from his garden. But she hasn't seen him in weeks. She assumed he was away on a research trip, like Amar.

He makes no move to get out of his car.

Its headlights make two yellow circles on his shiny garage door. How long has he been there? It feels like he's butting in on a private moment. Taking up space in her nighttime. Of course, he thinks he's alone. Maybe it's her who's interfering with his private moment, and when she thinks about it like that, staring at him through the window feels uncomfortably intimate.

Leah's almost asleep now. Her mouth moves halfheartedly. Cass pulls her upright, pats her back with a firm thump, and a series of small burps ripples through her body. Her eyes close. Her little puffs of breath make warm, wet patches on Cass's skin.

She's about to start the slow process of rising, walking to the crib, and laying Leah down, when the baby starts to wriggle. Cass stands and bounces her in her arms, trying to get another burp out. But Leah cries out, and lifts her head up with a strength Cass hasn't seen. She arches her back and her little body looks like it's curled the wrong way, like a backward C.

As her cries turn to open-mouthed wails, Cass's breasts tingle and spark. A tender spot below her diaphragm contracts. The dog wakes and lumbers up from the floor. She bounces Leah more energetically. She sits down and rocks her. But the baby only cries harder. It's painful to watch her pink, squeezed face; even her scalp is flushed. Cass swings her in her arms, which calms her for only a few seconds. She tries to nurse her, but Leah won't latch. She walks her around the house, slowly at first, and then faster. She thinks about what she ate and drank that could be bothering Leah. Only one cup of weak tea. She had two tomato slices on her sandwich at lunch — could that be it?

In her next circuit, she retrieves her phone from the bedroom and taps out an email to Amar while holding the baby over her shoulder and swaying side to side as if she's being buffeted by a windstorm.

Dear Amar,
   The baby won't go back to sleep. The baby won't go back to sleep! It's almost 1 A.M. I've been pacing the house for forty-five minutes. How long can a baby cry? An hour, two? THREE?

Love,
Cass

Every time she slows down, Leah starts back up. She can't do this all night — can she? Wet spots form in the cups of her nursing tank. Her arms are weary, her bare feet cold. At the bottom of her throat there's a panicky tightness.

Time passes; how much she's not sure. The baby's high-pitched cries surround her, corner her. She recalls Leah's birth, near the end, when she crouched in the birthing pool like a trapped animal. When the uneven waves of pain transformed into a wild, fiery hurt that gripped her hips and tailbone and wouldn't let go.

She paces through the nursery. Out the window, Mark's still there, but his Jeep is running now. Exhaust billows from its tailpipe. Cass thinks of setting the baby in her crib and leaving the room, if only to find out what will happen. She whispers in her ear, "It's sleepy time, Leah. Mommy's sleepy, Bear's sleepy, now it's time for Leah to go to sleep." She begins to lay her down, but before her hands reach the mattress the baby lets out a shriek like someone's poked her with a pin, and Cass scoops her up again.

The headlights of Mark's car sweep across the cul-de-sac. It pulls away.

Ten minutes later she's in her own car, wearing a jacket and rain boots over her pajamas. Leah's buckled into her car seat, still wailing, her arms flapping up and down. Cass backs her car out into the silent cul-de-sac. Behind her house the tall pines tremble in the wind.

She accelerates down the hill, and the noise of the road dampens — by a little — the sound of Leah's shrieks. They pass dark houses and storefronts, and as they drive through Woodland Park, eerie in the dark, the baby's cries finally begin to wind down like a toy that needs new batteries. Cass loosens her grip on the steering wheel; she unclenches her teeth. In the mirror attached to the backseat, she watches Leah's eyelids droop.

But at the stoplight her bawling starts again, and Cass takes the turn toward the highway. Driving ten miles over the speed limit, she passes three dark-windowed coffee huts, a farm stand surrounded by the shapes of pumpkins and gourds, and a pot shop with a glowing reader board that says TASTE OUR NEW EDIBLES.

As she nears the highway, a Jeep just like Mark's pulls out from the Shell station. It is him — she recognizes his mop of dark hair as she tails his car through the twisting on-ramp. She drives east around the base of the mountain, its jagged snowy top just visible in the light of the thin moon, and soon Leah's whimpers become halfhearted and

90

punctuated by stretches of silence. Mark's Jeep is a few cars ahead.

The baby's silent now. In the mirror, her face is tiny against the padded car seat. Her eyes flutter closed, and then snap open. Then closed again.

In her head Cass composes another email to Amar:

Dear Amar,

It's 1 A.M. and I'm driving down the highway, following our neighbor Mark. Well, not really. That sounds crazy. But, the baby's asleep.

Love,
Cass

At every exit she hesitates, intending to turn around, but she keeps going. She relishes the steady whine of the car's tires on the highway and the monotony of the scenery. Trees, mountain, road. Trees, mountain, road. She thinks of Robby, his eyes bright and his hands in the air, the warmth in his voice when he called on her in class, "What do you think, Cassandra?"

Red brake lights fill the darkness. The cars ahead slow. A sign flashes at the side of the road: RECK AHEAD.

She brakes and stares at the sign, confused

by the missing W, and Leah stirs. She realizes a second too late she's missed the only exit before the backup. While her side of the highway is full of cars, the westbound lanes are strangely empty. Rounding a bend, she sees why: a tractor-trailer, splayed across the highway, blocks traffic in both directions. The bumper of a crushed sedan sticks out from some brush at the roadside.

Another flashing sign informs her there's a DETOUR AHEAD.

As traffic slows to a crawl, Leah's eyes blink open and she whimpers. She starts to wail. Cars jostle for a place in the right-hand lane and Cass searches the road for a way out, any means to keep her speed up. But the line for the detour barely moves. The only car not in line is Mark's. He's in the left-hand lane. Where's he going? There's a space between the guardrails marked EMERGENCY VEHICLES ONLY and his Jeep makes a U-turn onto the westbound highway. As Leah's cries grow louder, Cass quickly changes lanes and follows him. She pulls through the emergency turnaround, her tires crunching over gravel, and accelerates to catch up.

But the turn is futile. The detour from the westbound side of the highway is being routed ahead of her, and she sees more red brake lights in the distance. She's going to be stalled on this highway with a screaming baby no matter what she does.

Mark's Jeep turns onto an exit ramp marked with a state forest sign. She hesitates for a second, and then jerks the steering wheel to follow him, hoping he knows another way back to Clearing. The road climbs toward the mountain. She winds through dense forest and fog appears. The baby's cries slow. Her little face turns peaceful again in the mirror.

But Cass soon regrets following Mark. They aren't driving closer to civilization, but farther away. She can't see more than a few yards in front of her. The fog is dense and deep and chalky white. Long, moss-covered tree limbs crowd the narrow road. She's got to turn around but there's no place to stop. She'll have to wait until the road forks, whenever that might be. She checks her phone — no cell service. Her teeth begin to chatter even though the heat's on.

She thinks of every news story she's read about people in Oregon driving down the wrong road and getting stranded, their cars broken down, stuck in mud or snow, buried by an avalanche of rock or ice, or swept away by a quick-rising flood. Broken Mountain is notorious; every weekend someone falls off of it or into it. She remembers the sign she saw at the trailhead near her house that warned her to BEWARE OF YOUR SURROUNDINGS. To watch out for cougars, bobcats, and bears.

Dear Amar,
    I'm lost in the woods. Off Exit 42. Somewhere on Broken Mountain. It's dark, it's cold, and there's nothing but trees.

Love,
Cass

She concentrates on the hazy road, alert for wild animals. She's not sure she's even following Mark anymore, although every so often she glimpses what she thinks is the outline of his car. Then she stops short — Mark's Jeep is suddenly right in front of her. He turns onto a dirt path toward the shape of something, a building of some sort, a cabin maybe. Her teeth chatter harder as she turns her car around as quickly and quietly as she can. It feels awful backing up into total darkness. She could be in the middle of outer space for as much as she can see in any direction, left, right, up, down.

Outside the driver-side window, a beam of light wobbles across a broken-down A-frame cabin with peeling yellow paint and a tangle of birds' nests in its eaves. It's Mark moving around with a flashlight. The car points in the right direction now, but Cass's foot hesitates above the gas pedal. The quivering light comes to rest on a patch of forest floor. Mark gets down on his knees. The light from a camping lantern grows around him.

Now he's up on his feet. He scurries back and forth from the A-frame to the circle of light. She waits for him to turn in the direction of her car, to notice her watching him through the window, but he doesn't. He carries the shapes of things in his arms. His head is down, focused on his task. He screws together tent poles and tamps them into the ground. He tugs blue fabric, shiny with moisture, over the top. He takes the lantern by its handle and stoops to crawl inside.

Then he pauses, turns, and squints toward the road. He lifts the lantern above his head. His face is filthy, streaked with mud. His clothes are torn and ragged.

He takes a step toward her car, the lantern still in his outstretched hand, and another step, and she panics, pressing her foot down hard on the gas. The car lunges forward, away from Mark, and Leah hiccups awake. Cass speeds down the mountain, through the tunnels of pine trees, through the thick fog. Leah's face is pink and annoyed in the mirror: she shrieks, hiccups, and shrieks again.

The road winds tightly to the right. Then the left, until they've nearly reached the bottom. *"Shhh, shhhh. Shhh, shhhh,"* Cass says, until her own skipping heartbeat slows.

The road straightens out, but the fog doesn't clear. It's descended down the mountain and into the valley. She turns onto the westbound highway and joins the traffic moving slowly through the murky air. She weaves around cars, and finally breaks through the haze. Leah's crying slows. Cass rounds the mountain, the fog a white cloud trailing behind her. Clearing is up ahead, a cluster of bright lights in a sea of dark green.

The image of Mark's dirty face surfaces in her mind. She shivers when she recalls his scurrying, jerky movements. She recognized something in his darting, wild eyes. Something she felt in the last minutes of Leah's birth, when she pushed her out of her body and it seemed like she would be split in two — that she feels when Leah wails and her cries seem to come from inside Cass's own skin.

EIGHT

From the living room window Ginny watches Mark and Noah drive off into the soupy fog that appeared overnight. It feels odd being at home by herself — it's such a rarity. Three turkeys emerge from the gloom. They strut across the cul-de-sac, and their beaks nudge the air. One of the cats is stalking them from the Mehtas' bushes. Ginny sets down her coffee and calls out the front door, "Pinky!" She walks outside and the turkeys scatter.

Ashmina's daughter comes out of her house and squints through the haze.

Ginny regrets coming outside now. Seeing Samara brings her back to the morning Ashmina died, to the fluorescent lights of the operating room and the beeping warnings of the monitors.

"Hi. I was trying to find our cat," Ginny says. Samara's taller than Ginny in her heeled boots. She always forgets how old

97

she is; still thinks of her as the teenager who babysat Noah a few times, on a rare Friday night when Ginny wasn't on call. But she must be twenty-four or twenty-five now.

"How's your dad?"

"He's all right." She keeps looking past Ginny, at a spot on her front lawn. But nothing's there. Just bright, wet grass.

"Everything okay?"

"Yeah." Samara walks toward her car, still staring at the same spot. "I've got to go —"

"You'll let us know if you need anything." She wants to say something more. Something like, I miss her too. But it doesn't feel right.

"Okay." Samara climbs into her car.

It occurs to Ginny that Samara's angry with her. She watches her drive away. Her face is serious behind the wheel of her small Honda. Ginny waves but Samara doesn't wave back.

Ginny stays on her front porch after she's gone and replays Ashmina's surgery in her mind again, step by step. She's done this hundreds of times, trying to figure out what she could have done differently. But she comes up with nothing, not a single thing.

She could talk to someone about it, a colleague, her husband. But she's out of the habit. The first time one of her patients died she tried to talk to Mark. To explain what it felt like, how the decisions she made in the OR would gnaw at her. The second-guessing followed her everywhere — work, home, during a hot shower, during sex. But it was too much for him. He started asking her obsessively about her day, and his worry weighed her down more than her own. So she stopped talking to him about it at all.

The turkeys have disappeared into the haze, and Pinky jumps up onto the porch and rubs his back against the front door. She lets him inside, picks up her coffee, and starts toward the stairs. She takes a sip from her mug, and the coffee tastes terrible. The ground shakes, like it does sometimes. She hears Noah's voice from the kitchen —

He must have left something behind. But that's not right. Mark and Noah drove away ten minutes ago, and they haven't come back. But that *is* Noah's voice. She steps into the kitchen. Her son stands in the middle of the room with a Wiffle ball in his hand. He rolls the ball across the counter and his feet slide on the tile as he runs to catch it before it falls off the other end.

"What are you doing back?" she asks, but he doesn't answer. As he grabs the ball, he bumps into another person, a woman who is small but solid-looking, with serious gray eyes. She wears a gray sweater exactly like the one that hangs, still wrapped in dry cleaner's plastic, in Ginny's closet. She is . . . Ginny's mind works hard to compute what she is. Her replica, her twin. Except she's softer, somehow, than the woman Ginny sees in the mirror every day. Her face is fuller, her hips rounder.

"Cereal or oatmeal?" the woman asks Noah. The fog is thick in the window behind her.

"Can I have toast with peanut butter?"

Ginny already knows what her twin will say: "Toast, coming right up for a hungry guy," because these are the words she spoke to Noah just a few minutes ago.

Noah sits down at the kitchen table and gulps his milk. Ginny's twin takes a plate from the cabinet and sets it down on the counter. She lays two pieces of bread in the toaster oven and presses the button to turn it on. She strokes Noah's hair as she crosses the kitchen to get the peanut butter from the pantry, and he tilts his head to smile at her with ruddy cheeks. The toaster oven beeps. Ginny's twin crunches a knife across the toasted bread, and the smell of peanut butter fills the room. When she sets the plate in front of Noah she kisses his forehead.

Like a video recording of her morning,

everything she and Noah said and did is the same. Almost the same. All the same things happen, but there's a feeling of warmth she doesn't recall. A sense of affection between her and her son that reminds her of when Noah was younger, when they would snuggle on the couch together and watch *Sesame Street.*

Ginny's twin retrieves her jacket from its hook. Noah brings his empty plate to the sink and searches the ground for his sneakers. She knows what happened next, just a few minutes ago, when it was her and Noah in the kitchen. Noah sidled up to her and she took his head in her hands, looked into his gray-blue eyes, and thought, It won't be long until you're taller than me, and I'll have to reach up to hug you. Then Mark's footsteps sounded on the stairs. He and Noah shrugged on their coats and Ginny pulled out her phone to check her clinic schedule. Mark said, "See you later" to her and "Grab your soccer bag" to Noah. She was focused on her phone when Mark hastily pressed his lips to her temple.

Now the woman, her twin, and Noah stand together by the coat hooks. She has Noah's head in her hands, just like Ginny did. "It won't be long until you're taller than me," she says. "And I'll have to reach up to hug you."

"That's because you're so short," Noah says, and they laugh.

Footsteps thump on the stairs. But it's not Mark who appears. It's Edith. Her hair is bright under the kitchen lights, her freckled face pink, like it's just been freshly washed. In her hand she holds a mug with one of Noah's baby pictures on it. She pauses at the sink to splash water into it, gestures to the window, and remarks on the fog.

Noah still can't find his sneakers. He leaves the kitchen, and now the two women are alone by the coat hooks. They wait for Noah to return. Edith says something in a low tone to Ginny's twin. They giggle and the laughter transforms her twin's face. It's her own short nose, her own slightly down-turned mouth, but enlivened and happy.

Her twin reaches for Edith's hair, trapped underneath her jacket, and pulls it free. They lean close to each other and their noses almost touch. They smell like soap and sugar and coffee. Light bounces off their shiny faces.

Noah reappears, sneakers on, and Edith opens the door to the garage. She steps out of sight and Noah follows. Ginny's twin is right behind. She's nearly through the door. Ginny reaches out, and gasps when she feels the slippery fabric of her twin's sleeve. The woman looks behind her, confused. She pulls her arm away and the material slips from Ginny's fingers. Her twin's eyes search the air for a moment. She smooths her sleeve. Then she snaps off the light.

A dense fog floats outside The Great Outdoors Store, a squat gray building near the entrance to the highway. Mark's driven by hundreds of times but has never been inside. He parks the Jeep, and makes his way through the mist. Inside is a dimly lit, cavernous warehouse. He thrusts his hands into his pockets as he follows a brown-carpeted aisle. The store is warm, especially for such a large space, and smells of citronella and WD-40. A simulated birdcall sounds out from somewhere. He doesn't know why he's here, not exactly. All he knows is the Other Mark's dirty face propelled him here.

Above his head tents hang like bulging stalactites, gray and dark green and camouflage. To his right, a wall of guns seems to stretch for miles. Rifles stand at attention, secured to the wall. Glossy handguns lay still in glass cases. A revolving carousel — the kind Mark has seen in diners, full of pies and cakes — contains a collection of hunting knives.

Although the parking lot was deserted, at least eight people mill around. Do they all work here? He keeps his head down and avoids eye contact with the salesperson leaning on the gun counter, a man with thick black eyebrows, who wears what appears to be an orange prison jumpsuit. Mark can feel the man's gaze. He shuffles into an aisle of camping lanterns and pretends to inspect one that's solar powered.

The next row is marked HOME SECURITY, and he steps in that direction. Door and window locks, alarms, security lights, and signs that say BEWARE OF DOG and SMILE, YOU ARE ON CAMERA fill the shelves. He picks up an emergency ladder, and it unfolds with a clatter that echoes across the store. He hurriedly tries to fold it back up, but the metal rungs slide out of his hands and unfold even farther.

A sign on the floor spells something out with crooked adhesive letters: ARE YOU PROTECTED? But Mark misreads it, thinking it says: ARE YOU A PROTECTOR? An image surfaces in his mind, of him and Ginny fifteen years ago, huddled against a tree, when they set out on a day hike in the Tongass National Forest, got lost, and spent a paralyzingly cold night cowering in the root system of an old-growth hemlock tree. They planned to walk for just a few hours and brought only a backpack with a couple of granola bars and a single bottle of water.

It was the one and only time he'd seen Ginny frightened beyond rational thought. She wanted to get up and move, to walk in some direction, any direction. But he knew they needed to stay put if they had any chance of finding their way back onto the trail at first light. It got darker and they slept in fits and starts, Ginny's head in his lap, her cheek pressed against his puffy coat. He slept with both his and her hands tucked inside his jacket, terrified that hers would become frostbitten, that she would lose a finger and her career as a surgeon would be over before it got started.

It was incredibly stupid to set out like that with no supplies, no in-case-of-emergency plan, and he has never again gone into the woods so ill-prepared. He's also never forgotten what it felt like, crouching together under the massive tree in the dark, its roots hard against their backs. Not just because of how scared they were. But because it's one of the few times in his life he felt Ginny truly needed him.

A man's voice interrupts his thoughts. "Are you interested in making your home more secure?" He appears beside Mark, bringing the sweet smell of pipe smoke with him. He wears jeans and a green Carhartt sweatshirt; a full brown beard covers his chin and cheeks. He holds out his hands for the ladder, dexterously folds it up, and sets it back on the shelf.

Mark returns his hands to his pockets.

"It's hard to know where to start," the man says. "The important thing is you're here."

"Right . . ." Mark sneaks a glance at the guy's beard — he couldn't grow a beard like that if he stopped shaving for a year.

"I'm Lee." The man holds out his hand for Mark to shake. "Why don't you start by telling me your concerns." He crosses his arms over his broad chest. "Whenever you're ready."

Mark hesitates. The Other Mark's wild-eyed face looms in his mind. He lowers his voice. "Have you ever had the feeling something bad is about to happen, but you're not sure what?"

"All the time." Lee says this like it's the most natural thing in the world.

"What did you do about it?"

"I got my butt in gear. I got prepared." Lee looks him in the eye. "Do you want to get prepared?"

"I want to keep my family safe."

Lee nods like this is the right answer, and this makes Mark feel good, like he made the right decision coming here.

Lee waves him toward the back of the store. "Follow me."

They walk through a thick hanging wall of sleeping bags that partitions the middle of the store. Behind a large sign that says survival gear, shelves contain packets of freeze-dried food, first-aid kits, fluorescent orange whistles, heavy-duty flashlights, compasses, and old-fashioned-looking emergency radios with metal dials. Also complicated water purifiers, sturdy folding shovels, silvery Mylar blankets, and ropes and cords of every color and length. Even rubber gas masks, radiation detectors, and jars of potassium iodide.

Lee holds up a yellow plastic suitcase. "We have some kits. They come in three sizes, for a family of two, four, or six. They have all your basics: food, water, light, shelter, survival tools, first aid, and toiletries for up to three days."

Mark picks up one of the suitcases and frowns at the label printed in at least eight different languages.

"But that's just the bare minimum." Lee surveys Mark. "And you're not the bare minimum kind of guy."

"I already have basic disaster supplies." He sets the suitcase down. "Everyone should."

"You want something more."

Mark thinks. "I want someplace I can take my family. Someplace secure."

"A safe room or a shelter."

"A shelter." Just the word makes Mark feel better, makes the image of the Other Mark recede from his mind. He has a feeling of sturdy walls protecting him and Ginny and Noah. The sense of their warm bodies close to his own.

"They aren't cheap. But peace of mind is worth the cash."

"How do you go about building something like that?" Now that the possibility has entered his mind, he's impatient for details.

"Two ways of doing it. Hire someone to build it —" Lee pulls a three-ring binder from a rack of catalogues nearby and opens to the first page. "But we're talking upwards of fifty thousand dollars for a professionally installed fallout shelter. Or build it yourself. A couple of companies, like Hard Top Structures" — he flips to the end of the binder — "have do-it-yourself models." He folds down the top corner of the page and hands the binder to Mark.

108

Mark's eyes land on random phrases:

Marine-grade access hatch.
48-inch diameter emergency escape tunnel.
Subterranean long-term food storage shelter.
War gas filtration system.

"I'll let you take a look at the options." Lee rubs his hand through his beard one more time before ambling toward the Fishing section.

"Thanks," Mark calls after him without raising his eyes from a brochure for Arizona Shelter Systems with the slogan BECAUSE SURVIVAL IS OUR HIGHEST PRIORITY. But on the back page he reads the small print: it will take thirty days just to schedule an estimate, and there's no mention of the cost. He flips to the bookmarked page for Hard Top Structures. The top sheet has a logo in the shape of a fortress, followed by a series of questions in bold black font:

Are YOU concerned about natural disasters, such as

Hurricanes, Tornadoes, Tsunamis?
Earthquakes, Forest fires, Floods, Landslides?
Or Invasions: Foreign, National, or Alien?
Or Nuclear War: Blasts and Fallout?

Or <u>Terrorist Attacks</u>, including Biological or Chemical?

On the next page a red inset presents "THE BUNKER ROOM. The Only Do-It-Yourself, Underground Blast-Resistant Bomb/Fallout System that Includes an Engineering Pressure Rating. By Hard Top Structures, The Only Name You Can Trust in Underground Shelter Design/Build." Then there's a big picture of what's included in the shelter kit, shown packed on a pallet, ready to be loaded onto a flatbed truck.

For the Series 100, measuring twelve by twenty feet inside, the cost is $9,500. But he isn't worried about the money. He's only concerned with how fast they can get the kit to him. He finds photocopies of the shelter's schematics, complete with materials list and project time line, tucked into the back of the binder. He strides to the counter, credit card in hand.

NINE

Samara inches her small car through the heavy white fog. She counts streets — the haze has obscured even the street signs — and slowly makes the turn for the Kells house. Inside, the house is unchanged since her last visit, empty and still. There's no reason for her to be here again so soon. But she can't be home right now. Yesterday she saw her mother hammering a FOR SALE sign into the front yard. Her mother who died a month ago. She can't figure it out, what she saw. What it was, what it means.

She reaches behind the living room drapes and feels for the cord. She pulls and they give way with a squeak. She sneezes. The streaked and cloudy windows make the backyard look like it's under water.

She locates a roll of paper towels and a bottle of orange-scented cleaner in the kitchen. She intends to give the living room windows a quick wipe down, for the sake of the pictures she needs to take for the MLS listing, but a strong odor of mildew comes from the enamel kitchen sink. She sprays it with the orange liquid and the *huuf* of the nozzle between her thumb and forefinger is so satisfying she quickly moves on to the speckled Formica countertops. The smell of chlorine and orange peel fills her nose.

There's no one she can talk to about what she saw. She imagines trying to tell her father about it, asking him if he's seen her too. Her mother, out in the front yard. She pictures the expression on his face.

She picks up the spray bottle and starts again. After a while the counters gain an indifferent sheen, but the sink looks exactly the same. She starts opening cabinets until she finds a bent fork, forgotten in a wax-papered drawer, and scrapes clean the rings of black around the faucet and its ancient sprayer. Her eyes migrate to the vinyl floor, to the dark, sticky outline where the fridge used to be.

She searches the house and finds a mop and bucket in the laundry room. She lugs them upstairs and closes the blinds in the kitchen. She turns up the thermostat, unbuttons her shirt, shivers, and steps out of her skirt. Wearing only a cotton camisole and underwear, she fills the bucket with hot water and some of the orange soap. She submerges the mop in the orange-tinted water and drags it across the floor. Over and over, until her muscles burn.

An hour later she has mopped the kitchen and bathroom floors and Windexed the aluminum-framed windows. She has shaken dust from all the blue curtains — miles and miles of blue curtains, all made from the same nubby material that holds an astonishing amount of dust. She has wiped down the wooden mantel and the bathroom sinks and the tops of the pastel-colored toilets.

She has sneezed and sneezed and sneezed. She has peeled and peeled and peeled her feet from the sticky vinyl floors. Her hands are red from the hot water, her underarms and the backs of her knees sweaty. But she keeps going from one thing to the next because it feels so good to do it. Better than being at home among all her mother's things, her clothes and her books and her dishes and her plants. Much better than being anywhere near the spot where she appeared, like magic, in the front yard.

She's up on a step stool in the dining room, attempting to wipe the dust from a chandelier with four white globes, when the doorbell rings. She jumps. She's forgotten she's only wearing her underclothes, and she never locked the front door.

She hears Shawn's deep voice. "Hello?"

It must be noon already; she asked him to come by to give her an estimate on refinishing the hardwood floors. "I'm here," she calls. "Lock that door, would you? I didn't mean to leave it open."

He walks toward her, grinning. His head is only a few inches shorter than the hallway ceiling. "Are you planning on showing the house in your underwear?" He takes off his hat, embroidered in red thread with the words HARRIS CONSTRUCTION.

She twists her hair away from her damp neck and lets it fall back down. "I started cleaning and I couldn't stop." She climbs down from the step stool.

She shows him where she pulled up the carpet, and the hardwood hidden underneath, and he takes measurements. His manner is relaxed, confident. She envies him, the assured way he goes through the world. She sees very little of the teenage boy she used to know. He's become something entirely different in the intervening years. He's grown up, while it feels like she's hardly changed at all. What difference is there between her and the girl that stood elbow to elbow with him at the Ping-Pong table in his basement? That girl had a mother and she doesn't. That's all.

"Can I show you something else?" She leads him through the house and into one of the bathrooms. The overhead fan whirs to life when she turns on the light. She points out some cracked tiles. "Can these be replaced?"

He frowns. "Whoever buys this place is probably going to rip all this out." He waves his hat across the room. "It's a shame. This house is pretty great as is."

"It is, right?" She reaches for one of the sparkly melamine pulls on the vanity.

"It takes time and money to find replacements for vintage tile like that." He runs his fingers over one of the cracked tiles. He shrugs. "You never know, you could find some buyers who appreciate pastel tile and tiny pink toilets." He laughs and the sound echoes in the small room.

Shawn pokes his head into rooms as they walk back to the kitchen. "It would be a fun project," he says. "Getting it to look like it did in 1959."

"Yeah . . ."

"You thinking of buying it?"

"Of course not."

"Why not?"

She hears her mother's voice in her head, and she uses her mother's words. "Moving back home was only temporary." Onward and upward, Sammy, to better things. "This job was only temporary."

"Oh yeah? What would you rather be doing?"

Her mind scrolls through the list of suggestions her mom has made over the years about her future: graduate degrees, certificate programs, internships abroad. But she answers him honestly. "I don't really know." She'll never hear another one of her mother's schemes for how she should live her life. This should feel like a relief, but it doesn't. It feels awful, and unfair.

"Oh, hell. I'm sorry." He puts his arms around her. "What else can I help with?" he asks in her ear.

She wipes her nose with the back of her hand. "There's one thing." She shows him the closet in the master bedroom, how its door rattles loosely off its track. He bows his head to step inside the closet, picks up the door easily, and snaps it into place. He pushes the door open and closed.

Then he grabs her and pulls her inside. "Don't be sad," he says. His breath is hot against her cheek.

"I've been cleaning — I'm all sweaty."

"You smell like oranges."

He presses her body against the closet wall

and kisses her, his hands on her hips. She hesitates, briefly, and then reaches her arms around his neck, pushes his hat from his head, and kisses him back.

Their breath grows loud and quick inside the small space. His fingers pull at the waistband of her underwear. She tugs his belt open, unzips his jeans. She kisses him harder, feels his teeth behind his lips. He picks her up, his hands under her bottom, and she wraps her legs around him. She gasps as he pushes himself inside her. There's the briefest second of pain and then they are moving against each other. She grips him tight with her thighs. Their bodies thump against the closet wall, and she stifles a laugh. And then everything feels like it's speeding up, and she loses track of where her body ends and his begins, and she doesn't care. She cries out, and a moment later he does too.

Her mind is blank when she retrieves her clothes from the kitchen. She picks up her shirt, pulls it on, and starts buttoning it. Her phone buzzes, and when she answers an unfamiliar, accented voice asks for Ashmina Mehta. "This is Samara Mehta, her daughter. How can I help?"

Shawn emerges from the bedroom, his cheeks flushed and his eyes sheepish. Samara holds up her hand. "One second," she mouths.

"Has your mother retired already?" the voice on the phone asks. "That's wonderful."

She turns away from Shawn, toward the front of the house. "What's this regarding?" Through the glass front door she watches the hazy shapes of a bike and child trailer move through the fog.

"I'm calling about the house in Sarapiquí."

"The what?"

Papers rustle in the background. "The one-bed, one-bath house — well, more of a cottage really — I sold your mom in Sarapiquí, Costa Rica."

"A house in Costa Rica." Samara laughs. "My mom didn't own a house in Costa Rica."

"Is your mother available?"

"There must be some mistake."

"Maybe you better put her on the phone."

"She had cancer. She died."

"Oh I'm so sorry." There's a long pause. Then, her voice slightly embarrassed, the woman tells Samara the lot adjacent to the home has come up for sale. "That's why I called," she says. "There are lovely forest views —"

Samara cuts her off, tells her she'll have to call her back. She hangs up the phone, her eyes still fixed on the fuzzy view of the road from the front door.

"Everything okay?" Shawn stands behind her.

"My mom bought a house in Costa Rica." The peaceful, blank feeling she had a few minutes ago has disappeared. "Why would she have done that?"

"An investment?"

She shakes her head. "If it was an investment I would have known about it."

"Maybe she was going to retire there?"

"No way." The image of her mother hammering a FOR SALE sign into the front lawn springs up in her mind. "She didn't have any plans to retire."

"People can surprise you. When my dad told me he was getting remarried I just laughed. Took him three times to convince me he wasn't joking."

"That's not the same thing."

He shrugs. "Seems pretty similar to me."

"Well, it isn't." She walks to the sliding door and closes it hard. "I have to go. I have an appointment downtown."

He's quiet for a minute. "Right. I guess I'll see you later."

He tucks in his shirt and gathers his tools.

She ought to say something to him, something nice. But she keeps thinking of her mom, out there in the yard. Her long brown braid swinging down her back.

"I'll call you," she says.

He puts his hat back on and nods.

She hears the rumble of his truck driving off into the fog as she switches off the lights and draws the curtains. With all the lamps off, the house feels old and dark. Her mother bought property in a foreign country. A place Samara's never been. A place her mother, as far as she knows, had never been. She retrieves the keys from the top of the stove. It's a puzzle, about the house in Costa Rica, and she waits for her mother's voice to offer up an explanation. But for once Ashmina's voice is silent. She can't think of a single thing her mom would say.

TEN

Mark calls to his son from a thicket of blackberry bushes at the top of the yard, where the edge of his property meets the state forest. He holds a can of yellow spray paint in one hand and a tape measure in the other. "Up here." Fog floats between the trees; the air is thick with the smell of pine needles and decomposing leaves.

Noah kicks soccer balls into a net on the lawn below, and his sandy-haired head bobs between the misty green fringe of some hemlocks. It's his third day off from school and he's cranky and bored. He climbs into the brush. "What are you doing?"

Mark points to the blackberry bushes. "This is where we're going to build something."

"What?"

"A shelter."

Noah frowns. "Like in World War II?"

"Sort of. More like an underground room

121

where we could go in an emergency."

"What kind of an emergency?"

Mark hands his son the end of the tape measure and points to a spot on the ground. "Stand right there." The tape measure crackles as he pulls it open. "Hold it tight."

"An emergency like you talked about at work? The mountain erupting?"

"I hope we never have to use it." Mark doesn't want to say any more than that. "But if we do, it's here. Ready to go." He walks backward, slowly because of the uneven ground, until he reaches twelve feet. He shakes the spray can and draws an X on the ground.

"We're going to build it ourselves?" Noah asks.

"Yup."

"How?"

Mark measures out twenty feet, and then another twelve. The sharp smell of the paint overpowers the pinesap and wet earth. "We're going to use a kit."

Noah looks interested now. Besides playing sports, he likes building things. K'nex and Lego sets, with complicated directions for constructing space stations or pirate ships.

"It'll be like one of your Lego sets, only a whole lot bigger." Mark draws the last X.

"Your turn." He gives Noah the can.

Noah draws shaky yellow lines connecting the X's over the pine needles, twigs, and bolete mushrooms that cover the ground. "Now what?"

Mark pulls the plans for the shelter from his pocket and shows them to Noah. The sheets are creased because every time he thinks of the Other Mark and his dirty, terrified face, he takes them out, unfolds them, and reads them again.

The top sheet has the fortress logo and the words

THE BUNKER ROOM
by Hard Top Structures
The answer to the "WHAT IF'S?" of modern life

A long list of hypothetical worst-case scenarios takes up the first page: tornadoes, hurricanes, tsunamis, earthquakes, forest fires, mudslides, dirty bombs, nuclear apocalypse. Mark flips past before Noah can read the list, and finds a black-and-white picture of a floor plan. A few smudged notations in his cramped handwriting dot the page. "See here," he points to the back wall of the structure on the piece of paper, and then to the corresponding line on the ground. "This part of the shelter will be completely underground. Only the front wall will be visible. The rest will be built into the slope of the yard."

"How are we going to get it underground?"

"We'll rent a backhoe."

"You know how to use a backhoe?" Noah is skeptical.

"I've used one once, when I helped with a watershed project in California." Well, he watched someone use it, anyway.

"Does Mom know?"

Mark waves the sheets of paper in the air to dismiss the question. "Don't worry about Mom." He points to the plans. "This is called a blast door, made of reinforced steel. Like the door to a bank vault."

He faces the spray-painted outline and makes a motion as if to open a door. "It'll be right here." He walks inside the outline, and it feels good. He imagines strong cinder block walls all around. A feeling of security and calm. "Come inside."

Noah follows his dad into the pretend shelter. "What'll it be made of?" he asks quietly. "Wood?"

"We'll build it with concrete and steel. It'll have a good air filter, too, to keep the air inside clean and safe." Mark turns the pages to show the pictures of the different components that will be delivered to their house: steel trusses and rebar, ventilation pipes of different sizes, concrete blocks.

Noah scratches his arm where it brushed up against a blackberry bramble. "Would we sleep in here?"

"Sure, if we needed to. There will be enough room for a few cots."

A misty rain starts to fall; it patters against the dead leaves on the ground.

"What else would we have inside?" Noah pulls up his hood and walks around the imaginary room.

"Whatever we want. Anything we think is important. Food and lots of water, enough for several days. A first-aid kit."

Noah thinks for a minute. "No TV, right? No PlayStation."

"Nope. There won't be electricity. We would be using flashlights and battery-operated lanterns."

"It would be just you, me, and Mom? And the cats —"

"Exactly. Just us. And the cats."

"Mom will want books. A bunch, because she's a fast reader."

Mark laughs. He takes off his glasses and wipes them with his shirtsleeve. "Good idea."

Noah is silent for a minute. "When are you going to tell her?"

"Soon."

Noah doesn't say anything.

"She may not be super thrilled with the idea," Mark admits. "She thinks I worry too much."

"But she won't notice," Noah says. "Not right away. Because she's so busy."

Mark nods. It's true. "But we can't do anything until we get these blackberry bushes cleared out." He steps outside the pretend door. "I'm going to Home Depot to buy a chainsaw. Want to come?"

"Can we pick Livi up on the way?"

"You think she'd want to come?"

"Yeah. She's by herself —"

Mark thinks for a minute. "What about Peter?"

"He's in Portland with his nana until we go back to school."

"Okay. Sure. Livi can come."

Samara waits until her father leaves the house to start searching. It doesn't take her long to discover something. She opens desk drawers in the room her mother used as her home office. Inside the first: a stack of index cards with Spanish sayings printed in her mother's handwriting. In the second: a

126

multicolored mountain of buttons. The third: a sheaf of papers including a bill of sale for a small house in Sarapiquí. The papers are dated over a year ago.

"Sarapiquí," Samara says out loud, and the unfamiliar syllables sound strange in the quiet room. She types the word into a search engine on the computer and images of the rainforest fill the screen: dark green leaves covered in droplets of rain, striped beetles with impossibly long antennae, tiny neon-green frogs. Birds the size of a cat or small dog. Monkeys with heart-shaped, tomato-red faces.

Sarapiquí, Wikipedia tells her, is a small town at the edge of the rainforest in the northern plains of Costa Rica. Birdwatchers travel there from all over the world to see great green macaws and sunbitterns and Muscovy ducks. In the winter in Sarapiquí, birds that have migrated from the United States and Canada — western tanagers and yellow warblers and Baltimore orioles — mingle with tropical birds like scarlet macaws and agami herons.

She tries to imagine her mom in Sarapiquí and pictures a woman with long, damp hair wearing a yellow dress. She climbs smooth stone steps with bare feet and raises a small pair of binoculars to her eyes. The woman is like her mother but also not like her mother. She is a younger, healthier version of her mother. She has bright eyes. Her skin is tan and smooth; there's no port scar underneath the straps of her dress.

Samara opens another drawer and finds a file folder containing an unpublished MLS listing for her parents' house.

LISTING:

1041 Pine Cone Court	$349,000
Clearing, OR	LS#: 54289
Bedrooms: 3	Square feet: 2,215
Bathrooms: 2.5	Year built: 1959
Garage size: 2	Taxes: $4,685/yr
Number of rooms: 8	Heating/cooling: Gas heat, no cooling
Lot description: Level	
View: Trees, obstructed valley	Basement: Partial; crawlspace
Schools: Niels Bohr Elementary Linus Pauling Middle School Clearing High School	
Notice: Owner is listing agent	

Enjoy the beauty of nature from your backyard. Don't miss this three-bedroom, 2.5-bath woodland retreat. Single-level living on a rare cul-de-sac perfect for families, retirees. Minutes to the university and downtown. Fireplace in the family room for cozy winter evenings. Backyard features drip irrigation and four raised garden beds. This well-maintained home won't last long. Presented by: Ashmina Mehta, Broken Mountain Realty.

She shakes her head at her mother's description of her own house. The picture she paints is appealing but also impersonal. *Anyone would love this house,* the ad seems to say. But not just anyone loved this house. Her mother loved this house. She loved it, but she was going to sell it. Why?

She goes into her parents' bedroom. It looks exactly the same. In the light from the window dust motes float through the air. Her mother's soft robe hangs from a hook on the closet door, and a tall stack of books sits on her bedside table, *The Cancer Survivor's Workbook, Planting an Edible Garden, Organize Your Life!, Superfoods for Cancer Prevention.*

She rests her hand on the footboard of the bed. Her father made the bed neatly this morning, pulling the cover smooth. It's hard to imagine her parents ever planning to leave this room.

The closet door whines when she opens it. She thumbs through a rainbow of suits and scarves and dresses, and her mother's sweet and earthy perfume fills her nose. Everything she touches is familiar — the geometric print dress her mom wore to her college graduation, the oversized blue button-down she used for gardening, a tasseled scarf she wrapped around her head when she lost her hair.

But when she reaches deeper into the closet she finds a neon-yellow jacket that looks like something a mountaineer would wear. Also, three pairs of nylon pants that zip off into shorts, tags dangling from their back pockets, and two floppy hats lined with mesh.

She reaches into the closet again, and when she finds another yellow jacket, identical to the first, she thinks her mom must have bought one for herself and the other for her dad. But no, they're both women's jackets; the only difference is their size. One is a large and the other a medium. Next to it is yet another jacket, exactly the same, only this one's a small. There are also six more pairs of nylon pants, one identical to the next, except in size.

Samara shakes her head. But then she understands. She kept buying them. That's why. The sicker she got, the smaller she became. Every time she shrunk a little more, she bought another size.

Samara turns to her father's sparser side of the closet. To his suits and shirts. Some old moth-eaten sweaters that ought to be thrown out. Her father who has never willingly gone on a hike in his life, who doesn't even like sitting out in the backyard. She's heard him complain the breeze ruffles the pages of his book, that he prefers to watch the birds through the kitchen window. She rifles through the stuff piled at the top of the closet, but finds only a bunch of T-shirts with paint spattered on them and a pair of ancient sneakers with no laces.

She thinks of the woman in the yellow dress, climbing stone stairs in the humid air of Sarapiquí. She tries hard to imagine her father beside this woman, but his image stays stubbornly fixed to the here and now. Her father does not live in a rainforest; he sits in his puffy chair in front of the television with his slippered feet propped on top of the coffee table. He mows the lawn in an old T-shirt and shorts. He organizes groceries in the kitchen pantry with NPR on in the background.

She takes the smallest of her mother's neon-yellow jackets from the closet and puts it on. She pulls on the next size, and then the next. She puts on the pants, too, until her body is muffled in slippery fabric. She finds other things with tags, and she puts these on too: a pair of thick-treaded sandals that smell like new rubber, an ugly reflective vest, an orange backpack with zippered pockets. Last she puts one of the mesh hats on top of her head.

She regards herself in the mirror. The hat sits crookedly, and she straightens it. She pulls the backpack's straps taut, and puts her hands on her hips. She looks like an explorer, an adventurer, a scout.

This plan of her mother's to change her life — it was so important she held on to it until the very end. She wants to ask her mom, Why was it so important? She wants to ask her, What was wrong with what you already had?

She walks to the kitchen, her body laden with all the gear, fabric hissing as she moves. She grabs a handful of trash bags and brings them back to her parents' room. She takes off the backpack and hat, balls them up, and pushes them into a bag. She removes the reflective vest and the coat and the jackets and presses them into the bag too. Then the pants and the sandals. Also a pair of birding binoculars she finds in a box under the bed and some books from the bedside table, *Pocket Guide to the Birds of Costa Rica* and *Into the Woods: Memoir of a Rainforest.* Anything that looks like it belongs to this version of her mother she doesn't know. That she doesn't want to know.

She's breathing hard by the time she's done. She pulls the trash bags through the house and they slide across the floor with a sound like *shhhh.* When she tugs them down the hazy front walk, the thin plastic catches on the concrete and tears, but she keeps going. She hauls them into her trunk and closes the lid, hard. She stands there for a second, her hand on the top of the car, droplets of rain pooling under her palm. Then she turns around and stares at the spot on the grass where she saw her mother. She wills her to appear again. Come out, she wants to say. Come out and explain yourself.

ELEVEN

Ginny fidgets in her chair in the Imaging waiting room. She picks up a magazine, a battered copy of *Good Housekeeping,* and puts it back down. She checks her phone, and stares at the receptionist and tries to gauge how long it's going to take. She picks up the magazine again, flips through its limp pages. But she doesn't see the print on the page. Other words and phrases rise up in her mind:

brain tumor
it could be benign, but
Noah, Mark
a side effect from her new beta-blockers
a mass
Noah, Noah, Noah

They finally call her name and an MRI tech wearing brown scrubs leads her to a small dressing room. He reads off his clipboard. "Mrs. McDonnell, we've got you scheduled for a head scan, is that correct?"

She frowns at being called Mrs. McDonnell, but stops herself from telling him she's the chief of surgery and signs more orders for MRIs than any other doctor in the hospital. He hands her a gown to change into and she takes it reluctantly. "Be sure to remove any metal on your person — jewelry, keys, etc." He consults her chart. "To confirm, you have no pacemaker, metal screws, or plates in your body?"

"No, nothing."

"You can put your valuables in that locker."

Once he's gone she pulls off her scrubs, her wedding band. She pushes her arms through the light-blue gown — the fabric has been washed so many times it's translucent. Did the tech tell her to wait in the room or come out when she's done? It's cold, and she hates standing here in the kind of gown her patients wear.

There's a knock at the door.

"Hold on." She's forgotten to secure her gown at the back. As she fumbles with the ties, the door opens, but instead of the tech in brown scrubs, it's Edith.

"Hi," she says. Her freckles are bright under the fluorescent lights.

"Um, hi?" Ginny grasps the back of her gown. Her cheeks burn. She remembers Edith and the other Ginny — her twin — pressed together, nose to nose, in her kitchen.

Edith steps into the room and closes the door behind her. Ginny is painfully aware of her polka-dot socks, a Christmas gift from Noah, and her washed-out underwear that sags in the back.

"What's going on with you?" Edith asks. The room is so small Edith's face is only inches from hers. Her breath smells sweet. "You've been acting weird."

Ginny lets go of the back of her gown long enough to reach for her pager. "What do you mean?" She reads an old page so she doesn't have to look Edith in the eye.

"I waited for you after our case the other night. I wanted to tell you about Dr. Pierce and this crazy patient from the coast. But you disappeared —"

"I had to deal with something."

"Okay." Edith pauses. "What are you getting scanned? Got a bum knee or something?"

"Something like that." Ginny tightens her grip on the back of her gown. "It's a head scan," she adds, and then wishes she hadn't.

"Oh."

She can see Edith wants to ask for more details.

"It's nothing serious."

"Have you ever had an MRI?"

"No."

"You're not going to like it."

"Why do you say that?"

"Because you have to lie there and let someone else be in charge."

Ginny can't help it. She laughs. "Wow. Tell me what you really think."

"Seriously. It's tight in there. Claustrophobic . . ."

Edith keeps talking, but Ginny is only half listening. She likes standing close to Edith in the small room. They've known each other for a long time. They've spent hundreds of hours looking at each other across the operating table. But they've never been this close.

Edith has an expectant expression on her face. She's said something and is waiting for a response.

"Sorry, repeat that?"

"I said Gary's a friend of mine."

"Who's Gary?"

"The MRI tech."

"Right."

"I can sit in the booth during the scan, if you want. Keep you company."

"Yeah, okay. Thanks."

"One more thing."

"What?"

"You don't know how to put on a hospital gown."

Ginny laughs. "I guess not."

"I'll tie you up the back." Edith puts her hands on Ginny's shoulders and turns her around. Her touch is light, but Ginny can feel the pads of her fingers through the gown's thin material. When Edith brushes the nape of her neck it feels like every tiny hair on her body has come alive.

"You're cold. Let's get you in there quick." Edith reaches for the last tie, but Ginny keeps her grip on the bottom of the gown. Her hand won't open. It can't. For a second it seems Edith will stop and leave the last tie loose. Then Edith closes her palm over Ginny's clenched hand. Her fingers are warm and firm. Ginny says a silent prayer Edith won't notice her underwear and lets go.

The MRI machine, a big white box with a long tube at its base, sits in the center of a starkly white room. Her whole body has to fit inside that narrow tube. Edith waves behind the glass in the observation room. The window is tinted, making her appear like she's in black-and-white.

Gary tells Ginny to hang the locker key from a little hook on the wall, and explains how the MRI will work. He says how long each scan will take, describes the loud beeping and rumbling noises she'll hear, and points out the bulb she can press if she starts to feel claustrophobic. The noise inside the machine is so loud, Gary says, they won't be able to hear her during the scans, even if she screams — that's the purpose of the bulb. But he'll talk to her through a speaker between scans. She has to be careful not to move, and she must keep her head in the same position the whole time. He says swallowing is fine but she should avoid blinking too much. Most people find it's best to keep their eyes closed.

He helps her onto the platform and puts a blanket over her legs. From the observation room, Edith smiles and puts her thumbs up. Gary straps a plastic helmet-shaped cage over Ginny's face. He hands her the bulb, and presses a button and her body glides slowly backward into the tube. She keeps her eyes open, and this is a mistake. She feels a rising panic as the outside room . . . slowly . . . disappears. Her breath is hot against the walls of the tube, only inches

139

from her face. It's like being trapped in a coffin. That's what Gary should have said: "It's going to feel like you're being shut inside a coffin." She closes her eyes tight.

Words and phrases intrude her thoughts:

tumor
Noah
got to buy new underwear
where else does Edith have freckles?
a mass in my brain
Noah

Her breath grows hotter, like there isn't enough air. She's not going to be able to do this. She wants to press the bulb. She can feel it in her hand — all she has to do is squeeze. Then she hears Edith's voice, loud and tinny, coming from a microphone somewhere behind her head. "You okay in there?" Edith asks.

"Yes," she says, trying to respond in a way that moves her face as little as possible.

"Try not to say too much, so the scans come out right. But if you need something, tell me. Or squeeze the bulb."

There's a pause, and it feels excruciatingly long. Ginny doesn't want to think about the walls of the tube pressing against her arms, or the lack of air, or the word *tumor,* so she

140

thinks about the feeling of Edith's fingers on the back of her neck.

Edith finally returns. "Gary's still getting the scan set up. That was a tough case the other night. You know, I looked him up afterwards. Robert Kells. He's some kind of famous philosopher. Did you know that? Wait — don't answer. Gary needs you to be really still." There's a short pause, and then Edith's voice is back. "What else can I talk about. The fog's been crazy, right? I just about drove my car into my neighbor's front porch this morning."

Edith's voice is calming. More than Gary's, that's for sure.

"Crazy weather makes me think of the time my house in Tennessee got flooded. Did I ever tell you about that? I bet you're wondering if the house had a big front porch, and if I sat out there drinking iced tea in a rocking chair." She laughs. "I did have rocking chairs on my porch, but I never had time to sit in them. I worked the whole time I was in nursing school. I lived with someone then, and we bought a house together and planned to —"

There's a pause. "We're ready for your first scan. It'll be three minutes. Get ready for some *loud* beeps." She says this like the beeps are something funny she can't wait

141

for Ginny to hear.

A rumble begins near her left ear. It sounds a lot like she's on an airplane, in a window seat, resting her head against the plane. A vibrating thrum. Then six throbbing gongs followed by six clacking beats. The sounds *are* kind of funny. As long as she doesn't think about how she's listening to them from inside a coffin.

The noises stop and Edith returns. "You're doing great — just stay as still as you can. Anyway, we bought the house together and we were going to fix it up. Then Lisa adopted this dog —"

Ginny blinks, and tells herself, Stop blinking. She knows Edith is gay, but Edith has never mentioned Lisa, or any other girlfriend.

"— and it all kind of went to hell. She spent all her time walking the dog and training the dog. We had started painting our bedroom this really pretty yellow, and it just stayed half-painted for months and months. I couldn't finish it because of my schedule. I mean, I couldn't paint the room when Lisa was sleeping in it." Edith laughs, but Ginny can hear the hurt in her voice.

"And then Lisa —" There's a click and Edith's voice disappears for a second. "We're ready for the second scan. Two minutes, okay?"

This time the beeping and clacking is on the right, and it sounds like her head is inside an eighties-style synthesizer. This strikes her as funny too. Her nose twitches and she has to concentrate to keep her face still.

"I like dogs, you know, but this dog Lisa got was a big, surly rottweiler." Edith's voice is back. "He never liked me. I would come home, dead tired from work and school, and he'd growl at me when I tried to sit on the couch next to Lisa. I mean, you want to be able to sit down on your own couch, you know? Wait — okay, this next one's three minutes."

After more electronic beats Edith returns. "So then Lisa goes off to a dog agility championship. I mean, what *is* that even? I think it's dogs competing over who can catch a Frisbee or jump over boxes . . . While she was gone, we had four inches of rain in two days and our backyard got flooded. The water was up to the back steps and I didn't know what to do. I ended up calling my dad and he drove all the way from Memphis to help me. That's a five-hour drive. I was so pissed at Lisa because she wouldn't come home early."

Edith sighs into the microphone, and then

there's a pause. "Gary's setting up the last two scans now."

Ginny tries not to move inside the tube.

"So where was I . . . Oh, the flood. So my dad helped me put sandbags up against the foundation of the house, to keep it dry. We basically spent the entire weekend covered in mud."

There's a click, and a long pause.

She wants to know what happened with Edith's flooded house. She wants to hear more about Lisa and the dog. She has a picture of Edith in her mind. She stands in a half-painted bedroom wearing a sundress. She's barefoot and her toes are painted bright red. Who would choose a rottweiler over Edith?

"We've got one more scan to go," Edith says.

The airplane thrumming returns in her left ear, and then the noises stop. She feels her body moving again, sliding out of the machine.

Back in the dressing room, away from Edith's voice, she pulls on her scrubs with a sense of dread about what the scans will show. She could duck into the MRI observation room and take a look herself — she doesn't need to wait for radiology. But she doesn't want to scroll through the images of her brain with Gary standing over her shoulder. She'll drive down the street to her office and read the scans on the hospital's internal server instead. At least then she can be alone with the bad news.

Outside the fog is dense and it smells like wet leaves. Rain mists her cheeks. She tells herself she'll feel better once she has all the facts, whether good or bad. She passes her new neighbor — she can never remember her name — who smiles and says hi as she moves slowly past, her hands on her large, pregnant belly.

It starts to rain harder. Edith stands at the end of the path under some large cedar trees, hazy with mist. She wears a bright blue jacket with a large hood that partially covers her face. "Hey," she says. "I brought your scans." She holds open her jacket; she's tucked the envelope inside.

"Thanks." Ginny's voice sounds leaden. She holds out her hand for the envelope, although now it's come to it, she doesn't want to look inside.

Edith keeps hold of the folder inside her jacket. "They'll get wet if we stay out here."

"My car's just there." Ginny motions a few yards away.

"Great," Edith says and walks that way.

They climb inside Ginny's Acura in the doctors' parking lot. The air inside the car is chilly but dry. It smells of leather and the dregs of her morning coffee, left behind in a paper cup.

As soon as they shut the heavy doors, the tapping of the rain becomes a muffled patter. Edith is very close. Her jacket crackles and sends flecks of water against the dashboard as she settles her tote bag on the floor of the car.

She hands the scans to Ginny. "There's nothing in there."

"Nothing at all?" Ginny tears open the envelope.

"See for yourself."

Ginny flips through the scans, quickly at first, and then slowly and deliberately. Edith's right. She feels intense relief. She reaches for the steering wheel, runs her fingers along its stitching. She's completely fine. Noah won't grow up without a mother. Her life will continue, just as it is.

She waits for a rush of gratitude for all the good, solid things in her life. But it doesn't come. Her life will continue just as it is. She'll go home and figure out what to make for dinner. She'll have a glass of wine, feed the cats, and talk with Mark about what to do if school is canceled next week.

She'll iron a shirt for clinic tomorrow.

Inside Edith's hood a few pieces of wet hair cling to her neck, dark red against her pink, freckled skin. "I'm not sure what you thought you'd find." She leans closer to look at the scans and blinks her translucent lashes. "There's nothing there but a healthy brain."

Ginny closes her eyes. She doesn't want her life to continue just as it is. Her life can't stay the same, because she's not the same. She's full of wanting when she wasn't before.

She hears Edith's soft breathing, and when she opens her eyes, Edith's face is full of . . . what? Concern? She doesn't want her concern. She pushes the hood away from Edith's face, sending droplets of water everywhere. Edith's hair is a frizzy tangle in her fingers. Her breath is humid and sweet. Ginny pulls her warm mouth over her own.

■ ■ ■ ■

II
COUNTERFACTUALS

■ ■ ■ ■

TWELVE

Today Leah doesn't want to be rocked or nursed. She hates her swing, slow or fast. Even when Cass bounces her in her arms, she's red-faced and angry. But if Cass stops bouncing, she turns from angry to enraged.

Cass moves through the house, jogging Leah in the air, and Bear follows close behind. She tries to put the baby down on different surfaces, and then quickly picks her back up again. A blanket on the floor, her car seat, a laundry basket full of clean towels. Leah doesn't like any of them. Cass paws through boxes, sweating, looking for something, anything that might help. A different-shaped binky? No. A vibrating bouncy chair? Good for about five minutes. A bath in her baby bathtub? Hates it.

Dear Amar,
    The baby's crying again. And you're not here. Remember when you said you

wanted a big family? And I said maybe? Well, Leah is it. No more. One and done.

Love,
Cass

She considers the car again. She could drive in circles around town, go past Robby's house — it's not that far away — and see if his car is in the driveway. But when she looks out the window the cul-de-sac has transformed overnight. A dense white fog covers everything — trees, houses, grass, road. She can't imagine driving through that again. She's so tired her eyes feel pasted open. She'd probably run off the road, like the car she saw last night on the side of the highway.

She continues her search. She's pulling a violet baby wrap from its bag when the doorbell rings. Leah stops crying. She looks around, a quizzical expression on her face. The silence opens up, cool and empty, better than anything. Bear doesn't even bark.

When Cass opens the door it's Noah, Mark and Ginny's kid, and she feels a ridiculous relief at seeing another person. An image flashes through her mind — of herself, handing Leah to Noah, and running, hard and fast, out the cul-de-sac and down the street.

But then another image replaces it — of Noah's dad, Mark, in the woods, a wild look in his eyes.

Bear wags his tail and tries to get past Cass.

"Hi." Noah looks at his sneakers. "I don't have my key."

"Oh no. You should come in," Cass quickly steps aside, and Bear crowds the doorway and licks Noah's hand.

"That's okay. I just wondered —"

Leah starts fussing and Cass bounces her, but the bouncing does nothing.

"Mrs. Bloom, who used to live here —" Noah pets Bear on the head. "She had a key, and I thought maybe it was still there."

Leah's cries grow shrill and Cass reaches, experimentally, to press the doorbell. At its buzz Leah stops. Again, she looks around. Again, her red face softens and her eyes turn quizzical.

Noah laughs. "Does your baby like the doorbell?"

"That's literally the only thing she likes today." Cass transfers Leah to her other shoulder and waves him inside, out of the fog. "We'll look for the key."

"It used to be above the cabinet in the kitchen," Noah says once they're inside.

"Why aren't you in school?"

"There's mold."

"Oh."

"And your parents are . . ."

Noah's face changes. "My mom's at work."

Cass wants to ask, Where's your dad? But she doesn't. She pulls a step stool from the pantry and tries to unfold it with one hand.

"I can hold her," Noah says. "I've held my cousins before."

"Why don't you sit," Cass says. "It's easier. She can be wriggly."

She settles Noah on the couch and he knows how to position his arms like a cradle, so she lays Leah in them. Leah looks up at his face and grimaces, but she doesn't cry. Bear settles on the floor at Noah's feet.

"What's her name?" Noah asks. "I think my dad . . ." He pauses. "I think he told me but I forget."

"Leah," she says. "If she starts crying, we'll ring the doorbell again, okay?"

Noah smiles.

She climbs up the step stool and feels around on the top of the cabinet. But when her fingers brush something cold and hard she hesitates. She looks down at Noah and the baby, and she can't do it. It's only 11:00 A.M. The day stretches out before her, long and loose, exactly the same as yesterday, punctuated only by bouts of crying, vigorous rocking, dirty diapers.

She climbs down. "Sorry, it's not there."

"That's okay." Noah holds Leah out for Cass to take her. "I'll just go hang out in my backyard until my mom comes home."

"No," Cass says quickly. She doesn't take the baby. "You should stay. Leah likes you. You can watch TV, or whatever you want —"

Noah eyes the door. "Are you sure?"

"Absolutely. Your mom would be upset if she knew you had no place to be."

"Yeah . . ."

"I'll get you something to eat. Are you okay holding her a little longer?"

Cass and Noah watch half a movie on the Disney Channel in blissful silence, the baby content in Noah's arms. When Leah gets hungry, Cass takes her upstairs to nurse, and leaves Noah with a PB&J and a glass of milk. She settles in the rocker and watches Leah's face, smoother and calmer now, her cheeks pink rather than red. At first she's hungry, determined, and then her eyelids begin to droop. Cass can't believe it, but her eyes close and stay closed, even when she lowers her to the crib, even when she tiptoes out of the room and down the hallway.

When she goes downstairs she brings the violet baby wrap with her. "Do you think you could help me figure this out?" she asks Noah. She tugs the wrap from its bag and it slithers to the floor. It's a long stretchy piece of fabric, the color of a spring crocus. Just fabric, no buckles or straps or snaps.

"What is it?"

"It's a baby carrier. Infants are supposed to like it."

Noah's eyes are on the TV. "Can I finish this episode? I've never seen this one. I only get to watch an hour of TV a day —"

"Oh, should we turn it off? What would your mom say?"

"No. She's not here. You're in charge."

She leaves it on and finds the instruction booklet for the carrier. There are six different wraps you can do with the fabric. She starts reading the directions for the "Easy Wrap," but soon her eyes grow heavy. She rests her head against the back of the couch, lets the booklet fall from her hand.

She wakes to a commercial break. Noah's show has ended. She stands up, looks around. The baby monitor is still quiet.

Noah picks up the booklet and pages through it.

Cass smooths the wrinkles from the wrap. "If I could figure this out," she says, "I could have my hands free, get some things done . . ."

"What do you want to get done? Maybe I could help."

Cass feels like hugging him. Will Leah be sweet like this when she's eleven years old?

"Some things you could help me with. Folding laundry, sweeping the floor. But other things I have to do for myself —"

"Like what?"

"Reading. Writing."

"What do you write?"

"I used to be a scholar. A philosopher." She thinks for a minute. "That's someone who figures out the meaning of things . . ."

"Like Plato and Socrates."

Cass smiles. "Exactly."

"So you're really smart. My mom's smart too. She saves people's lives."

"I know. She's an impressive person." Cass stretches the wrap between her two hands. "Your dad is too."

Noah nods and reads from the instructions. "It says fold the fabric in half, pull it like a belt across your stomach, and wrap the tails across your back and up and over your shoulders."

Cass threads the ends around her waist, crosses them over her shoulders, and ties them in a thick knot — then frowns at the twisted, sagging fabric hanging from her chest.

"I think you have to keep it all going one direction . . ." Noah shows her a picture of a smiling woman wrapping her pudgy baby.

Cass unwinds the fabric, tries again. This time she keeps the fabric smooth, front and back. But she's tied it too tight. Small as she is, Leah will never fit. Her next attempt is better, and she thinks it might actually work.

"What's next?" Noah asks.

"Now we wait for Leah to wake up, so we can try it out."

"Can I hang out a little longer? My mom doesn't get home until after six."

"You can stay as long as you want."

They watch the TV in silence for a few minutes. "With the baby asleep, I don't know what to do with myself," Cass says. She gets up and checks the dryer. She can't remember if she started a load of laundry yesterday or not.

She did. She gathers Leah's pajamas and burp cloths into a basket, brings them back to the couch, and she and Noah fold them, making little piles of her daughter's tiny, sweet-smelling clothes on top of the coffee table. Cass lets her mind wander as she folds, thinking of Robby and her old paper.

Thinking of the boxes full of books upstairs, and the ideas inside them.

When Leah wakes, not with screams but with happy babbles, Cass brings her downstairs and tries putting her in the wrap. She tucks her into the inner flap of fabric, and then the outer. Noah reads the next set of directions, and shows her another picture, and she lifts the loop around her waist up and over Leah's bottom and back. She leans forward and takes a few tentative steps. She walks around the living room until she's used to the feeling. It's amazing, really, to have her arms free. Bolstered to her chest, the baby's weight feels like nothing at all.

"She likes it," Noah says.

He's right. Leah settles her warm cheek against Cass's chest, and after a few minutes her body goes slack and her eyelids droop. Her little hand curls around the top of Cass's breast, as if to assure herself it won't go anywhere while she sleeps.

She stays tucked inside the wrap while Cass finishes folding the laundry, loads the dishwasher, and makes a pot of soup for her and Noah. And then it's nearly six o'clock. Noah will have to go home soon.

Cass has a thought. The fog is still thick outside, but it's not raining anymore. The street is dry. "I'm going to take Bear for a walk. Want to come?"

They walk through the cul-de-sac, under the towering pines cloaked in mist, and wind downhill through the neighborhood. Noah holds on to Bear's leash. The wrap hugs Leah tight. Cass has put her oversized rain jacket over it and Leah snuggles inside the layers of fabric. They stay on the sidewalks, wary of cars emerging out of the gloom, and squint in all directions when they cross the street. The way the fog has settled is uneven. It has depths and eddies, like a stream. It encircles houses and trees, giving the uncanny impression of roofs and treetops hovering in midair.

Cass counts the streets. Robby's house is only two more blocks away. They pass fifties-era ranches and cottage-style homes with bikes leaning against their front porches, an empty pocket park, a community garden overgrown with tall sunflower stalks and furry green sage. At the corner Bear lunges at some turkeys that strut out of the mist. But Noah keeps hold of the leash and laughs. Bear barks, and the turkeys scamper into the bushes.

When they get to Arden Street Cass slows. Something occurs to her. It's true that she didn't call Robby all summer. But he didn't call her either. He must have remembered the baby was due in August. Was he really so angry not to get in touch, even then?

His house is up ahead, a blue ranch with fog blanketing its front lawn. No lights on. "I'm just going to see if someone I know is home," she tells Noah. She shifts Leah in the wrap and walks to the front door.

She rings the doorbell. No answer. She peers into the windows but can't see past the blue curtains. She's been inside a few times, when she was Robby's research assistant her first year in graduate school. She remembers the walls lined with bookcases, the piles of papers on every surface — on the dining room table, on top of the piano. The house was full of stuff and yet it felt empty and still. One time she peeked into Robby's bedroom and his wife's things were still on top of the dresser, a brush, a paperback novel, some bobby pins in a dish.

Leah whimpers and Cass runs her hands over the wrap to warm her small body. She moves around the side of the house, along a moss-covered path, and tries to get a look inside the garage. It's empty. And clean. So clean it's almost as if no one lives here at all. There used to be a key under an urn — she used it a few times when she dropped off books Robby had requested from the library. She turns over some pots but finds nothing.

She goes back to the front door and rings the doorbell again, calls out, "Robby," but there's still no answer.

"Who lives here?" Noah asks.

"My advisor. He's a philosopher too."

"I don't think anyone's home." He points. All the other houses on the block have their recycling bins on the curb, but the sidewalk in front of Robby's house is empty. "Maybe he's away."

Cass hugs her jacket around Leah. It's getting dark, and the temperature has dropped. "It's late," she says. "Your mom will be wondering where you are." She turns back the way they came, up the hill, the murky early evening light disappearing behind the mountain, Leah heavier now than she was before.

THIRTEEN

Ginny snaps on the light in Mrs. Carlyle's hospital room and her residents file in after her. She's shorter than both of them but her voice fills up the cold, quiet room. This is exactly what she needs. The sight of the two of them, her chief resident, Patrice Dawson, and her intern, Seth Harper, in their white coats and scrubs. They look like they do every morning. Like nothing's happened and it's business as usual. She kissed Edith in her car yesterday — the memory is like a flash of color in a dark room. That's why she needs work. Cold, clearheaded, chlorine-scented work. The regimented routine of the surgical floor, the methodical pace of the OR. She needs to hear the sound of her own firm voice, and the expression on her residents' faces as they listen to what she has to say.

"Mrs. Carlyle is post-op day three. Status post, open cholecystectomy." She taps some keys on a computer that displays her gall-bladder patient's electronic records. "Positive flatus overnight. White count dropped from 14 to 12. We've started her on clears. And her Foley is out."

Mrs. Carlyle squints at Ginny. "I'm blind without my glasses." Her quavering voice is almost inaudible. She reaches out a thin arm to pull the wheeled bedside table closer and gropes along its surface. Her face is sallow; her lips and cheeks the same color.

Ginny hands her the glasses, and Mrs. Carlyle puts them on and adjusts them. "That's better." She lays her head back down.

"Dr. Harper, do we have cultures back?"

Her intern stands with his hands stuffed in his pockets. He appears confused by this basic question. "I don't know."

Normally she would tell him: Get it together, and while you're at it, take your hands out of your damn pockets. But instead she lets Dr. Dawson explain that they're waiting on results from the lab and will keep Mrs. Carlyle on broad-spectrum antibiotics for now. Ginny taught him how to speak this way, how to convey confidence and deference at the same time. Now if he could just teach Dr. Harper the same.

She moves closer to Mrs. Carlyle. The

whites of her eyes are yellow-tinged. "What about her bilirubin?"

"It's normal, 2.1," Dr. Harper says. "Which is weird, right? She still looks jaundiced."

"Is something wrong?" Mrs. Carlyle asks.

Ginny pulls out her stethoscope. "Everything's fine." She opens the top of Mrs. Carlyle's gown and listens to her heartbeat. "I'm going to have you sit up a bit —" She slips the stethoscope between the pillow and her patient's narrow, birdlike back.

She listens to her lungs and helps her lay back down. "Let's repeat the bilirubin. Something's not adding up."

Mrs. Carlyle grabs Ginny's hand and she can feel the bones in the woman's fingers. "Am I going to be all right?" Her brown eyes are large and shiny behind her glasses.

Ginny blinks, feels an unexpected wave of emotion. She pats her patient's hand.

"You're getting the very best care," Dr. Dawson says in a firm voice.

But Mrs. Carlyle holds Ginny's gaze. "Thank you, Dr. McDonnell," she whispers.

When Ginny speaks her voice is thick. "No thanks required." She moves to the sink, rolls up her sleeves, and turns on the hot water. She squeezes pink soap into her hands, rubs her palms together under the tap, and feels the steam from the hot water on her cheeks. She recalls the fogged windshield in her car yesterday. The weight of the MRI scans in her hands. The feeling of Edith's wet hair under her fingers and the melting softness of her lips. And she remembers the woman she saw in her kitchen, her doppelgänger, her twin, who stood nose to nose with Edith and smiled.

She wipes her face with a wet paper towel. When she moves back to the bed Dr. Harper gives her a curious look. She grabs a pair of blue latex gloves, size small, from a box by the door, and the gloves make a satisfying snap as she pulls them on. She makes sure her voice is steady. "I'm going to check under your dressings," she tells her patient.

She pulls the sheet down and opens the woman's hospital gown. Mrs. Carlyle shivers; goosebumps appear on her stomach. Layers of gauze, secured by surgical tape, cover the right subcostal incision. Ginny presses her fingers against the skin, pulling it taut, before tugging the white surgical tape loose. The skin around the incision is puckered and shiny with antibiotic ointment. The staples are clean. Ginny replaces the dressings and gown, and pulls the sheet back up. "Looks good."

Mrs. Carlyle nods, shivers again, and closes her eyes. Ginny reaches for the blanket at the foot of the bed but it's not there.

Dr. Dawson holds up his buzzing pager. "That's my Whipple."

"Go ahead. I want you to see Dr. Jory's approach. It's different from mine."

The door closes behind him, and Ginny looks under the bed for the blanket.

"What are you doing?" Dr. Harper points to the button to call the nurses' station. "I can call the nurse."

She finally finds the blanket under a chair and spreads it over her patient. "She looks cold."

Out in the hallway Ginny tells Dr. Harper to find the floor nurse. "Remind her that Mrs. Carlyle needs to be ambulatory today."

One of the internal medicine doctors types at the nurses' station computer, and once Dr. Harper's gone, Ginny taps him on the shoulder: "I have a question for you."

"Sure." He has a small cut on his chin that looks like it's from shaving.

"I saw a patient in clinic yesterday. A follow-up visit." She pauses for a second, distracted by the smear of blood on his chin. "She says she's been hearing and seeing things. There's no history of mental illness or substance abuse. The only medication she's taking is a beta-blocker. Inderal."

"Hearing and seeing things —"

"— that aren't there. Hallucinations."

"How long has she been on the blocker?"

"About a month."

"Vivid dreams are a common complaint. And every once in a while I get someone who says they were drinking coffee in their kitchen, or whatever, and suddenly their dead brother appeared. Or their dead dog. Some variation on that."

She lets out the breath she was holding. "No kidding."

Dr. Harper hovers behind her. "Which patient is this?"

"Don't worry about it."

The internist asks, "Why is she taking the Inderal?"

"High blood pressure."

"Is this Mrs. Wong we're talking about?" Dr. Harper asks.

"No, it isn't."

"Tell her to follow up with her PCP, and they can switch her to a different blocker," the internist says, "and that should solve the issue." He stands up from the computer. "Make sure she knows she shouldn't stop all at once. The dosage will need to be reduced gradually, and the side effects could continue for a week or two." He shrugs. "Better hallucinations than a heart attack."

"Right. Thanks." Of course there's a medical reason for what she saw. The world is made of concrete causes and effects. She motions for her intern to follow her down the hall. Then she turns back: "You've got a bit of blood on your chin." She grabs a tissue from a box on a nearby cart and hands it to the internist.

He frowns at her and takes the tissue. "Thanks."

As they walk down the hallway she reminds Dr. Harper about tests that need to be ordered, consults that need to be called. She feels better, more in control, more like herself. "I want you to keep a close eye on Mr. Morales's breathing," she tells him.

He pulls half a bagel out of his white coat pocket and takes a bite. "Got it," he says with his mouth full.

Her stomach rumbles. "Where did you get that?"

"They're in the doctors' lounge." He frowns when he sees her exasperated expression. "Did you want one?"

"No."

He stuffs the rest of the bagel into his mouth.

"If Mr. Morales's sats keep dropping, he'll need to be tubed. Have you done a chest tube yet?" A flash of red appears at the end of the hallway. Edith walks toward them, taking the shortcut to the OR through the surgical floor.

Ginny stops short, but there's nowhere to go. Dr. Harper's ahead of her now. "Hold up," she calls after him. "We need to go over the new electronic inventory system." She waves him behind the nurses' station and around the back of a tall glass cabinet.

"Really?" He looks confused.

"Come on." She's talking very fast, or maybe it just feels like she is. "Quickly now."

Dr. Harper glances behind him, as if sensing there's another reason for her sudden interest in proper protocol for the clean utility cabinet.

"Go ahead, take me through it," she prompts.

He starts jabbing at a touch-screen computer attached to the cabinet. There's only about four square feet of space and she can smell the raisin bagel on his breath. She hears Edith say hello to the floor nurse. They start talking about a patient on the sixth floor whose finger was bitten off by an alpaca. Edith laughs, soft and melodic.

As Dr. Harper narrates how he would

input two rolls of nonwoven elastic bandage, Ginny watches the little squares of Edith that show through the glass shelves of gauze, tape, and tubing: the freckles above the V-neck of her scrub top, the gold watch band that squeezes her wrist, the pale pink strip of scalp where she parts her hair. Looking at that pink skin, Ginny's face feels warm and her body soft. She remembers the invertebrate animals she studied in college, comb jellies, trumpet anemone, and orange cup coral. Their pulpy, transparent forms.

Dr. Harper waves the bar-code scanner through the air, trying to get it to work. He shakes it, blows on it.

Ginny takes it from him and shows him how it works. She hears Edith saying goodbye to the other nurse. "I suppose it's going to take some practice," Ginny says, her eyes on Edith, who's now walking away from the nurses' station.

She regrets hiding now. She ought to go say something. But once they are out from behind the cabinet, Edith's already halfway down the hallway. She turns the corner, her ponytail floating behind her like some kind of rare bird taking flight.

Ginny watches her go, and Dr. Harper watches her watching Edith. "Are we waiting for something?"

"No." She readjusts the stethoscope around her neck. "Let's go."

Fourteen

Standing in the lobby of the Department of Philosophy, inhaling its familiar scent of photocopier ink and soggy windowsills, Cass fights the feeling she doesn't belong here anymore. It's so strange to be back here with Leah. The last time she stood in this spot she was pregnant, and Leah was balled up inside her belly, instead of curled against her chest in the baby wrap. She walks past a line of bookcases displaying faculty publications, where the foreign translations of *Counterfactuals* take up a full shelf:

Contrafactuales

Гипотезы

反事实

Kontra

Αντιπαραδείγματα

Tényellentétes

Controfattuali

反事実

Alternatívy

Kontrafaktiska

Phản thực

It's oddly quiet as she weaves through the maze of cubicles and offices irregularly carved from the building's original 1950s floor plan. She pauses at her own cubicle, one of several brown boxes in the middle of a yellow-carpeted hallway. There are still papers on the desk, graded essays that students forgot to pick up. Tacked to the cubical wall is a postcard portrait of Anne Conway, and a snapshot of Amar and Bear on the porch of her old student apartment.

She keeps going. All the faculty office doors she passes are shut. At the end of the hallway metal heaters blast warm air. With Leah's body pressed against her own, she feels sweat collecting under her arms and between her breasts. She takes off her coat and shifts Leah's weight inside the wrap.

She thinks of the relative cool of Robby's office. He always kept his window cracked, even on icy January days. When she reaches Office 707, she wants to knock, to wait for Robby's answer. The room's dark — and tidier than she's ever seen. She turns to the adjacent office, belonging to Robby's secretary, Mrs. Trevy, but it's dark too.

She returns to the lobby. The big clock on the wall above the bookcases says 9:55. Almost ten on a Thursday. That's why it's so quiet. Everyone's in the weekly department meeting. In just a few seconds they'll all stream out of the conference room across the lobby. She turns quickly toward the graduate student lounge because she's not ready to say hello to everyone all at once.

But then the conference room doors open with a shrill creak and Leah startles. She chokes and sputters, and spits up curdled milk down Cass's chest.

As people spill from the conference room, she pulls a blanket from the diaper bag and, wiping furiously, turns away from the crowd even as she sees recognition in two or three of the approaching faces. Leah's sputters turn to *ah, ah, ah*s, and Cass hurries to the women's bathroom.

The heavy bathroom door is on a spring and it closes . . . so . . . very . . . slowly.

Inside the yellow-and-white-tiled bathroom, she pushes her hair away from her sweaty face. Pink powdered soap has made little messes on top of the sinks. Quiet drips escape from the faucets. She searches the diaper bag for a change of clothes while Leah cranes her neck to gaze at the globe-shaped lights above the streaked mirrors.

After Cass has pulled Leah from the wrap, she lays her down on the green vinyl sofa in the corner, positioning her own body so Leah won't roll off. Leah's eyes find the lights again. Cass peels off her damp clothes and changes her diaper. "I only have one change of clothes for you, teacup, so please" — she holds her hands together in prayer — "please keep these clean." Leah wiggles in her diaper on the slippery couch and watches Cass's face.

Once Leah's dressed, Cass uses wipes to clean her own sour-smelling shirt. She's waving the baby wrap through the air, in an attempt to dry it out, when Ellen Porchet bumps into the bathroom with two over-stuffed tote bags. Cass hurries to gather up the pile of dirty wipes, but the linguistics professor, who wears a fluttering, asymmetrical shirt and woolly gray clogs, doesn't look in her direction. She heads straight for a toilet stall. The door shuts; there's a sigh and a long stream of urine.

When Professor Porchet comes out of the stall, she sets her totes on the ground, and turns on a faucet. Her dangling earrings wobble as she washes her hands. She finally nods in Cass's direction. "I'm glad I ran into you." She dries her hands, taking no notice of Leah. "My research fellow has won a lectureship in Germany, which is great for him but terrible timing for me. Could you help me out? It's just ten hours a week."

"I would love to, but —" Cass clears her throat. She's spoken to practically no one in days, aside from Noah, and her voice sounds slow and thick.

Professor Porchet interrupts her before she can begin again. "Because I'm in the middle of correcting the galleys for my new book on morphemes, and I just know they're going to stick me with some first-year graduate student who'll be no help at all." She scowls and digs in one of her totes, finds a stick of Blistex, and rubs it over her lips.

"I'm not actually enrolled this term." Cass stands up and holds Leah with one arm and stuffs the wipes into the trash can with the other.

Professor Porchet seems to see Leah for the first time. "You've quit the Ph.D. program?"

Leah wriggles in Cass's arms and she turns her around so she can stare at the lights. "I didn't say that. I plan to come back."

"Good."

"I'm available next year. If you'll need an assistant then —"

"Possibly." She drops the Blistex back into her bag. "What's the name of your friend? He sat next to you in class. Andrew something —"

"Andrew Morrison."

"I thought his paper on split ergativity was solid . . . although not as good as yours." She fluffs her hair in the mirror and her earrings swing. "I'll ask him if he's interested in the assistantship."

She eyes the door to the hallway and Cass moves aside to let her pass.

"Don't take too much time off." She wags her finger at Cass before she goes. "I had a graduate student a few years ago. Very talented. Brilliant even. She took a year off to have a baby. Or maybe it was to take care of her sick baby . . ." She tilts her head to one side. "Doesn't matter. The point is, the year turned into two years. And then I never heard from her again."

Once she's gone Cass winds the wrap around her body and tells herself she doesn't care what Professor Porchet thinks. She's not her mentor or her friend. What she has to say doesn't matter. She remembers Robby's words in her head: I expect great things from you, Cassandra.

She pulls the fabric over her left shoulder, and over her right shoulder, and ties it around the back. This time she manages to get the tautness just right. She tucks Leah in, puts her coat on so it'll cover the wet spot on the wrap, and shoulders the diaper bag. Then she walks back to Robby's secretary's office. This time the light is on.

"Cass. And your baby. A girl?" Mrs. Trevy leans across her desk and smiles.

"Yes. Leah." Cass steps inside. Unlike

Robby's office, Mrs. Trevy's is full of plants and tidy piles of paper. No books.

"Listen, I can't get ahold of Robby," Cass says. "He's not answering his phone. They say he's on leave —"

Mrs. Trevy's smile disappears. "I left you a message months ago. You didn't get it?"

"We moved. I had Leah." It's hot under her coat, with Leah pressed close. "I didn't."

Mrs. Trevy gestures to Robby's office. "I found him on the floor." There's panic in her gold-flecked eyes, and behind that, something else. Anger maybe. "I thought he was dead."

"What was wrong with him —"

"He drank himself into a coma."

"Oh my god." She covers Leah's head with her hands. "When was this?" She has an awful feeling she knows what Mrs. Trevy is going to say.

"The end of spring semester. You saw him that day, I think —"

"Where is he now?"

"His sons moved him out of his house. He's living with one of them now. Ben." She turns her gold rings around on her fingers. "He's been in and out of the hospital all summer."

"That's why his house is empty."

"I think they're planning to sell it."

Cass pulls off her jacket, not caring about her stained shirt. Leah presses her face against Cass's chest and squashes her nose; her mouth makes little wet circles against Cass's skin. "She's hungry," Cass says. "She's always hungry —"

"Sit. I'll shut the door."

Cass sets the diaper bag on the floor, sits down in a chair. She loosens Leah, unhooks her bra, and covers the baby's head with the wrap. "I can't believe I didn't know about Robby."

Mrs. Trevy sighs. "He's never been what other people want him to be. But at least when Lillian was alive he took better care of himself."

"He never talks about her."

"He's heartbroken, even all these years later."

"I only know two things about her — that she played piano, and read all his drafts."

"She did. Every word. That's probably why he can't seem to finish that second book." She pauses. "But the last few years something's brought him out of his funk."

"What?"

"You."

Cass peeks at Leah under the wrap. Her sucking has slowed.

"He thinks you're going to be the next

181

him," Mrs. Trevy says. "But do you want to be?"

"I thought I did." Cass unlatches Leah, pulls her from the wrap, and lays her against her chest. "But now I don't know."

Mrs. Trevy gets up from her desk. "May I?"

"Sure." Cass pulls a cloth from the diaper bag.

Mrs. Trevy takes the baby in her arms and lays the cloth over her shoulder, like she's done it many times before. She pats Leah firmly on the back. "She's beautiful."

"She's small."

"Waste of time to worry about stuff like that," Mrs. Trevy says. Then her face softens. "It's not easy." She strokes Leah's patchy hair. "I remember."

"I love her. But everything's different since she was born."

"I remember that part. It doesn't last forever. Well," she laughs. "Maybe it does." She hands Leah back.

The sound of rain comes from the window, pinpricks of water against the glass.

"Mrs. Trevy, were you the one who sent me my old paper?" Cass asks.

"Oh, yes. I did."

Leah kicks at Cass's hip. "Why?"

"After you met with Robby . . . he told

me he needed to get something to you, that it was important. He said he'd leave it on his desk." She sits back down. "I left before he did that day, and when I arrived the next morning —"

"That's when you found him."

"I started tidying up his office, after the ambulance took him away, after I phoned his kids. I don't know why. I just needed something to do. I knew he was in bad shape, but I never thought . . ." She presses her hands together on top of the desk.

"Then I remembered what he said about leaving something for you," she says. "I found the folder under a pile of sophomore exams."

Leah wiggles in Cass's arms, and she tucks her back into the wrap. "He wrote something on that paper — a note." She *shh shh*s in Leah's ear. "But the last page is missing."

"That doesn't surprise me. His office was always such a spectacular mess. I've finally got it into some kind of order —"

"I've been trying to find the lost page."

"Go and see him. He's in Room 507 at the hospital. Ask him what he wrote. Isn't that better than reading it?"

She's right of course.

"I should have tried calling you again," Mrs. Trevy says. "I knew it wasn't like you to not call back."

"It's my fault. I've been . . . I don't know. Preoccupied. Not myself."

"You've been taking care of your baby, and that's what you should be doing."

"I don't know if Robby would agree —"

"He would." Her smile is rueful. "Even if he wouldn't admit it. I know he would."

FIFTEEN

Ginny closes herself in a bathroom stall, sits down on the toilet seat, and rests her head in her hands. It's the first time she's sat down in fifteen hours. Her arms ache from reaching over the operating table; her throat is bone dry. Her lap chole case started late because of an OR scheduling delay, and then she discovered her patient's belly was full of scar tissue. She doesn't like the boundary lines she got around the mesenteric vein, but it was the best she could do without jeopardizing the pancreas. Not good enough.

She hasn't seen Edith again, and what happened in her car yesterday feels far away. She rubs her hands over her face. She hasn't eaten all day. It's been several days, really, since she ate a real meal. Her stomach feels concave.

She stays inside the bathroom stall and pulls her phone from her pocket. She dials her husband, and when he answers she asks to talk to Noah.

"He's already asleep," Mark says. "He was so beat."

"Damn. All right." She feels a surge of disappointment that she can't hear her son's voice. That it was Mark who tucked him in and turned on his night-light, not her. "How did his game go?"

"He did great. They won. Listen, I was working outside and found a leak. The water company can't come to fix it until morning, so you better shower before you come home."

"Really?" She groans and the sound echoes against the tile walls. "All right. I'll be home in a few hours."

After she hangs up she pulls her scrub shirt away from her chest and smells sweat and antiseptic. She doesn't have any soap or shampoo at work, so all she has to look forward to after rounds is a lukewarm rinse in the moldy hospital locker room.

At rounds her residents are beat down too. Blood splatter dots the hem of Dr. Dawson's scrub pants. There's a dent in Dr. Harper's hair from the elastic band of his scrub cap. She lets them do the talking as they wind through their patients' rooms. She asks only a few questions.

A floor nurse waves at her chief resident from down the hall. "Your patient's blood pressure isn't looking good."

"My Whipple?"

"Go ahead," Ginny says. "We're nearly done anyway."

"What about the chest tube for Mr. Morales?" Dr. Dawson asks.

Ginny rubs her forehead. "We'll do it. Another hour isn't going to make a difference."

He hurries away.

"We'll check Professor Kells's vitals again," she tells Dr. Harper, "do the tube, and then go home."

Dr. Harper takes an energy bar from his pocket. "Sorry," he says with his mouth full. "I haven't eaten . . . I don't know, since this morning I think."

When they get to Professor Kells's room, he's still chewing. She waits. "Do you see me eating right now?"

"No . . ." He hesitates. "But maybe you should be."

She stares at him.

"When was the last time you ate anything? You look like you're wasting away."

"Dr. Harper, I'm not your friend."

"Sorry?"

"We aren't friends. I'm your boss."

"I just thought —" He stands up straighter. "I'm sorry. It's none of my business. I shouldn't have said anything." He throws the half-eaten energy bar into a trash can. "I'm going to stop talking now."

"Good idea."

In Professor Kells's room his sons stand by the window talking. One wears jeans and a gray checked shirt and the other a loose-fitting suit. Both have thick hair like their dad, and both are tall, over six feet. She glances at her patient's long legs underneath the sheet. She's never seen him upright, but he must be a tall man too.

She says a quick hello and checks the bandages covering the incisions in Professor Kells's abdomen. His eyes are sunken slits below his bushy eyebrows; his lips are colorless around his endotracheal tube. But his vitals are good — strong for his age and what his body's been through over the last four days. He doesn't have the look of someone who's about to die. His cheeks have some color in them. His body still has bulk in the bed. Again he reminds her of her father. Something about the shape of his head, and his body's stubborn will to live.

The two sons are arguing about something. The one wearing jeans addresses

Ginny: "When are we going to see my dad's doctor?"

"That's me."

The man in the suit reaches out his hand. "Hello again. I'm Ben. We met the other day. This is my brother, Greg."

"Because there have been ten different people coming in and out of this room," Greg says, "we're getting confused —"

"Don't mind Greg," Ben says to Ginny. "Hospitals stress him out."

"Was there a specific question you had about your father's care?" Ginny waits while Greg walks over to his dad's bed.

"I want to know how my dad's doing."

"I think he's doing surprisingly well given his age and history of liver disease. His vitals are good, but we need to get his bladder pressure normalized."

Greg gestures at his father's gauze-covered belly. "He doesn't look like he's doing well." His face contorts. "I mean, good god." He reaches out, tentatively, and squeezes his father's limp hand.

"When will you take that out?" Ben gestures to his dad's endotracheal tube.

"If he does well overnight, we'll extubate him in the morning," Ginny says.

Greg pulls a chair close to his dad. "He wasn't around a lot when we were growing

189

up. We've seen him even less since our mom died," he says. "His work was always more important. Now he's finally taking a break. He says he wants to get to know us." He turns to Ginny. "But you don't really know what's going to happen to him. Do you?"

There's a pause, in which she would normally repeat the speech she's made hundreds of times, about the challenges of making an accurate prognosis when there are so many variables involved. About the strength of the care provided at University Hospital. But instead she looks at Professor Kells the way his son sees him, at his sunken eyes and pallid skin, at the needles and tubes that snake from his nose and arms.

That's what she saw when it was her own father lying there. She hated the thin hospital gown that barely covered his broad chest. She hated the nurses and doctors standing over him, checking and prodding and poking, taking up every minute of whatever life he had left. She tries not to think about her dad at work . . . or her husband, or her son. She keeps things separate, home and family on the one side, and work on the other. But tonight she can't seem to help mixing up the two.

The spell is broken when Dr. Harper starts talking. He makes the speech about the difficulty of prognosis, using all the words and phrases she tends to use. His tone is compassionate but matter-of-fact. He gets to the point quickly and doesn't diverge into further conversation. He does a good job. She has taught him something after all.

Once Dr. Harper's done, Greg nods and sits down heavily in a chair. Ben thanks them, and she motions to her intern to open the door. "We'll be monitoring your father's intra-abdominal pressure closely overnight," she says. "Good night."

Outside she tells Dr. Harper to set up Mr. Morales's chest tube, and then ducks into the doctors' lounge, where it smells like popcorn and dirty socks. One of the anesthesiologists snores on the sofa, in spite of CNN blaring from the wall-mounted TV. She opens the fridge and stares at the tiny bottles of water and soda, and the brown paper sack labeled THIS IS VANESSA'S DINNER, NOT YOURS. She takes a Coke and drinks the whole thing. She reaches for one of the bananas on the counter, but the hunger she felt an hour ago has evaporated. She puts it back.

She's been letting things get to her today. She feels . . . thin-skinned somehow. Not herself. She throws the soda bottle into the recycling. It's because of what happened with Edith. She's got to stop thinking about it. She'll talk to her, tell her the kiss was a mistake. She grabs another Coke and drinks it as she walks to Mr. Morales's room. At the nurses' station she pauses. "Can you call down to the OR and find out if Edith is still there. I need her to stop by Room 509 on her way out."

SIXTEEN

Dr. Harper has everything laid out at Mr. Morales's bedside: topical anesthetic, a chest tube, Kelly clamps, and a needle driver. In his gown and mask, his shoulders are set; his eyes are dark and close together under his puffy cap.

Mr. Morales lies back on his pillows. His worried eyes shift from Ginny to Dr. Harper.

"You've explained the procedure?" Ginny puts on a pair of gloves. Dr. Harper nods.

She leans close to Mr. Morales's ear, because he's a little deaf. "There's going to be some pressure right before we place the tube. We'll be as quick as we can."

"So I'm going to inject one percent lidocaine with epi" — Dr. Harper holds up a syringe — "with a 22-gauge needle." His voice sounds cottony from behind his mask.

"Yes."

"At the fourth intercostal space."

"Correct."

Dr. Harper pushes the needle in between the patient's ribs and Mr. Morales winces. He presses the needle's plunger and checks his watch. He picks up the scalpel. "I make a three-centimeter cut." He bends down and makes the small incision, and Ginny hands him some gauze. He holds it over the incision and picks up the Kelly clamps. Sweat shines on his brow.

"Take your time. Visualize the action before you perform it."

"I use the clamps to punch through the intercostal muscles and into the pleural cavity. Then I spread the clamps."

"Now, Matt —" She wants to warn him not to spread the clamps too fast, but before she can finish her sentence he's thrusting the clamps through the cut. He spreads them open and out, all in one swift motion, and Mr. Morales's body recoils. A spurt of pleural fluid gushes from the hole as the patient swears in Spanish and thumps his arms against the bed.

"Oh shit," Dr. Harper says.

"Don't stop now. Keep going." She holds Mr. Morales's arms steady. "Sweep with your finger to make sure the lung isn't in the way, and then get the tube in." She leans over the patient. "That was the worst part," she says loudly.

Dr. Harper sticks his finger into the incision and squints at the ceiling. He inches the tube through and hooks it up to the Pleurevac. "Whew." He wipes his forehead with the back of his gloved hand and grins. Ginny feels fluid seeping into her scrub pants. She's soaked from the waist down.

She leaves Dr. Harper to deal with the cleanup and grabs a handful of paper towels on her way out. In the hallway, she bends down to wipe off her clogs. Fluid has dripped into her left sock and the wet cotton sticks to her heel. She is so done with this day. But the thought of home doesn't improve her mood. There's nothing to look forward to there. Noah's already asleep, and Mark will be sitting in front of the TV. She'll eat leftovers in the kitchen by herself and go to bed.

When she straightens up Edith's right in front of her. Her freckles are bright under the fluorescent lights. "You wanted to see me?"

Ginny's empty stomach flips. "Yeah, I wanted to tell you —" But she can't bring herself to say what she intended.

"What happened to you?"

"I took a bath in pleural fluid." A trickle runs down her arm and she wipes it with the paper towels. "Just a little something extra to end my disaster of a day."

"That bad?"

"Listen, thanks for keeping me company" — Ginny's face warms — "during my MRI."

"That's all you wanted to talk to me about?" Edith's tone is playful, teasing even.

There's an awkward pause. Finally Ginny gestures at her soaked scrubs. "I'm going to head home and take a —" She frowns and squashes the wet paper towels into a ball. "A shower."

"What's wrong?"

"Oh, the water's out at my house. I have to brave the second-floor locker room."

Edith makes a face. "It smells in there."

"It does." Ginny sighs. "But no worse than me right now, I guess." She throws the ball of towels into a nearby trash can, and then wishes she hadn't, because now she doesn't know what to do with her hands.

"You could come borrow my shower," Edith says softly.

Ginny thinks again of Mark, at home in front of the TV, and Noah, asleep in his room.

They look at each other.

"Do you remember where I live?" Edith asks. "Right by the university."

"Yellow house on Starker Drive."

"That's right."

Edith's house is a tiny bungalow the color of honeycomb. Its porch is clear of all the stuff heaped on her neighbors', like gardening tools and watering cans and extra bike wheels. Two pots of rosemary stand on the steps and a single beach-cruiser-style bicycle rests against the porch railing.

"Hello?" Ginny calls through the half-open front door. The rain patters against the porch steps. She's nervous. She's been here a couple of times, when Edith needed a ride to work. But it feels completely different this time.

She hears Edith's voice from inside, telling her to come in. She waits in the entryway on the hardwood floors. She can hear water running. A slipcovered sofa, its bright pillows pressed flat, divides the living and dining room. An open paperback perches on one of its arms. The front curtains are drawn.

Edith appears with a green towel in her hands. Her crinkly hair is down around her shoulders.

"I don't want to touch anything," Ginny says. Her scrubs are still damp, her left sock gummy. In the car she sat on a couple of surgical towels to keep her seats clean.

"I'm running you a bath," Edith says.

"Oh, that's okay."

"No arguments — it'll be just the thing."

She follows Edith through a narrow, yellow-tiled kitchen that smells, faintly, of burnt toast. "Where's your cat?" Ginny asks.

"Oh he's around here somewhere. Probably hiding behind the couch."

Ginny thinks of Fisher and Pinky asleep on Noah's bed, and looks back at the front door. She hesitates. What if Noah wakes up and looks for her and she's not there? But he doesn't do that anymore. He hasn't since he was three or four.

"Are you hungry?" Edith doesn't wait for her answer; she reaches for a plate sitting on the counter and unsticks its Saran wrap. "I made jam cake." She cuts a thick slice and puts it on a napkin. Then she leads Ginny down a short hallway and into the bathroom.

In the small green-and-white room, steam hovers above the half-filled tub. Palm fronds sway and twirl across the wallpaper, and a square of rug the color of new grass covers the black-and-white tile floor. For the second time in two days, the two women stand together in a confined space. Edith hands Ginny the towel and she hugs it to her chest. Then Edith sets the piece of cake on the sink and stoops to dip her hand into the water. She adjusts the faucet handle by a fraction of an inch. "It's temperamental. Let me get it just right."

She straightens up. "That one." She points to one of the bottles sitting near the tub, a container with flowers on its label. "That's the antidote to being doused in pleural fluid." She picks it up, squeezes some of it under the tap, and leaves the room, closing the door behind her.

Ginny eats the cake — dense and sweet with orange peel and powered sugar — in three bites, and wishes there was more. She undresses, pushes her stained scrubs into a corner with her bare foot, and steps into the hot, fizzing water. She scrubs her whole body with a washcloth and the tropical-smelling soap, quickly, listening for sounds outside the room. She hears the rattle of dishes in the sink, the faint noise of the radio.

She lays her head against the porcelain and feels the heavy air settle on her skin. She looks at each object in the room and thinks: that belongs to Edith. A single toothbrush set atop the shallow sink. Three hair ties in a silver dish on the windowsill. A pink razor balanced on the rim of the tub.

When there's a knock at the door, she startles, splashing water onto the green rug. She sits up and the gauzy shower curtain billows.

Edith calls, "I have a glass of wine. A glass of wine and a beer. Whichever you like. Can I come in?"

Ginny sinks down into the bubbles so only the tops of her knees poke out. She runs her hand over the pucker of skin just below her belly button — her C-section scar — and says, "Okay."

Edith keeps her eyes on Ginny's face and sets the beer down on the side of the bathtub. "You look good, relaxed." She sits on the toilet seat and begins talking — about work, about her house, and about the road trip she took to the redwoods this past summer. Ginny sips her cold beer and says little in response, but Edith doesn't seem to mind.

They've talked like this before, in the staff room at the hospital, or standing outside in the parking lot, the hoods of their jackets shielding their faces from the rain. But it doesn't feel like it did those other times. Edith relates the entire plot of the last movie she saw, in minute detail, even standing up to act out some of the scenes. She goes on and on. Ginny wants something to happen, but she doesn't know how to make it happen. She stops following Edith's words and just listens to the way her accent stretches out the vowels in words like *you* and *do, wonder* and *drawer.*

The bubbles dissipate. Edith is laughing about something, revealing three silver fillings in the back of her mouth. When she stops laughing the room goes quiet. The only sound is the gentle *tunk tunk* of the tub stopper's chain. Edith sets her glass on the windowsill. "That water must be cold by now," she says, and Ginny nods, even though it's not true. The water, the air, and her body are all the same temperature.

Ginny sits up and folds her hands over her breasts. She waits for Edith to hold open the towel for her. But Edith kneels next to the tub instead. She lowers her hand into the soapy water, like she did earlier to check the temperature, and her fingers skim the hollow of Ginny's knee. "Lay back," she says. "I'm going to warm you up."

Ginny sinks back into the water; she closes her eyes. She trembles as Edith's hand follows the curve of her thigh, up, up . . .

When Edith's fingers dip inside her, they are soft, then hard, grazing, kneading. Slow, too slow. Ginny turns her head away, arches her back, but Edith braces her with the heel

201

of her hand. She can hear her own breath, loud against the tile. Edith's fingers keep moving. Faster. Until it feels like everything inside her body is being scooped out. All of it — skin, muscles, blood, bones. Until she's all hollowed out, and there's nothing left. Nothing but a last, choking breath.

SEVENTEEN

Samara reaches for the kettle in her parents'
kitchen, pauses, and looks around the room
with a feeling of disorientation. The blend-
er's gone from its spot on the counter. So is
the basket full of restaurant napkins and
hot-sauce packets her mother would never
throw out. The prescription and vitamin
bottles have disappeared from the lazy
Susan, and there's a bare spot next to the
toaster oven where an appliance used to be.
A juicer? A bread maker? She runs her
fingers over its faint sticky outline.

She starts pulling at cabinets and drawers
and they rattle open hollowly. She moves
into the living room: the bookshelf has no
books in it and the coffee table no magazines. Her mother's collection of porcelain
birds is missing from the mantel and her
classical music CDs are gone from the
stereo cabinet.

"Dad!" Samara yells, but he doesn't

answer. She searches the house. Then the extendable ladder rattles from the front yard. She pushes her feet into some shoes and goes outside. He's up on the ladder again, pasting squares of tinfoil to the side of the house, a supposed deterrent to the woodpeckers. She folds her arms across her chest and surprises herself by saying, to the heels of his worn-down ASICS sneakers, "Mom bought a house in Costa Rica. She was going to move there."

He turns, keeping his grip on the sides of the ladder. The sun appears from behind the clouds, and he squints. "I know."

She lets her hands fall to her sides. "You know?"

He doesn't answer until he's climbed down from the ladder. The tinfoil in his front shirt pocket sparks and flares in the light. "Of course."

"But, why? Have you ever been there?"

"No, never."

"Then why on earth —"

"You know how your mom would fixate on things. She watched a documentary on PBS about bird migration — about how birds from North America spend the winter in Central America. She started reading everything on the subject and announced she wanted to buy property down there. I thought she'd lost her mind."

"You and Mom were going to move to Costa Rica, together."

He bats a gnat away from his face. "That's right."

"You, in the middle of the rainforest."

"Yes."

"But the house, it's in her name only. And I found all this stuff . . . all this outdoor gear. All of it was for her. None of it was for you."

"The house was in her name for some tax reason. And all the gear —" He laughs, but his eyes are shining. "She wanted me to lose some weight before she bought anything for me." He frowns. "Did you really think your mom was going to leave the country without me?"

"So you know about everything. You know she was going to sell the house?"

He seems to hesitate. "That's why I've been sorting through her things. I want to carry out our plan."

Samara blinks. She tries to reorganize the facts in her mind. What she thought she knew about her parents, and what she knows now.

"You have your life to get back to, Sammy," he says. "You don't need to stick around just for me."

"I want to be here."

"I'll feel closer to your mother at the cottage in Sarapiquí than I do here. At least, I hope I will."

"There's no place more full of Mom than this house."

"I don't feel that way." His face is set, determined. "This house just reminds me of how she died."

"That's because of Dr. McDonnell." Samara gestures to Ginny and Mark's house, and then lowers her voice, because her neighbor Cass has come out of her house with her dog. "She should move, not us —"

"Sammy, you have to stop with this. Your mother's death wasn't Dr. McDonnell's fault. It was nobody's fault."

"She could have had more time with us. She didn't have to do the surgery."

"It was her decision."

"Dr. McDonnell talked her into it. She was the one —"

"Sammy, that's just not true. Dr. McDonnell was very clear about the risks."

Samara kicks the wet grass with her foot. "What were you and Mom going to do in the middle of the rainforest?"

"Watch birds. Learn how to grow tropical plants —"

"You don't know anything about those things."

"That was the point, Sammy. We were going to learn. We were going to try something new." There's an eagerness in his expression she remembers from childhood, when they would pack up the car and go on meandering road trips mapped out by her mother. She always got carsick on those trips.

"You're going to do all that by yourself now."

"I'm going to try."

"You'll hate it. You know you will —"

"Maybe it's a bad idea. But it's what she wanted. So I'm going to do it." He turns back to the ladder and starts climbing up.

"I want to know what you've done with all of it."

He turns around and the foil in his pocket flashes. He doesn't say anything.

"Her things, Dad. Where are they?"

"I donated them."

"To where?"

"The Sustainability Coalition Thrift Shop."

She starts moving toward her car.

"She didn't want you burdened by all of it," he calls after her.

"We don't have to do what she says," she calls back angrily. "She's not even here."

Cass waits at the bus stop a few blocks from the cul-de-sac. The fog has cleared. The mountain is a dark green shadow, its jagged peak hovering on the horizon. Leah snuggles against her in the wrap, with Cass's jacket over it. This morning she developed a sudden dislike of her car seat, and screeched when Cass tried to strap her in. So they take the bus to the hospital. Cass chooses a seat near the driver, and they watch trees and houses and cars pass by. The hanging flower baskets downtown are full of asters now, instead of marigolds; and pumpkins, shiny with rain, sit on people's front porches. By the time they get there Leah has fallen deeply asleep, her warm cheek pressed against Cass's chest and her hand curled on top of her breast.

Cass gets off the bus and pauses just inside the hospital's sliding glass doors. She hasn't been back here since she had Leah. She and Amar stood in this same spot the morning after her birth. A nurse had helped them strap the baby into her car seat, and they took the elevator from Labor and Delivery to the lobby, looking at each other nervously the whole ride. It didn't feel right, taking this new human being out into the world. Leah was so little, her pink face dwarfed by the padding in her car seat. She still had hospital bracelets on her tiny wrists. They hesitated in the doorway. The sun was shining and Cass blinked in its light. The cool air felt strange against her hands and her face, like her skin was brand new.

Cass moves through the lobby and her sneakers squeak on the waxed floors. She finds the elevator. The fifth-floor hallway is bright with fluorescent light. Leah sleeps on in the wrap.

She knocks when she gets to Robby's room, and two men stand up from chairs in front of the hospital bed. His sons. She's only seen pictures. They are tall, like Robby. They have his broad shoulders and thick hair.

"Hi." She hugs Leah close in the wrap. The room is small, with one narrow window and a blue curtain half-closed around the bed. "I'm Cass. I'm here to see Robby."

"It's only supposed to be family —"

"Greg, this is Cass. Remember?"

"Right." Greg frowns. "Brilliant Cass."

The other man reaches out to shake her hand. "I'm Ben."

Greg extends his hand too, although his face is reluctant.

"I can't believe I've never met either of you," she says, and immediately knows this is the wrong thing to say.

"He talks about you a lot," she adds, quickly, even though this isn't really true. "And your mom —"

"He's really sick," Greg interrupts. "He's not speaking."

"He's doing much better than he was," Ben says. "They're going to move him out of the ICU today."

"Maybe," Greg says.

"Come in," Ben says. "Hopefully he'll wake up."

Ben and Greg go to the cafeteria and Cass sits next to the bed. It's strange to see Robby this way, pale and prostrate, eyes closed. The sheet is pulled up, almost to his chin, as if he's a little boy who's just been tucked in.

Ben said he was doing better. But he looks awful. Old and drawn. Even his typically wild hair is flat, subdued. Tubes come out from under the sheet. A machine at the top of the bed hums and blips. But he is breathing on his own, slow and shallow. She watches his broad chest rise and fall.

The room smells like bleach and something else, like soap and cedar. She leans closer. Shaving cream. She can see a little on the side of his clean-shaven face. "Robby?" she says softly. But there's no change from the bed. The machine whirs and beeps. Out the window tall cedars encircle a wide expanse of wet green lawn. But the outside world feels far away, the room sealed in and still.

"I've come to talk to you. I'm sorry I didn't come sooner. I didn't know you were sick. I feel terrible about that." She pauses. "I've wanted to talk to you for months. I had my baby — Leah. She's here. If you open your eyes you can see her."

Robby's breathing stays the same. His eyes stay closed.

She takes the red folder out of the diaper bag, and pages to the note he wrote. "I know it's not the most important thing right now. But why did you keep this old paper of mine?"

His eyelids flutter. She can't tell for sure, but maybe he's listening.

Leah shifts in the wrap, whimpers. Cass pulls her out, lays her across her shoulder, and rubs her back. She presses her nose to Leah's warm, patchy head.

Then, in a hoarse whisper, Robby says, "It showed promise."

"What?"

He cracks open his eyes. "I kept it because

it showed promise."

She feels the prickle of tears. "I shouldn't have said those things, that day in your office. You lost your wife —"

He holds up his hand, but she keeps going. "I can't imagine how I would feel if I lost Amar or Leah."

"I don't want you to be me." He coughs, clears his throat. "You can do more than I ever did. And do it better. I know you can —"

She shakes her head. "I let you down." She leans closer to the bed, holding the baby's head in her hands. "I'm sorry."

Robby reaches out, slowly. He squeezes Leah's little hand. "Make it up to me."

"How?"

He points to the paper. His voice is even hoarser now. "Start here."

EIGHTEEN

Samara searches the aisles of the thrift store, a brightly lit, oblong shop empty except for a tall woman who sorts linens behind the cash register, and two older women who stand in the Household Items section, picking up teacups and bowls, turning them over, and setting them back down. Samara's eyes dart this way and that. She sees the ugly crocheted blanket that used to hang over the chair in her parents' bedroom, and a pile of brightly patterned pillows from the living room couch. She throws the blanket over her shoulder, scoops up an armful of pillows. The blanket is musty and the pillows smell faintly of crackers. She brings them to the cashier.

"Can I put these here? I'm going to buy them."

The woman looks up, surprised. "Of course. Take your time."

Samara hears her mother's voice in her

head, louder than it's been in days, as she gathers the rest of the pillows, squishy and floral-printed and woven with multicolored thread. Didn't you hear what your father said? I didn't want you to keep all my junk.

But Samara doesn't listen. She grabs a shopping cart from the front of the store and stuffs the pillows inside. She wheels it to the Kitchen section, where she finds the bread maker and the Tupperware, and Women's Clothing, where she spies her mother's gardening clogs and a tangled heap of her socks.

She pushes the cart up and down the aisles, filling it three times. The mountain of stuff at the cash register grows. Back in Household Items she spies her mother's glaringly orange Fiesta ware pitcher, but before she can reach it, another customer picks it up. "Two-fifty," the woman says. "This is real Fiesta ware."

Samara pushes past a rack of men's shirts and taps the woman on the shoulder. "Excuse me, are you going to buy that?"

"I was actually."

"Because it was my mother's. And I'd like it back."

The woman stares.

"Did it get donated by mistake?" her companion asks. "That's awful." She turns to her friend. "You should let her have it. It has sentimental value."

"All right," the woman says, reluctantly, and hands her the pitcher.

In her head her mother says, You don't want that old thing, Sammy. There's a chip on the bottom. But Samara does want that old thing. It's not an old thing. It's a portal to another moment in time. To a summer day on her parents' back deck. To the sound of ice cubes clinking in a pitcher of lemonade, and the heat of the sun against the backs of her hands and the tops of her thighs. To the taste of sour and sweet, and the pressure of her mother's cool fingers on her shoulder as she leaned over the table to pour her another glass.

She puts the pitcher in the cart, pushes toward the Books and Music section, and begins pulling CDs from a shelf. Vivaldi's *Four Seasons;* Bach's violin concertos; Mozart, *The Magic Flute,* with a sticky note on the back that says *call Claire* in her mom's looping writing. She drops them all into the cart, and something falls out of an old sweater of her mother's, cable-knit, with deep pockets that sag open. She picks it up. It's a photograph of a young woman standing on an airport tarmac, in front of a plane with the letters TWA on its side. She's wearing a purple sari and the wind has blown a piece of her hair across her face. She's very young, and she squints at the camera in an uncertain way.

Samara knows the story of her mother's trip to the United States to join her father — the second half of the story anyway. Her parents have told it dozens of times. There was turbulence on the last leg of her mom's flight, and she was sick on the plane. Once she landed at JFK she went into the first shop she saw to buy something to change into. So when she marched up to Samara's father in baggage claim she wore a huge sweatshirt printed with the words I LOVE NY.

Samara squints at the face in the photograph. The girl in the picture doesn't look like the main character in her mom's story. She doesn't appear confident and capable, able to laugh at herself. She looks like she's not ready. She looks like she might not get on that plane. Her mother was twenty-four when she took that trip, exactly the same age Samara is now. It was probably her own mother who took the picture. She wonders what Nanni said to persuade her? To convince her to go?

Samara pushes the cart to the counter, still staring at the photograph.

"Ready?" the cashier asks. The mound of miscellaneous things has grown almost as tall as she is. It looks heavy and dark and sad. You don't really want all that stuff, her mother's voice says. It was mine, and I didn't even want it.

The rain runs down the store windows in little streams. When her mom got on that plane, she changed her life. And she was planning to do it again, to get on another plane, with Samara's dad this time, and change it all over again. Samara looks at the picture once more and then puts it in her pocket. She takes the orange pitcher from the cart. "I think, after all, I'll just take this."

Cass leaves the hospital with the baby in her arms. She walks past the bus stop and keeps going. It starts to rain, and she pulls her hood up, wraps her jacket around Leah.

The baby's breath is warm against her skin as she flips to the first page of her old paper and starts reading. She winces at the typos and awkward writing style. She's mixed up *their* and *there* and used the word *century* when she meant *decade.* But the exposition of Leibnitz's *On the Ultimate Origination of Things* demonstrates real mastery of the material, and there's an almost relentless precision in the comparison of his views with those of Spinoza's, on the nature of possibility and its expression in the world. Hidden inside the paper's long expository paragraphs are sparks of original thought, circled or starred by Robby's black pen.

She remembers what it felt like when she first met Robby and they would talk for hours in his office — about the mind-body problem, the concept of utility, the idea of the good life. She would show up with a list of questions, and he would answer them, one by one. She would try to poke holes in his answers, and he would argue with her like she was a colleague, rather than a sophomore student. It was thrilling. Their discussions were expansive and open-ended; one topic led to the next, and the next. They would go on like that until late, until everyone else in the building had gone home, and the sky grew dark outside his office window.

She keeps walking and reading as Leah snores softly against her chest. Toward the end of the paper, the argument begins to meander. It references Robby's book *Counterfactuals* and discusses Leibnitz's assertion that there are an infinite number of possible worlds inside God's mind, but only one actual world, which God chose as the most perfect of all possibilities. She doesn't know what she was trying to get at in these paragraphs. Her thinking is a jumble of false starts and half-formed ideas. Here Robby has circled a paragraph, once in black ink and once in blue.

Every philosopher is looking for the idea that will solve all problems, a Theory of Everything, or TOE: Leibnitz, Spinoza, even you, Professor Kells, in your book. But your book didn't do it, not fully. Because the infinite possibilities you talk about, that we can understand through counterfactuals — they're hypothetical. It only truly works if they're real.

It only works if they're real.
This is the part of the paper Robby wanted to talk about the day they argued. There's something there, an idea, half-formed, inchoate. Robby's book proposed hypothetical alternate worlds as a way to solve problems, to answer certain questions about causality, and about false and idealized theories of nature. It was groundbreaking in that way. Only a handful of contemporary philosophical texts get close to a Theory of Everything. Robby's was one.

But at twenty years old she had dared to

ask if his theory could do more, if he could have pushed it further. Actually, she didn't ask. She stated. Robby's philosophy is only a true TOE if the alternate worlds described by counterfactuals are real entities. If parallel worlds actually exist, and our own world is just one of an infinite number of worlds in the multiverse.

And with that a lot of things reorder themselves in her mind — certain passages in Quine and Kripke and Plantinga. Certain unsolved problems, often rehashed in her graduate seminars, and during Robby's office hours. The shape of something forms. A grand, many-limbed idea. It expands and appropriates other things — thoughts, problems, questions. It gets bigger. It stretches, turns irregular and ugly, and then coheres again, and reshapes itself anew.

"Start here," Robby told her. He wanted her to go back to the beginning, to the first class they had together, to her old paper, full of typos and run-on sentences. To this paragraph he circled. He wanted her to question, head-on, the theory he so painstakingly laid out in *Counterfactuals.* But she's not the girl who wrote those words anymore — fearless and unselfconscious. Inexperienced, unrestrained.

Her life is smaller since she had Leah, and

less free. But it's also much more than it was, all at once, all at the same time. She has to be more than one thing now. She has to be two, three, four. It seemed impossible at first. But now . . . maybe it's not.

She pulls her jacket tighter. Leah murmurs and her eyelashes flutter against her chest. The first time she read Robby's book, it seemed to split open her brain. It changed the way she thought about philosophy, and the world. The girl who wrote this paper couldn't write something that did that, not really. But could she now?

She turns into her neighborhood. The rain has stopped. She's nearly reached her door when her phone rings. She's surprised to see Amar's number flashing across the screen.

"What's wrong?" she answers.

"Cass." His voice is deep and familiar. There's a strange clicking sound on the line. He raises his voice over the clicks. "I've been emailing you all week —"

The clicking grows louder.

"It's hard to hear you. There's this clicking." She lets herself into the house, and Bear runs to greet them. She drops the diaper bag to the floor, sits down on the couch.

"How is Leah? It's killing me, being away

221

from her. And you."

"She's good. Hungry." Leah's rooting against her chest. She unbuttons her shirt and the baby greedily latches onto her breast.

"You must be —" Clicks drown out his voice.

"I can't hear you, Amar."

"My phone barely works here —" In between clicks she hears "off the coast of Alaska" and "had to come to port because —" Then the clicking stops. "I got all your emails at once," he says. "The last message said you were driving around Broken Mountain in the middle of the night —"

"I didn't mean to send that one."

"We're leaving again in a few minutes," he says. "Right now I just need to know you're okay."

She shakes her head and laughs, but it comes out like a sob. "I wasn't before. But I am now."

"Because the messages you sent, Cass —"

"They sounded a little crazy."

"A lot crazy."

"I'm all right, I promise."

"I have to tell you something. When I couldn't get ahold of you —" He pauses. "I called Mrs. Mehta. She's going to help you with the baby. Just until I get back."

"I don't need help. I'm fine."

"Please."

Cass looks around the room, at the unopened boxes lining the hallway, the sink full of dirty dishes, the tufts of dog hair littering the floor. "Okay. Maybe it's not such a bad idea."

NINETEEN

Mark sits high on the seat of a rented backhoe. The control stick vibrates under his hand as he lifts the yellow boom up, up, and then forward. The machinery was unwieldy at first, but now he's got the hang of it. Even with earplugs the sound of the engine is tremendous. The noise, and the vibration, drives away every thought that comes into his mind.

He moves the boom forward again, his seat bucking underneath him, and drops its teeth into the wet hill. Then he pulls it back and scrapes away dark earth and looping roots. It's satisfying to watch the hole grow bigger with each gouge.

He follows the spray-painted lines he and Noah made. Every so often he kills the throttle, climbs down from his seat, and consults a small black notebook where he's organized his notes, schematics, and calcu-lations. He keeps his earplugs in. He steps inside the hole to check his work with a tape measure. He feels the grooves made by the bucket under his boots; he smells exhaust, wet earth, and crushed leaves. The far wall of the hole stands nearly as tall as he is. By the time Noah gets home, it will be as wide and deep as it needs to be.

Ginny wakes late in the day to a horrible racket, a deafening crunching coming from outside. She squeezes her eyes shut. In her mind Edith's face looms over her own in a wallpapered bedroom. Damp sheets the color of cantaloupe cling to her skin. She rolls over and presses her burning cheeks into the pillow. She's ashamed of herself; she's thrilled with herself. Her stomach turns with the thought of what she's done.

A high, whistling screech joins the crunching. She pulls herself out of bed and shuffles to the window. Her head throbs. She opens the blinds and blinks — her husband's out there, operating some kind of machinery. A yellow metal arm scrapes dirt from the top of the yard and makes a square hole in the ground. She can't see Mark's face, but dirt streaks his arms. He maneuvers the machine this way and that. Its bucket jerks up and down, and then sideways.

Two days ago he told her he was going to

build a potting shed in the backyard. "As long as it isn't ugly," she told him. She didn't ask why he wanted to build a shed, instead of just buying a prefabricated one from Home Depot. He was going to build it into the hill, he assured her. She wouldn't even know it was there. It would be camouflaged by the trees. Why did her husband want to build a camouflaged potting shed? She should have asked him why. But she hadn't.

Edith's pink, freckled body surfaces, again, in her mind, but she shakes it away.

She pulls on her robe and grabs her pager. The window in the hallway has a better view of the yard. The machine has left wide, muddy tracks across the lawn. One of the expensive boxwoods they planted in the spring, that Mark took such care to water and fertilize, is half-flattened. And the hole — it's bigger than it first appeared, like a giant has taken a bite out of their lovely wooded hill.

Downstairs everything in the house feels off. Noah's soggy boots have soaked the carpet at the bottom of the stairs. Her feet kick up little puffs of cat hair when she crosses the hardwood floors. She opens the back door, leans out, and yells at Mark, but his face is turned toward the trees. The backhoe's engine drowns out every sound.

She searches for a pair of shoes, and as she pushes her feet into some flip-flops, the crunching and screeching suddenly cease. She goes outside and finds Mark standing at the lip of the dark, wet hole. Black work gloves cover his hands and a smudge of rust-colored mud marks one of his cheeks.

The air is thick with exhaust and she coughs. "Mark, what on earth —" She pulls her robe tighter around her shoulders as she crosses the yard. Her feet squish in the muddy grass.

He shakes his head — he can't hear her. He takes off his gloves and pulls orange earplugs from his ears.

"What is this?"

"I told you. I'm doing a little project." Sweat darkens his shirt at the armpits. She can smell him from where she stands.

"You said you were building a potting shed. Not digging a huge hole in the back-yard."

"You look exhausted. Go back to bed."

She feels a flash of annoyance. How can she sleep with all this noise?

Mark walks the perimeter of the trench. "I've only got the backhoe for another hour. When I'm done I'll come in and make you some food."

She climbs after him and her feet slip around in her flip-flops. A tumble of dark earth, crushed grass, and upturned roots stand in her way. Inside are the snapped stems of a western bleeding heart they planted a few summers ago to attract hummingbirds to the yard. "I don't need food —"

But Mark isn't listening. He's already reached the other side of the trench. He stands with his legs spread wide and writes something in a small black notebook. In the puddle of muddy water inside the hole is her own reflection. Her hair sticks up at odd angles. Her robe bunches around her waist and its tie drags on the ground.

She straightens it. "I don't like it Mark," she calls. "I don't understand —"

"I'll clean it up. Replant. Don't worry." He puts the notebook into his pocket and starts toward the backhoe.

It begins to drizzle. She steps away from the pile of dirt and branches and her heels slip out of her flip-flops into cold earth. She starts to fall, but then Mark is there, reaching out to steady her.

She rights herself.

"What time did you get in?" He holds his gloved hands over her head to block the rain.

She forces herself to meet his eye. "Late."

"I was expecting you."

Her face warms. "My case ran long." She changes the subject. "Where's Noah?"

"At a friend's."

"Okay." She hugs her robe tighter.

"You're cold."

"I'm fine."

"You've got no socks on." He points to her feet. "Go inside. Have some coffee." He puts his earplugs in.

She gestures at the dark hole — she wants to know how much bigger it's going to get. But he's already climbed inside the backhoe. He flips a switch and it roars to life.

When Mark gets down from the backhoe to check his measurements, his wife is gone. She's upset with him now, but she'll change her mind. She looked small standing next to the excavation site, in her fluffy robe and plastic flip-flops. Sometimes he forgets how tiny she is. Small enough to pick up, if he needed to.

He's standing in the hole with his tape measure when he hears the rumble of a flatbed truck behind him. It inches its way, backward, into their cul-de-sac. When it comes to a stop, a man climbs down from its cab. Mark hurries toward him.

The man reads from an oversized clipboard. "I've got a Hard Top Structures underground shelter kit, Series 100. Plus a . . . what's that say? A 'riser blast hatch,' part number 366."

Mark grins. "It wasn't supposed to be here till Monday." He feels like jumping up and down.

"Tried calling you this morning, no answer."

A massive black tarp covers the bunker kit, held down by cables that look like huge rubber bands. Mark tugs on them to see how they're attached.

"I've got to go through this whole list," the man says. "Get your signature at the bottom."

"Okay, sure." Mark takes off his gloves, tucks them under his arm, and wipes his sweaty hands on his jeans.

"A ventilation pipe add-on kit, and a blast protected NBC air filtration system." He pauses. "What the heck is an NBC air filtration system?"

"A nuclear, biological, and chemical overpressure air filtration system," Mark says solemnly.

The man's eyes widen. "Okay then. Just need your John Hancock right there." He presses the bottom of the page with his finger.

"What about the backup hand-crank pump for the air filtration system? It was an add-on item."

The man takes the clipboard back and flips through the paperwork. "Says here it's on back order. Won't be shipped till December first."

Mark folds his arms over his chest. "Shit, I need that crank."

As Ginny pulls on a pair of jeans and an OHSU sweatshirt, a loud sound erupts from the front yard, different from the noise of the backhoe engine, a diesel-powered rumbling. She stands on tiptoe to look out the bathroom window. A flatbed truck inches backward into the cul-de-sac. A black tarp, shiny with rain, covers its cargo. Someone's having something big delivered; the neighbors are going to love that. As if the sound of the backhoe wasn't enough.

Her husband appears beside the truck. He gestures with his arms.

What the hell? She stomps down the stairs, pulls on a raincoat and boots. Outside Mark stands at the back of the truck, his arms full of rebar. "Mark —" She moves toward him through the wet, overgrown grass. "You need to tell me what on earth is going on. Now."

"The delivery was supposed to be Monday. I planned to tell you about it this weekend."

"Tell me about what?"

"I'm not building a potting shed." He lifts the metal rebar over his shoulder. "I lied."

"Then what's all this for?"

The rebar clatters in his arms. "I'm building an emergency shelter for our family. It cost $9,500. That's a lot of money, I know, but I'm saving a lot by building it myself."

She stares at him.

"This stuff's heavy," he says. "Let me set it down."

"Wait." She holds her hand in front of his chest. "What do you mean an emergency shelter?" She shakes her head. "Like a . . . what? A doomsday bunker?" It's too absurd. She laughs.

Mark glares at her. "Go back inside. We'll talk about this later." He stalks toward the backyard.

But Ginny doesn't go inside. She stays on the front porch, her hands on her hips, and watches, with growing exasperation, a bewildering procession of metal beams and trusses. Mark helps the deliveryman carry a curious-looking metal tube, about eight feet long with a tapered end. Its smooth sides glow in the overcast, afternoon light. Next is a tumble of blue plastic hoses and a netted sack full of brackets and bolts.

Every item carried or rolled past adds to her mounting sense of disorientation. Who is this person wheeling a giant saran-wrapped drum? Hefting an armful of four-pronged metal rods? Not her husband. Her Mark would be out grocery shopping right now. Her Mark would be mowing this overgrown grass.

At one point her new neighbor opens her door, frowns at the strange items being unloaded from the truck, and then closes the door again.

Now Mark inspects a gray metal slab on the truck. He and the deliveryman struggle to lower it to the ground. Grunting, Mark manages to tilt it onto the dolly. It's a metal door, thick as the length of her arm, with a circular handle like the hatch of a submarine. There are red letters painted inside: DANGER. KEEP CLEAR OF BLAST DOOR.

The deliveryman holds the dolly steady as Mark turns the wheel on the door, to the right and the left. He nods to himself and smiles.

"Mark." Ginny starts toward them.

He leaves the metal door where it is and

climbs onto the truck. He pushes another crate closer to the edge.

"Mark, stop." She's forced to look up at him because she's barely taller than the truck's wheels. "Stop unloading."

He peers over the side of the truck. Now that she has his attention, she steps back onto the grass. "No more metal piled in our backyard. Not until you tell me why."

"I told you."

"I know what you're building. Now I want to know *why* you're building it."

"I'll explain everything, I promise."

"Great. Explain. Now."

He gets down from the truck. "We're almost done. Just a few more —"

"No." Her voice rises and the deliveryman stares. "Now."

Mark lowers his voice. "I'm doing this" — he gestures to the truck and the muddy tracks in the grass leading to the backyard — "for you. And for Noah."

"We're supposed to be a team, you and I," Ginny says. "We're supposed to tell each other the important stuff." She thinks of Edith and her cheeks turn hot, but she presses on. She points at the metal door. "That there. Whatever the hell that is. It looks like something pretty fucking important."

He puts a protective hand on the top of the door. "It is fucking important." His chin juts out in a ridiculous way.

"You're acting like you've lost your mind."

He steps closer. "Why can't you trust me?" He grabs her shoulders. "Why is that?" A wild look flashes across his face. And then it's gone, and his eyes dart away to something behind her. She turns, and Noah stands a few feet away. He wears his blue rain jacket with the hood up. There's a girl with him. Her skinny legs are clad in neon-green jeans. She stares at the thick metal door with the submarine handle.

Noah won't look at Ginny. Standing a head taller than the girl, he's sturdy, all muscle and no bone. He looks older than he actually is. Or maybe she hasn't been paying attention to how grown up he's become. He'll be twelve in January after all. But his face, framed by his blue hood, is still soft. In it she sees the toddler who cried out for her from his crib, and the little boy that gripped her legs when she dropped him off at preschool.

Noah, her sweet boy. They've embarrassed him, her and Mark, yelling at each other in the front yard. And that's just the start if she keeps . . . keeps doing what she wants to do with Edith.

"It came early," Mark says to his son. He's excited again. "It's all here." He counts out items on his fingers: "The riser hatch and ladder, the air filtration system, ventilation pipes —"

"Noah," Ginny interrupts, "why don't you introduce me to your friend?" Her pager buzzes in her pocket as she steers Noah toward the house.

"I'm Livi." The girl holds out her hand and Ginny shakes it.

Mark climbs back up onto the flatbed of the truck, and calls to Noah: "Once I'm done unloading, we'll go to the hardware store to pick up the cement mix."

Ginny's pager flashes with a 911 call from the fifth floor. "I don't think Noah's friend is interested in that, Mark," she says quickly. She motions for Livi to follow her and Noah. "Why don't you two have a snack?"

She dials the surgical floor, but no one picks up. It rings and rings.

"I have to go into work," she says to Noah. "Do me a favor and stay in the house. You can play PlayStation if you want."

"What games do you have?" Livi asks.

"It's not the weekend," Noah says to Ginny.

"I know it's not the weekend." The phone still rings in her ear. "But I'm making an exception."

Noah's face is dubious. "Why?"

"I have to go." Out the window her husband is pulling the black tarp off a white metal box with grooved sides. "Promise me you'll stay in the house." She grabs her car keys. "Okay?"

TWENTY

Samara has never been to Shawn's house, but she knows where it is, a narrow two-story with a shady yard, about ten blocks from her parents' house. It's late when she arrives. His street is dark and deserted; the neighbors' porch lights are out. Overhead the pine trees sway in the wind. She's still not sure how she feels about Shawn. He wants something from her, and she's not certain she's ready to give it. But she feels bad about the last time they saw each other at the Kells house. He was trying to help, and she didn't want to listen.

She rings the doorbell and a chorus of muffled barks erupts from inside. Then, the sound of many legs running. When Shawn opens the door two big dogs crowd around him, wagging their tails and nosing Samara's knees. One has copper-colored hair and a white patch near her nose; the other's coat is gray and black and bushy. They smell like mud and wet leaves.

"Wow." She holds out her hands, and the dogs lick them. "They're huge! And muddy."

"Sorry. I took them out to Split Ridge earlier."

Samara wipes her hands on her jeans. "No worries."

He herds the dogs back inside.

"What are you doing here?" His face is guarded.

"Can I come in?" She cranes her neck to see inside. The floors are nice, hardwoods the color of honey.

"It's late. I was about to give the dogs a bath —"

"I'll help you."

His face is skeptical. "Really?"

"Yeah."

"You'll get your clothes all dirty."

She steps through the door. "I don't care."

Shawn's house is warm and smells like lemon-scented wood polish. It's tidy, too, except for a stack of mail on a side table, and some muddy dog prints in the hall. The kitchen has open shelving and concrete countertops. In the living room a dark leather couch sits in front of a large stone fireplace; a woven rug covers the floor. The dining room has a half-built bookcase in it, instead of a table.

Shawn gets a paper towel from the kitchen and wipes the dog prints away.

She points at the hearth. "Did you build that?"

"Yeah." He gets hold of the dogs' collars. "Got the stones out of a creek on Broken Mountain."

"I like it. And the kitchen?"

"My dad helped."

"What's this?" She walks over to the book-case.

"I'm building it out of wood leftover from work."

She runs her hand along one of the shiny cherrywood shelves. "I can't believe I've never been here."

"I've invited you. A bunch of times —"

"I know." She's not sure what else to say.

He waves her up to the second floor, and the dogs' tails hit her on the knees as they climb the stairs. One of the bedrooms has a treadmill in it, and nothing else. The other has a wide bed with wooden posts, and three large dog beds.

"How many dogs do you have?"

"Two." The copper-colored dog leans against him and he rubs behind her ears. "This is Maple." He points at the fuzzy one. "And Ruff."

"You have a dog named Ruff?"

He shrugs. "My niece named him." He opens the door to the bathroom and pulls the dogs inside. "I had three. But Ladybird was really old. Had to put her to sleep last year." He turns on the water in the tub and the dogs try to escape the room.

Samara steps in front of them and shuts the door. Dog hair flies through the air, and she coughs and laughs. She sits with her back to the door and the dogs lick her face.

This room's not renovated like the rest of the house. The sink is seventies yellow; the shower tile is brown-and-white and smells faintly of mildew. A pile of old towels sits on the back of the toilet.

The bathtub fills, and the dogs quiet. Their ears turn down and they side-eye the water. Steam fills the air.

"You're going to put them both in there at once?"

"No, one at a time. But they try to hide when the other's getting bathed, so I started trapping them in here together."

He pats the side of the tub. "Come on, Maple." She turns around in a circle, and then tries to nudge Samara away from the door with her nose.

"Nice try," Samara says. "Go on."

Maple makes a little skip toward the tub,

stops, turns around again.

"It's a long process." Shawn laughs. "Come on, girl —"

She jumps in and stands in the few inches of water, looking miserable while Shawn sprays her down.

"Should I wash?" Samara asks.

He hands her the shampoo.

She moves closer to the tub and Maple wags her tail, but only a little. The dog's breath is hot against Samara's face as she lathers Maple's coat, working the mud out from under her legs and chest, and in between the pads of her paws. The smell of soap and wet dog fills the room.

Once both dogs have been washed and released from the bathroom, they dash wildly through the house. Shawn runs after them with a towel but eventually gives up.

"It's late," he says. "Do you want to stay?"

Both of their shirts are splattered with water, their fingers pruney.

"Do you want me to?"

"Up to you."

"Then, yes."

The dogs are shaking themselves and rolling around on the carpet in Shawn's bedroom. They try to jump up on the bed, but he shoos them off.

He offers her a T-shirt and she peels off

her wet shirt and jeans. He gets two beers from the kitchen, and they lie on his bed.

"That day at the house," Samara says. "I was acting weird."

"You were."

"I've been . . . preoccupied."

"I remember what it was like." He takes a sip of his beer.

"When your mom died."

"Yeah."

She remembers from high school. Breast cancer. His sister missed two months of school. Samara brought books and worksheets from their teachers to her front door. But she wasn't invited inside. She's ashamed to admit she hasn't thought about it since, even after she and Shawn started seeing each other. Even after her own mom died.

Maple has settled herself on the floor. Ruff stands at the side of the bed and wags his tail.

"I've never asked you about your mom. I should have . . ."

Ruff sets his head on the covers near Shawn's pillow. "I used to wish her back," he says softly. "I'd picture her in my room at night. She would sit on the edge of the bed watching me. Sometimes she'd brush my hair from my face." He motions, and his voice trails off.

"I'm sorry, Shawn."

He pats the bed and Ruff jumps up, wedges himself between them. His fur is still damp. He pushes his wet nose into Samara's hand.

Shawn strokes the top of his head. "Could be worse. You've got your dad. I've got mine."

They sit back and drink their beers in silence for a while. The window's cracked open, and a cool breeze ruffles the dog's tail.

Shawn nudges Ruff. "Back to your bed."

The dog reluctantly gets down, looks back at them with mournful eyes.

"Which is his?"

"The blue one." Shawn turns off the light and they get under the covers. "I tried taking Ladybird's bed away. But they like sleeping on it. So I kept it there."

He puts his arms around her. Maple is snoring now.

"What have you decided?" His voice is low and sleepy in the dark. "Are you going to stay or go?"

"Stay." As soon as she says it she knows it's true. She doesn't actually want to go back to Seattle. She likes her job, even though she never planned to do it for more than a few months, even though she's not as good at it as her mom was. "But I'm going to have to find a place to live."

He laughs. "Don't want to keeping living with your dad?"

"He's selling the house, he's going on an adventure —"

"Good for him."

She sighs. "It is good, for him." She tucks her head between Shawn's arm and his chest. Heat radiates from his skin. "Maybe it'll be good for me too."

TWENTY-ONE

Saturday morning Mark and Noah drive north to buy a hand crank for the shelter's air filtration system. The late morning sun flickers across the windshield of the Jeep; ahead the mountain hides behind shifting, white clouds. Mark's thumb crawls around on the steering wheel. He needs the back-ordered crank to finish the bunker. Picturing it completed in his backyard is the only thing keeping him sane, the only thing keeping the Other Mark's constant questions at bay. When he called The Great Outdoors, Lee said his uncle, Harry, might have an extra. He isn't sure what he's getting into, and getting Noah into, driving to Lee's uncle's house — which Lee called *a compound* — in the middle of nowhere with three hundred dollars inside his jacket pocket to pay for the part. At least he convinced Noah it wasn't a good idea to pick Livi up on the way.

He turns onto the highway, going east, and follows the directions written on a note stuck to the dashboard of the Jeep. The sun disappears as they turn onto an exit ramp marked with a state forest sign, and then wind up and around Broken Mountain on a service road. Moss-covered pines and firs crowd the road on both sides. He thinks of the Other Mark and imagines his dirty face hovering, supersized, on the horizon. His mouth opens and closes, mouthing the words What's going to happen, Mark, what? What? What?

Noah pauses his handheld video game. "Where are we?" In the rearview mirror his cheeks are smooth and pink. He's wearing his soccer uniform, a blue nylon shirt and loose-fitting black shorts. He's such a solid, healthy kid. It comforts Mark, looking at him.

"On the other side of the mountain. Can you help me find this left? There's a mile marker, 23, just before the turn." He passes Noah the note from the dashboard.

The trees grow dense and dark around them as the road climbs. Noah is quiet for a while, and then he asks, "So . . . does Mom think you're nuts?"

"Why, you worried your old man's going crazy?" It doesn't occur to him until he says it that this could be true.

Noah appraises his dad, and Mark tries for a casual expression. "I guess not," he decides.

The road climbs farther.

"There," Noah points. "That sign says 23." Around the next bend, nearly hidden by blackberry brambles, a dirt and gravel path forks to the left. There's no route or street marker, only a large PRIVATE PROPERTY sign nailed to a cedar tree.

Mark slows the Jeep. He hesitates. He cranes his neck; the road is only wide enough for one car.

"What has your mother said? About me?" He suddenly wants to know.

Noah looks at his dad and at the road behind them. "We're in the middle of the street."

"Just tell me what she said."

"She doesn't want me working on the shelter." Noah lowers his eyes and kicks the back of the seat. "She says it isn't appropriate."

Mark imagines his wife's supersized face joining the Other Mark's on the horizon. His wife's lips are pressed together. She shakes her head. "Do me a favor and don't talk to your mom about the shelter." He turns onto the gravel road. "If she asks, tell her to talk to me."

They creep along the road through a tunnel of flame-colored tamaracks and bushy grand firs, and Mark watches for mule deer or wild turkeys that might cross their path. Gravel pops under the Jeep's tires. The road doesn't widen. If another car comes from the other direction, they'll be at a stalemate. There's no place to go but forward. More PRIVATE PROPERTY signs appear, one every few trees. A few are nailed to the sides of Oregon ashes, and this annoys Mark. One of the signs has a few holes in it. They look like bullet holes, but he doesn't point them out to Noah.

"This place is creepy." Noah peers out the window.

"It is." Mark pictures his wife's disapproving face, now under the gold tamaracks. He ignores it. Eventually a metal gate, the kind used to keep horses in their pasture, appears, blocking the road. Over it someone has draped a large yellow flag with a black, coiled snake and the phrase DON'T TREAD ON ME. To one side of the gate is a realtor's yard sign, spray-painted white and stenciled in large green letters:

YOU ARE ENTERING THE SOVEREIGN REPUBLIC OF STAY THE FUCK OFF MY LAND

Noah turns to Mark. "Wow, Dad."

He knows this is the moment to figure out how to turn the Jeep around and drive home. But he needs that crank. He pads his thumb against the steering wheel. "We'll be fine." He puts the Jeep in park and turns off the ignition. The car rocks on its tires for a moment and then goes still.

Noah reads from the sticky note. "Untie gate."

Sure enough, a thick rope secures the gate to a towering western red cedar. Mark gets out of the car. "Wait here."

"No way, Dad. I want to see."

"I mean it. Wait here."

Mark tries to untie it, but it's harder than it looks. He tugs it this way and that. This is ridiculous. There must be a way to . . . He digs his fingers into the tight loops. Well, hell. He stands back and surveys the length of the rope.

The car door squeaks open and Noah comes to stand next to him. "Why don't we just leave the Jeep, hop the gate, and walk in?"

The fearlessness of his son irritates Mark, and also makes him proud. "No. We're not doing that."

"Why not?"

"Because we just aren't."

"But we need that thing, right? The crank thing. For the shelter."

Mark takes one of the loose ends of the knot. "Let me just figure this out."

There's no way he's going to reverse the Jeep all the way back to the main road because he can't untie this fucking knot. He twists with the grain of the rope's fibers, and pulls hard at the knot's loops. He puts his whole body weight behind it. His feet are hot inside his hiking boots, and he starts to sweat. He's pulling so hard he slips on the damp ground, falling hard in the mud.

Noah erupts into laughter. Then he stops. "Dad, are you okay?"

Mark gets up and brushes dirt and twigs from his pants. "Very funny. I fell on my ass." Then, "Don't repeat that."

"What, the word ass?"

"Yeah. Don't repeat it."

"Okay, Dad."

Mark goes back to twisting and pulling the rope. Noah stands nearby and watches him.

"Noah, seriously. Go find something else to do."

Noah walks around the Jeep a few times. He grabs the gate and shakes it, and the DON'T TREAD ON ME flag ripples and flaps against the metal. "We can jump this, easy," he says.

"Can you go stand by the car?" Mark keeps working at the knot. He gains a quarter of an inch, then a half an inch. A bird warbles from a nearby tree. "Hear that, Noah?" He tries to draw his son's attention from the gate. "That's a chestnut-backed chickadee. Never hear those in town."

Noah puts his foot on the gate and tests his weight.

"Hear it? The *tsee-dee, tsee-dee*?"

The knot finally gives way, and the gate groans as Mark opens it. He congratulates himself. He fucking did it.

Noah looks disappointed.

Mark takes off his glasses and wipes his face with his shirtsleeve. "Come on, back in the car."

They drive until they see a group of structures, all painted a shade of dark green that uncannily matches the surrounding trees: a farmhouse, a trailer, a barn, and a couple of outbuildings.

They get out of the car slowly. The matte green paint is even stranger up close — the color of a green maple leaf without its shine. Everything in view is painted, the house's porch and stairs, its mailbox. The trailer and the barn and the chicken coop, all the same.

"This place is weird," Noah says.

A pickup truck is parked in front of the trailer. No, not a pickup. A sort of disassembled pickup. The back of the cab is open, revealing two headrests covered in a dark camouflage print. On the roll bar is a black-and-white sticker that says GET READY.

Mark tells Noah to stay in the driveway, and he climbs the farmhouse steps. He knocks on the door and listens. It's very quiet. He hears only the sound of the wind in the trees, the creak of insects. He wishes it wasn't so quiet. He knocks again, and Noah starts toward the trailer. Mark tells him to wait.

He catches up to his son. Blackout curtains darken the trailer's windows and an X of duct tape covers the doorbell. Mark knocks and Noah hovers behind him. Again there's no answer. Mark peers in the windows, feeling stupid and, he has to admit, scared. He puts his hand on his son's shoulder and they walk around the back of the trailer. Beyond the small yard the shadowy forest looms, dense with moss-covered pines and firs. A strange scent he can't place fills the air, damp and flowery.

It's already past the time Mark agreed to meet Harry. He doesn't know what to do.

"It smells like something," Noah says.

Mark peers into the woods. "Yeah, I know."

Noah climbs a pile of firewood, jumps off it, and then wanders toward the trees.

"Noah, hold up," Mark calls. "We're going to wait here."

But his son has disappeared behind a cedar tree. "Dad, there's smoke."

"What do you mean?" Mark sniffs the air. "Where?"

Noah's right. Between two western red cedars a column of smoke seems to rise from the ground itself. When he reaches his son, Noah's bent over a sort of exhaust pipe coming up from the ground. One of Noah's eyes squints shut as he looks down the pipe.

But it's not smoke coming from the ground; it's steam. Mark gets down on his hands and knees, flattening the wood sorrel that surrounds the pipe. He peers down the dark metal tube, one-eyed, like Noah did, and gets a nose full of moist, sweet-smelling air. There's a sound, a metallic backbeat, *tun tunt, tun tunt,* that reminds him of something.

"Laundry," Noah says. "It smells like laundry."

Mark sits up and wipes his fogged glasses. There's a bunker right under their feet. He's sure of it.

"Hello?" Mark says, tentatively, into the pipe.

"Is there someone down there?" Noah asks. He bends over the pipe again and the tops of their heads touch. "In the ground?"

Mark sees his own excitement reflected back in his son's face. They yell into the pipe together and it feels thrilling and ridiculous. "Hellllooooooo!"

A muffled voice answers. "Yeah?"

Mark calls back. "It's Mark."

"Who?"

"I'm here about the hand crank."

"About what?"

Mark bends closer to the tube, his lips brushing its cold metal grate, and yells again. "The crank!"

There's a pause. Then: "Door's open."

They're going to see inside a bunker. A real one. But where's the door? They walk farther into the woods and search the ground. This time Noah doesn't run ahead. He stays beside his dad as they weave around thick tree trunks and tangled black-berry bushes. The pines and firs grow dense and the light turns dusky. A small yellow marker indicates they've now entered the state forest. Surely they've gone too far.

Mark is about to tell Noah they must have

missed the door when his mouth goes dry and tinny, and the earth shudders under his feet. He reaches for his son.

"What the heck was that?" Noah says.

Mark squints between the trees —

About thirty or forty feet ahead, a campfire burns in a small clearing in the brush. A dark-haired man crouches over it. The Other Mark.

"Dad, why did the ground shake like that?"

Mark pulls his son back the way they came, his legs trembling and his boots clumsy on the uneven ground. Blackberry branches scratch his arms and pull at the fabric of his pants, but he doesn't stop until they've reached the pipe. "Stay here," he says.

Noah protests. "What's going on?"

"Everything's going to be fine." Mark swats a bramble from his elbow. "Just stay in this exact spot." He points at the pipe and charges back into the brush.

He barrels through the forest. He stomps over a disintegrating log. His shoulders snap the branches of fir trees. He's had enough. The clearing is up ahead.

The Other Mark's still there, sitting cross-legged in front of the fire, about forty feet away. He leans over a heap of smoldering twigs and the firelight illuminates his mud-streaked face. A broken-down A-frame cabin with peeling yellow paint stands nearby, nearly hidden in the trees.

Mark holds up his fist. "Hey." His voice is more breath than sound. "Hey, you." He trips over a root and his hand scrapes the furrowed side of a cedar tree. "You." He can't bring himself to call out his own name.

Nothing happens. The Other Mark's expression doesn't change.

Mark starts to run. "What do you want?" He pumps his arms. His voice is louder: "Tell me what you want. Tell me or go away!"

He's only twenty feet away now, and he's charging the Other Mark as fast as he can get footholds in the soft ground. He careens around one tree trunk and then another. Faster and faster. But there's something uncanny about the trees surrounding the Other Mark, and the light too.

"I said, *go away*!" His double's only ten feet away. Then five. But it's not right. Something's not right. *Whack.* There's the sound of wood against skull, an explosion of pain above his right eye; and the feeling of the back of his head bouncing against the damp ground, and then nothing.

A man's large, sunburned face appears.

Mark's head throbs. Somewhere high up and out of focus, the trees sway. He reaches up to touch his forehead, the tender lump above his right eye. His glasses are gone. An old-growth fir rises up a few inches from his feet. Its roots are hard under his back. He waves the sunburned man away and says his son's name. Then he yells it.

"I'm here." Noah kneels beside him.

Mark sits up and inhales sweet, loamy air. He peers into the forest, but there's nothing to see. Just trees, earth, and sky. He reaches for Noah and squeezes his arm. His chest swells. He told the Other Mark to go away, and he did.

The man stands up. "I'm Harry." He's clean-shaven, with graying hair buzzed close to his pink head. He wears gym shorts and athletic socks pulled up to his knees. His arms are short and muscular.

Mark feels around for his glasses and pine needles prick his fingers. Noah holds them up. "They were like this."

Harry shakes his head. "You smashed them up good. What the heck were you doing?"

Mark twists his glasses back into an approximate shape and puts them on. A crack in one of the lenses makes the world appear folded over onto itself. "I tripped."

"Looks to me like you ran headlong into that tree." Harry juts his thumb at the old-growth fir.

Mark scrubs his forehead, and bits of dirt and bark fall to the ground. The break in his glasses makes Harry's head look like it's attached to his waist. "Why would anyone run into a tree?"

"Well, I don't know why." He holds out his hand and pulls Mark up from the ground. "Got to be some reason."

"I'm fine now."

"I don't know if you're fine or not. But I don't want to stand around gabbing about it." Harry starts walking away.

"Wait." Mark calls after him. "What about the hand crank?" Harry's white socks are already disappearing into the brush.

"Come on," he says to Noah. "Help me." He puts one arm around Noah's shoulder and they hurry after Harry. The way the world bounces through Mark's cracked glasses makes him feel queasy, but he concentrates on Harry's socks a few yards ahead of them. Finally Harry pauses in front of a thatch of western hemlock. He elbows his way through the bushes, pulling branches this way and that.

Mark and Noah follow. Beyond the hemlock is a metal door, set into the sloping, moss-covered ground. Harry reaches to turn its circular handle, once, twice, and it moans like an animal in pain. He presses a code into a keypad lock in the door and sets his feet wide to pull the door open with both hands.

He climbs in. Mark prepares to follow, but Noah hangs back. His face is pale. Brambles have torn his uniform at the elbow. "Dad, I want to go home."

"We will. This will only take a minute." Mark puts his hand on his son's back and stands aside so he can climb in first.

But Noah doesn't move. His eyes shine with fear. "I don't want to go in there."

Mark hears a faint hum from the shelter, feels a slight draft from inside. "It'll be fine. I promise."

TWENTY-TWO

Inside it's warm and dim. Interior noises replace the sounds of the birds and the creaking of the trees: the *tummm* of a heating vent, the watery whir of a washing machine. Mark steadies himself as the room bounces through his cracked glasses. He smells WD-40 and laundry detergent. Noah stands close, his shoulder pressed against Mark's side. Metal walls curve around them; the ceiling hovers just above Mark's head. A large puffy couch sits low to the ground along one wall, and there is a small table and chairs at the far end of the tunnel-like room. Shelves full of objects crisscross the walls.

Harry closes the hatch and locks it. The bolt slides into place with a scrape, sealing them in. He turns to Mark and Noah. Despite the walk through the woods, his socks remain high on his calves. "So."

"So," Mark replies. A clipboard hangs on

a nail next to the door. A checklist, many pages long. Mark has been working on some checklists himself. He closes his left eye and tries to read the page from where he stands.

Harry points at Noah. "Your boy's bleeding."

Mark adjusts his glasses. He's right — Noah has an angry scrape along his jaw.

"I'm fine," Noah says.

"He needs to wash out that abrasion. Put some Neosporin on it." Harry's sunburned face is serious.

"Thanks. If you've got some."

"You don't have any with you."

"Ah, no."

Harry points at the sofa. "Why don't you sit there." He walks to the rear of the tunnel, past two sets of bunk beds made up with white sheets and wool blankets. He goes around a corner.

Neither of them sits down. Noah stays close to the hatch and Mark reaches above his head to touch the curved ceiling. On the shelves are canned foods and paper towels and batteries — AA, AAA, C, D, E. Tight, dark rolls of bedding, a shiny tool chest, three shovels. Sandbags, each the color and size of a fat hare. Binoculars and fishing poles. Jumbo tubs of bleach and a portable kerosene heater. A thick nest of bungee cords and zip ties.

"We don't need a lock like this, do we?" Noah peers at the keypad lock in the door, a flat silver box with tiny yellow buttons.

"No, why would we need that?"

"I don't know." His voice wavers. "Why would we need that?"

"We wouldn't."

"Why does this guy need it?"

"Because he's —" Mark lowers his voice. "Because he's not like us."

"You mean, he's —"

Harry reappears with a bottle of hydrogen peroxide and a metal tin containing tufts of cotton, a tube of Neosporin, and a few Band-Aids. "Thanks so much," Mark says a little too loudly.

"You'll need the sink first," Harry says to Noah. He points the way he came. "To the right."

Noah looks at his dad.

Mark nods and smiles to show him there's nothing to be afraid of. "Yeah, sure. He's right. Wash it out first."

Noah moves slowly to the back of the shelter and a few seconds later Mark hears water running.

Harry asks him if he wants a beer.

"Sure." It's the middle of the day, but he guesses no is the wrong answer.

Harry nods and walks to the rear of the shelter again.

Mark notices a gas mask on the shelf above the table and chairs. He hesitates, and then picks it up. He squeezes his left eye shut so he can read its orange label. It's in Hebrew, but a tag stapled to its elastic strap is printed in English.

Export Sensitive Item: This item has been identified as potentially requiring formal authorization or licensing to export under U.S. government export control laws, including but not limited to the International Traffic in Arms Regulations (ITAR) and the Export Administration Regulations (EAR).

He's about to try it on when Noah returns from the bathroom, drying his hands on his shirt. "There's like twenty guns back there," he whispers.

"There are not twenty guns." Mark replaces the mask on the shelf and steps toward the rear of the T-shaped shelter. He peeks down each end. To the right a door stands ajar; inside is a large metal sink and a toilet with a fuzzy blue cover. To the left, a rack of guns. His stomach lurches. Five rifles, their wood sides polished and gleaming, stand upright. Two handguns, as glossy as mink, hang on hooks, their black muzzles pointed to the floor. Past the guns is a small kitchen, where Harry stoops in front of a refrigerator.

Mark creeps back to his son. He picks up the peroxide and dabs Noah's cheek.

"Ouch."

"You're fine. Everything is going to be fine." He opens a Band-Aid with a picture of Spider-Man on it. "We used to have these," he says absently.

"Does he have kids?"

"No," Mark says quickly. He glances at the two bunk beds. "I mean, if he does, I'm sure they're all grown up."

Harry comes back holding a laundry basket full of clean clothes, with two IPAs tucked inside. He holds out the basket and Mark takes one of the beers. Harry sits down on the couch and begins folding gray underpants, the same kind Mark buys in a twelve-pack from Costco. "So you're a friend of Lee's."

"Not a friend, exactly. I met him at The Great Outdoors Store."

"And you're building a bunker."

"Yes."

"Why?"

Mark takes a sip of his beer. He doesn't want to answer.

Noah points to the Band-Aid stuck to his jaw. "Do you have a kid?"

Harry shakes out a white T-shirt and folds it carefully. "My grandson used to live with me." His eyes focus on the shirt in his lap. He lays it carefully beside him.

"Where did he go?"

"Noah, we don't need to ask —"

"You're familiar," Harry says to Noah. He picks up another shirt. "You play baseball?"

"Yeah, and soccer. And basketball."

Harry nods. "Basketball's a good game for you. You're tall." He sets the shirt on the pile. "I coached T-ball when I was the PE teacher at Pascal School."

"You taught elementary school?" Mark doesn't know why he's surprised — the man looks exactly like a gym teacher.

"I go to Niels Bohr," Noah says.

Harry taps his finger to his forehead. "We played your team a few times. I remember you were fast, with a decent arm." He looks at Mark when he says this.

"He gets that from his mother."

Harry nods, and then points across the room. "Got a dartboard over there," he tells Noah. "Let's see what you can do."

While Noah throws darts, Harry asks Mark again: Why is he building a bunker? It's the same question Ginny asked him yesterday. He didn't answer then, and he doesn't want to answer now. But he suspects the question, like the one about the beer, is a test. Harry's deciding whether he deserves the hand crank he's come to buy. And because he needs that crank, he takes off his glasses and says, in a low voice, "I had a dream. A very vivid dream. In the dream my family was in danger. Something awful was about to happen, and I was the only one who could protect them."

Harry's red face draws closer to Mark's. "What was going to happen?"

Mark shakes his head. "I don't know."

"Something awful, but you don't know what." Harry passes his hand over his face. "That's the rub, isn't it. The not knowing."

Their eyes meet and Mark feels that, even though he hasn't told Harry the whole story, even though they couldn't be more different, this stranger might understand him better than anyone in the world.

Noah has thrown all the darts into the cork and steps up to retrieve them.

"That's why we've got to prepare," Harry says and Mark nods in agreement. "That's what I keep telling Muriel — that's my ex-wife. She thinks I'm nuts."

"I don't think it's crazy to have a plan." Mark puts his glasses back on, and Harry's head wobbles above his torso.

"That's why I do a lot of reading," Harry says. "A whole lot of reading. Someone like yourself will appreciate that. Because we've got to be equipped for all the possibilities. Natural disasters. Nuclear or chemical attacks. Biological warfare. A terrorist attack on our water supply, for example. These are the things that keep me up at night." Harry presses his hands together. "And I'll tell you what really terrifies me . . . what really shrivels my balls? An electromagnetic pulse that fries every electrical circuit in the U.S. All that North Korea has to do is detonate a nuclear missile in the atmosphere above America and set off a shock wave of electricity. And then we're toast.

"Can you imagine?" Harry continues. "No cellphones, no computers. Half the population would be dead in a matter of months from starvation or disease." His voice is getting louder and Noah looks over from the darts. "It'll be every man for himself. That's why I've outfitted this space with low-tech backup systems. If a pulse happens, I'm not going to be caught with my pants down."

Mark doesn't know exactly what's going to happen. What exactly the Other Mark is warning him about. But he feels certain it isn't going to be an electromagnetic pulse.

Or anything to do with North Korea. He repositions his glasses on his face. "Doesn't it make more sense to put your energies toward the most probable disasters? Volcanic eruptions, earthquakes, tsunamis . . ." he says gently. "Statistically speaking, they're much more likely than a terrorist attack in the middle of Oregon."

"You're thinking like a scientist. I get it. But I'm not about that. I go with my gut. And my gut tells me I need to worry about *everything.*" The tendons in his neck bulge.

"If we lived on the East Coast, or in a big city —"

Harry pounds his fist into his knee. "I mean, everything." A wild expression crosses his face, and for a moment, he does look crazy. *"Every goddamn thing."*

And then the expression disappears; his shoulders tip toward the laundry basket at his feet and his muscly body goes soft. "My wife didn't like worrying about everything. She said it was exhausting."

Mark reaches out to pat Harry's shoulder, even though the gesture feels strange. "By any estimation, we're in the best possible spot for staying safe from all sorts of things." He aims at a reassuring tone. "Climate change, war, disease. The only real danger is from the earth itself. From the tectonic plates underneath us."

"Yeah." Harry doesn't sound convinced. He picks up a stack of folded shirts and puts them into the laundry basket. "Is that what you are? A seismologist?"

"Oh, no. I'm a behavioral ecologist. My current project investigates how geothermal changes in ground water affect the behavior of the northwestern spotted frog . . ."

But Harry doesn't seem to be listening. He looks at the hatch, as if to check if it's still shut tight. "You married?"

Mark nods.

"Your wife on board with your plans?"

Mark hesitates, and then admits, "Not exactly."

Harry nods; he looks like he expected this answer. He picks up the laundry basket. "Let me grab that crank for you."

Mark can't remember what he was going to say about his research ponds. He eyes the four bunks, the shelves packed with food, the massive brown plastic water tank as tall and broad as a black bear. He wants to know more about Harry's ex-wife. He wants to ask him if she left him before or after he built this bunker, before or after he started living down here, under the ground.

Harry returns with a shrink-wrapped package containing the hand crank, and waves Mark off when he tries to pay for it. "Nah, just take it."

Mark thanks him and Harry shakes his hand firmly.

"I don't go into town much, but if you need help with your installation, give me a call." He shakes Noah's hand too. "You take care of yourself, and your boy." He opens the hatch door, and Mark and Noah climb back out into the damp air.

TWENTY-THREE

Ginny parks her car in front of Niels Bohr Elementary, a brick building with a shallow roof and a throng of bicycles crowding its double front doors. This time on a Saturday afternoon she would normally be at her office catching up on paperwork and emails. A heap of stuff covers her desk — a paper that's overdue to the *Journal of General Surgery*, a stack of unread resident evaluations, a folder full of staff contracts that need her signature. She's at least a week behind on her dictations. But she needs to be here, at Noah's soccer game. With her son, and with Mark. She's been too absent.

Outside the air smells like wet pavement. She pulls her hood up, opens her trunk, and finds her rain boots and a folding chair. She balances on one foot, and then the other, to take off her clogs and pull on her boots. She hears the bleep of whistles from behind the school.

Niels Bohr looks exactly the same as the last time she was here. There's no evidence it's been closed for mold remediation for a week. Mark told her which rooms were affected but now she can't remember. The soccer fields are a mess of muddy, neon-green grass. Noah's game is on the field closest to the trees. Beyond that, the mountain rises up, dark green and ringed with haze. Its snowy split top nudges the gray sky.

She walks past the other games, past the buzzing energy of hovering, rain-jacketed parents and the too-serious faces of the coaches. When she finds the right field, she stops at the sideline. The two teams warm up on opposite sides of the field, the Monarchs in blue jerseys on the right and the Aphids in red on the left. The players' heads bob and dart as they balance balls on their knees and bounce them off the insides of their ankles.

She looks for her son's number, 14. At the shriek of a whistle, Noah's friends Peter and Gus move toward the center of the field, and their knee-socked legs shuffle in the wet grass as they form a circle around their coach: 8, 10, 4, but no 14.

A group of parents sits under the trees, their backs to the mountain. Mark ought to be there, sitting in a folding chair that matches Ginny's, his feet resting on a cooler with Noah's water bottle and some peanut-butter-and-jelly sandwiches inside. But he isn't. Seneca's father — she can't remember his name — stands close to the sideline with his hands aloft, ready to clap. Ginny nods at him and he smiles uncertainly, like he can't remember who she is. "Let's gooooo, Monarchs!" he yells.

Then she sees them, Mark and Noah, hurrying across the grass from the parking lot. Mark waves an apology at the coach.

The other team, the Aphids, has the ball. There's a scuffle for it in front of her, and the players' feet kick up bits of wet grass. Mark makes his way to where she stands, and greets the parents by name. He's acting like everything's okay. But everything's not okay — his glasses are broken. There's a raised, purple bruise above his right eye.

"What happened?"

He holds up his hands. "I'm fine. It's stupid. I took Noah on a bike ride. I ran over a branch in the road and fell off my bike."

"Is Noah all right?" She can see he is. Across the field he's waiting for his coach to sub him into the game. He bends down to reposition one of his shin guards. When

274

he straightens up he waves.

"It was just me being clumsy."

"Why weren't you wearing your helmet? You always do."

"I was." He shrugs. "The strap was loose and it got knocked off when I fell."

She reaches up to touch the contusion on his forehead. His skin is cool and slightly damp. She wonders if he's lying. "Don't you have an extra pair of glasses?" She's speaking to him like normal. But since they yelled at each other in the front yard, things are not normal at all.

"I didn't want to waste time trying to find them. We were already late." He takes off his jacket, sets it on the ground, and sits down. He puts his elbows on his knees.

She unfolds her chair and sits too. The whistle sounds. The coach calls for a substitution and Noah runs onto the field and into the striker position. They watch the game silently for a few minutes. The Monarchs gain the ball. A teammate passes it to Noah, and Mark's eyes follow him as he runs down the field. "He's playing well."

"He is." She listens to the trees rustle overhead. She shifts in her chair, crosses and recrosses her legs. She needs to be here, with her family. She wants to be here. But she wants to be somewhere else too — in her car, turning right out of the parking lot, driving to Edith's yellow bungalow, and knocking on the door. She didn't know sex could be like that. So electric, so all-consuming. When Mark touches her there's no urgency; it almost feels like nothing at all.

"Tell me about the shelter project," she says. "I want to understand."

Mark is quiet for a minute; he watches the game. "Those idiots in administration are never going to fund DAMN."

She suppresses a smile at the acronym. "This is about work?"

"No. Well, yes and no."

The referee calls time out and the Monarchs huddle around their coach.

"When we bought the house we brought the foundation up to seismic code. We have the generator, and all those crates of water in the garage —"

"It's not enough." He digs his elbows into his knees.

"Why does Noah have to be involved? It's not safe, Mark. He's only eleven years old."

"We can't protect him forever."

She's said this very thing to Mark so many times. When he didn't want Noah to try out for peewee football; when he wanted to go along as a chaperone for Noah's class hike into the lava tubes on Broken Mountain; when they had to put their old cat Pepper to sleep.

Mark repositions his glasses. "Besides, Noah and I are having fun working on it together. We're bonding."

This irritates her. "You and Noah are always together."

"That's because you're never home —"

The referee calls a time-out and Noah runs over and asks Ginny for his knee brace. His cheeks are flushed and his arms flecked with wet grass. "What are you and Dad talking about?"

"Nothing. Don't worry about it." She digs for the brace in Mark's bag.

"Are you arguing?"

"We're talking about how great you look out there." She reaches over to help him pull on the brace.

"Wrong leg," Mark says. "It's his left."

She shakes her head. "Of course it is."

The whistle blows and Noah runs back onto the field, with a backward glance at his parents.

Ginny and Mark stand together and watch the kickoff. "I should have told you about the project sooner," he says.

"You should have."

"But this is something I need to do, and I

277

want Noah's help."

Several players tussle over the ball in the center of the field. Mark claps and moves to the sideline. She looks at the back of his neck, where his pale skin meets his damp, curly hair. There's some dirt and bits of leaves stuck to his flannel shirt, evidence of the bike spill.

She ought to press him. She ought to find out what's really going on. But she doesn't. When Noah emerges from the knot of elbows and knees, he's got control of the ball.

"Okay," she says.

"Okay?" He sounds surprised.

"But I don't want Noah anywhere near that backhoe."

He smiles. "The excavation's done. We're on to the foundation."

They fall silent and watch Noah line up at the midfield line for the kickoff. Mark bounces on his toes and Ginny thinks of Edith, thinks of seeing her again, how she can make that happen, and she allows her eyes to wander from the game, to the parking lot and the road beyond.

■ ■ ■ ■

III
BROKEN MOUNTAIN

■ ■ ■ ■

TWENTY-FOUR

Cass carries Leah down the stairs and watches Mr. and Mrs. Mehta make coffee and search the kitchen shelves for a frying pan to make eggs. They bicker good-naturedly about whether to make the eggs with the yolks or not. They've been coming over like this for the last two days, to help with laundry or dishes, or to hold the baby so Cass can take a nap. Noah has shown up a couple of times too, and Mrs. Mehta cooks for him, always more than one kid could possibly eat.

This morning Cass has set her laptop bag by the front door. Inside are notes she wrote in the margins of her old paper. The notes are the start of something, her book, her answer to Robby's *Counterfactuals*. Her theory of the multiverse. For the first time since the baby was born, she wants to go out, to leave Leah for a few hours. To bend over her laptop, like she used to at the university library, and lose herself among half-formed ideas. To lose track of time, to lose track of her body.

Ashmina, as she's urged Cass to call her, scoops coffee into the coffeemaker. Her dark hair is pulled into a loose braid, her cheeks rosy with blush. Mr. Mehta cracks eggs into a bowl and hums under his breath. She can trust them with the baby for a few hours, can't she?

She goes into the kitchen, shifts Leah to one shoulder, and pours herself a glass of juice. Leah kicks her legs against her swaddle, grimaces, and loosens one arm.

"Ready to go?" Ashmina asks.

Cass drinks the juice and eats the eggs, still holding Leah. She puts the dishes in the sink. But then Leah's arms begin to flail. Her face scrunches, like something's hurting her. Cass carries her into the living room, circles the couch, bounces her in the air. *"Shhh, shhh,"* she says in her ear. *"Shhh, shhh."*

Ashmina follows, her orchid-print shirt fluttering behind her. She brings the earthy scent of her perfume.

"Maybe this is a bad idea," Cass says.

"Everything will be fine." Her slightly accented voice is kind but firm. "I promise."

Cass finds a pacifier in the baby seat and

offers it to Leah, but she bats it away.

"All I need is a bottle," Ashmina says. "And then you can get going —"

Cass *shhhh*s louder. "I just fed her." She tries the pacifier again and this time she's able to wedge it into Leah's mouth. Cass sways her in her arms until her wails lose some of their volume and turn into *eh eh eh*s. Leah sucks at the pacifier and her limbs go soft. Her eyes find the light fixture in the hallway, and her hand finds its spot on top of Cass's breast.

Mr. Mehta's voice comes from the kitchen. "We managed to keep our daughter, Sammy, alive. I think we can handle Leah for a few hours —"

Ashmina holds out her hands for the baby.

"If she starts crying, check her diaper," Cass says, quickly. "She doesn't like being even a *little bit* wet. Make sure you use diaper cream. She had diaper rash a few days ago —"

Ashmina's smile has gone a little rigid, but Cass presses on. "If a diaper change doesn't work, try the swing. Or you can put her in the stroller and push it back and forth like this." She moves Leah to one shoulder so she can move her arm in pantomime. She thinks hard about what else to say . . .

She hesitates. Leah's damp fingers clutch

the collar of her shirt. She slowly loosens her grip. She hands her over, puts on her jacket, and picks up her laptop bag. "Promise me you'll call if she's crying for more than ten minutes —" But Ashmina has already walked the baby to the living room windows, turned her toward the pine trees.

"Or . . . five minutes, even," Cass calls after her.

She picks up her keys. Her body feels strangely — unsettlingly — light without Leah in her arms, or attached to her breast, or wrapped against her body in the violet wrap.

Mr. Mehta waves her toward the door. "Go, go."

She stands outside the door. One of Mark and Ginny's cats emerges from the bushes, stalks across the cul-de-sac, and disappears into the trees. She thinks of the quiet table she'll sit at in a nearby café, and the hot coffee she'll drink while she works. She pictures herself typing up her notes and a list of questions she wants to ask Robby. She imagines the feeling of the computer keys under her fingers. But her feet won't move from the porch. She taps out an email to Amar on her phone.

Dear Amar,

The Mehtas have offered to watch Leah this morning, so I can write. But now I can't leave the front porch. How did you manage to do this? To leave her? It must have killed you.

Love,
Cass

She can't help it — she presses her ear against the door and listens. At first there's nothing, and then a muffled wail. Her throat tightens. She listens harder. The baby's cries become shrill, and her breasts turn prickly and hot. She's not good at this. She's not going to be good at this, not ever.

She barges through the door. Ashmina stands up from the couch with the baby, surprised. "She's hungry," Cass says.

"You said you just fed her —"

Cass takes the baby, her little body warm and heavy in her arms, and she feels instantly better.

"Babies cry, Cass." Ashmina smooths Cass's hair where Leah tugged it loose from its braid. "I thought you had work to do."

"I do." Cass presses her cheek to Leah's, feels her tender skin against her own. "I want to go work, and I want to stay here." She feels the sting of tears, and the wet spots in the cups of her nursing bra.

Ashmina's face softens.

"There need to be two of me," Cass says.

"It feels like that now. But it will pass."

Cass shakes her head. Hearing this doesn't help. It doesn't even feel true.

"This is a problem we can solve," Ashmina says.

Cass gestures to her chest. "I can't leave my breasts at home."

"You just need a pump."

"I have one . . ." It's in a box somewhere, a strange machine with tubes and wires coming out of it. "I just haven't figured out how to use it." Or even unpacked it.

"I sold thirty houses the year Sammy was born. I had to figure out how to be in two places at once —"

Cass presses her nose to Leah's head.

"Here's what I would say if you were my daughter. Everything will be okay. You're not the first person to go through this, Cass."

But it feels like I am, she wants to say.

When the Mehtas come back that afternoon Cass finds the heavy black bag containing her breast pump, dumps its parts onto her bed, and inspects the strange plastic shapes one by one: clear funnels, flimsy white discs, long thin tubes. The instructions fill a fifty-page booklet. After she's snapped everything together the directions tell her to *Center the assembled breast shields over your nipples. To begin pumping, turn dial clockwise.*

She holds up the funnels, now fastened to the pump by the plastic tubing, and she's grateful Leah's downstairs with Mr. and Mrs. Mehta. She unhooks her bra, pulls up her shirt, and presses the cold plastic to her breasts.

Your pumping session will start in the Stimulation Phase. While pumping, adjust the speed by turning the dial to your comfort level.

She frowns at the term *stimulation phase.* Okay, here goes. She braces herself, twists the little yellow dial the whole way, and gasps — it feels like someone's twisting her breast in their fist. Once she's turned the dial down the squeezing slows to something more tolerable, but she's horrified to watch her nipple being stretched to an incredible length inside the plastic tube.

To find your Maximum Comfort Vacuum, increase speed until pumping feels slightly uncomfortable (not painful), then decrease slightly.

Nothing has come out. The bottles attached to the funnels are empty. She turns the dial a little to the right. Then a little more, wincing. The pump's rhythmic growl, *weh ohh weh ohh weh ohh,* sounds like a panting animal. If there's anything more unlike nursing Leah — unlike the tender, pulling suck of her daughter's small mouth — it's this.

Finally a drop of white falls into the bottle attached to her left breast, and then another. She feels the familiar pins and needles of her milk letting down, and drops of milk begin to fall into the other bottle too. Measurement lines mark the sides of each bottle, and she watches, fascinated, as the drops slowly add up to a quarter of an ounce, and then a half of an ounce of yellow-tinged milk. It's spellbinding, really, to see it up close, this substance that's nourished Leah for the last two months. There's something exquisite about it, something golden, but also something off-putting, as if each drop of milk contains some echo of the pain it's taking to wring it out of her.

All so she can go work, all so she can be in two places at once. Maybe that's why, with each twist of the pump's suction, she feels something, a cleaving, a separation. Making two of yourself is vicious work.

She wishes she had a pen. She wants to write something down, something for her book, about this idea of splitting herself in two. But she has no pen, no paper. Her computer is in the other room. She checks the bottles. The drops of milk have grown smaller and the bottles have collected nearly two ounces on each side. She turns the dial all the way off, carefully detaches the cones from her breasts, re-hooks her bra, and springs from the bed to her laptop. It's on the windowsill at the top of the stairs, and she kneels down to open it. She starts typing as soon as the screen appears.

She hears the sound of Ashmina singing to Leah downstairs. She doesn't have to crouch here in the hallway. She can go out, she can be alone with her thoughts.

Dear Amar,

I've started writing again. A new project. It's too big to talk about yet. But I'm excited. I'll tell you more when you get home.

Love,
Cass

Downstairs the kitchen counters shine. It smells clean. The two or three boxes that crowded the fireplace in the living room are gone; the Mehtas have unpacked the books inside, put them away in the bookshelves that line the hallway. There's a bunch of sunflowers in a vase on the dining room table, and on the mantel, some framed photographs — of her parents, and Amar's parents and brothers. Ashmina must have found them in a box. They've been such a big help. She doesn't know how to thank them, or what she'll do when they move away.

She holds up the pumped milk and Ashmina nods with approval. Noah is here too. He comes out of the kitchen. He's sweeping up dog hair with a broom, and he smiles and waves. She takes Leah from Ashmina, presses her nose to her patchy head, and inhales her milky, soapy scent. "I'm going out for a little while, teacup," Cass whispers in her ear. "But I'll be back soon." She takes a breath and hands the baby back.

"Everything's under control," Ashmina says firmly.

"There's three of us and only one of her," Mr. Mehta says.

"Right. Okay," Cass says, "I'll be back."

Leah kicks her legs against Ashmina's hip. She isn't crying this time, but her dark eyes seem to search for Cass's face. And then, like she's done it a thousand times before, and it's the most natural thing in the world, she looks at Cass and smiles. She smiles like she's just seen the most beautiful, spectacular thing.

"Oh!" Cass hears herself say.

Mr. Mehta reaches out to squeeze Leah's cheek. "Aren't you a happy baby?"

Ashmina turns Leah around. "How about that. You love your mamma, don't you?" She picks up Leah's tiny fist and waves it in the air. "Now we'll wave bye-bye. Bye-bye, mamma. Bye-bye."

Cass thought she would be okay to leave. She wants to leave, to get back to the notes she just typed. She's going to leave. She's shouldering her laptop bag. She's waving goodbye. She's leaving. She's doing it, but it feels awful. Will it feel this awful every time?

Twenty-Five

On Tuesday morning Samara turns the key in the lock at the Kells house and hears the now familiar long scrape and faint click of the bolt sliding loose. "It's rare to find a house this untouched in Clearing," she says to her clients. "It's almost entirely the same house it was when it was built in 1959. Kind of like stepping back in time."

She stands aside so the couple can walk in first. The wife is small and plump, with delicate features and glasses. She has her phone in her hand and has already taken several pictures of the outside. The husband is tall and lanky, with a brown beard. He strides ahead of them into the living room.

His wife shakes the rainwater off her jacket and smooths her windblown hair. "Is it always this wet?"

Her mother's often-repeated answer to this question springs automatically to Samara's lips. "Perfect weather for drinking a cup of coffee by the fire —" She gestures toward the limestone fireplace.

"Is it gas?"

"No, woodburning."

The husband takes a small tape measure from his pocket and measures the mantel.

"I've sold several houses from this era," Samara says. "This one is the best maintained I've seen." She rests her hand on top of the mantel, its varnished wood cool and smooth to the touch. "It has a lot of soul, I think." She's not sure what this means, but feels it's true.

The wife eyes the yellow-and-gray stones critically. "We'd have to tear this out . . . There's no place to put the TV."

Samara turns away so she doesn't show her irritation. "I think the previous owners had a television here." She points to the far wall. "And a sofa there." She walks down the center of the room. She can't help but add: "I did see a mantel exactly like this one in *Architectural Digest* last month . . ."

She ought to say, Of course it might suit your family better to change the layout of the room. That's what her mother would say if she were here. But her mother's voice, speaking up inside her head, says something else: If you don't want them to buy this house, don't sell it to them. Show them the bungalow on Starker Drive instead.

Samara leads the couple down the hallway. "There's an amazing chrome vanity in the master bathroom. And the tile's in great shape." She reaches into the room and turns on the light.

"Oh my god," the wife exclaims. "It's the color of Pepto-Bismol."

"It's a decent size," the husband says. "Imagine it with white subway tile."

If her mother were here she would nudge her, and communicate with her upturned eyebrows that Samara should agree. That would look great, she ought to say. And, You have great taste. But again Ashmina surprises her:

You don't like these people, do you, Sammy?

No, I don't.

Why?

They have no imagination.

Is that the worst thing?

Samara thinks for a minute. Yes, it is.

The woman has turned to look at her with a strange expression.

"Let's see the lower floor," Samara says, quickly, and turns off the bathroom light. "By the way, there's a house on Starker Drive you might be interested in. A craftsman. Late thirties."

The husband waves his hand dismissively. "We've already rehabbed a bungalow. We want something different."

She shows them the rest of the house, but she keeps her comments short. She doesn't point out the things she loves: the telephone nook in the hallway, the built-in shoe racks in the downstairs closets, the storage cupboard under the stairs that smells like a Christmas tree.

She leaves them alone in the garage for a few minutes to talk, and as she walks back through the house, she's struck again with how similar it is to her parents', and also how different. Without all the junk, you can see the home's architectural lines. The symmetry of dividing an oblong dining room and square living room with a wide stone mantel. The good sense of a kitchen turned toward the morning sunlight, and away from the noise of the road. Without any furniture or lamps or overstuffed pillows or potted spider plants or stacks of hardback thrillers, you can appreciate the intention of the house. Its spirit, even. What it is, and what it wants to be.

She pauses in the master bedroom. The room still smells faintly like orange-scented cleaner. She thinks of Shawn's warm hands on her hips as he pressed her against the closet wall. He thought she should buy this house herself. Was that such a crazy idea?

She waits for her mother's voice to tell her, Of course it is. You're not supposed to live in Clearing, Sammy. You're meant to be doing something else. But instead Ashmina says, What you said about a house having a soul, do you think that's true?

When the man and woman come inside they say they're ready to write an offer. Samara's surprised. "I thought you didn't like it."

"The interior doesn't matter," the husband says. "The square footage is good, and it's in the right school district."

The number they have in mind is only five thousand under the asking price. She ought to be thrilled. She's both buyer and seller's agent, and will get the full six percent commission. But she moves slowly as she walks to her car to get the paperwork she needs. The wind has picked up and blows yellow leaves in circles around the front yard. Shifting white clouds compete with the sun in the sky. The bungalow, her mother's voice says in her ear.

When she comes back inside, she asks them, "Are you sure you don't want to see the bungalow first?"

"No, this is the house." The woman nods

at her husband, and they smile. They're so sure of themselves. So satisfied. Her mother's right; she does dislike them. They're going to take a hammer to the pink tile and wallboard over the telephone nook. They're going to throw the bathroom's sparkling melamine handles into the dumpster. When they're done, it will look like every other house. Generic. Easy.

She lays the forms on the kitchen counter and they scratch their signatures at the bottom of each page. She can see the spot on the carpet where Mrs. Kells's piano used to stand, and she pictures her there, now, her fingers swinging through the air in time to the ticking metronome. Through the sliding glass doors the sun flickers, and the trees wave in the wind. She remembers her mother standing outside identical doors in her parents' house. She wore a dress printed with sunflowers and held a pair of grill tongs in her hand. She swayed to some music and beckoned to Samara through the glass. "Leave your book, Sammy," she said. "Come outside into the fresh air."

In her bedroom Cass types on her laptop and Leah rocks in her baby swing, its white noise turned up loud. The pendulum of the swing creaks back and forth, back and forth.

Wind buffets the house; the sun appears in the window, and then disappears again. Cass is getting somewhere with her idea, her theory of the multiverse. She's been able to shepherd her thoughts onto the page, to begin to shape them into something another person, another reader, will understand. When she doubts her ability to accomplish something so big, so potentially ground-breaking, she imagines what Robby will say, how he will question her the next time she sees him. How he will urge her on.

Then the floor shakes like it does some-times, a small tremor from deep inside the mountain. Cass has a metallic taste in her mouth she remembers from pregnancy. A noise comes from down the hallway. A hum-ming. She listens, her hands poised over the laptop keys. It must have been the wind. But there it is again — a musical sound. It makes her think of the songs her dad would murmur to himself when he was down in the basement fixing something. "Tuesday Afternoon" and "A Whiter Shade of Pale."

"What's making that sound, teacup?" She picks the baby up from the swing, and Leah reaches for her ponytail.

"Ouch." She frees the strands of hair Leah has balled up in her fist. "Who could it be, who could it be?" Cass sings.

At the top of the stairs she stops. The noise comes from down the hallway, from the nursery. But that can't be. She and Leah are the only ones in the house, except for Bear.

The baby monitor. It must be picking up a signal from someone's radio, or another monitor nearby. It's on her desk. Little green bars light up its screen. She switches it off, but the sound continues, faintly. Is she imagining it now? Leah kicks her feet against her hip and gurgles. Cass strains to hear.

Still there.

A thread of fear tugs her body taut as she goes back to her bedroom and calls the dog. She points at his bed in the corner. "Bear, stay. Stay with the baby." She puts Leah back into her swing, straps her in, and returns to the top of the stairs. She listens. The wind is stronger now. The snap of hail hits the windows. But over the sound of the wind, over the hail — someone humming a melody.

At the end of the hallway, the door to the nursery is partly open. She takes a few steps and there's no mistaking it.

Tuesday afternoon . . .
Something calls to me,
The trees are drawing me near

For a second she has the fantastical thought that her dad has arrived on a surprise visit, has let himself into the house, and is now sitting in the nursery singing to himself.

But it's not a man's voice. It's a woman's. Whose?

She steps closer. She peeks through the crack in the door —

The woman sitting in the rocker isn't real. Cass knows that.

Because the woman is her.

The woman reads some loose printed pages with one hand, and with the other she rubs her stomach, her T-shirt pulled taut over her pregnant belly. Hail strikes the window behind her. *Tunktunktunk.*

Cass doesn't move, she doesn't call out. She just stands entranced. She notices things. First, the woman's dark eyes and thin nose. The crooked part in her hair. The way she tips her feet onto her heels when she pushes the rocker back.

The picture Cass has of herself — it doesn't match the woman in the rocker at all. When she thinks of herself the picture is colorless, all light eyes and skin and hair. Washed-out. Static. An overdeveloped driver's license photo that lives permanently in her mind. But this other Cass is a polychro-

matic wonder. Full of agile, assured movement, even in a routine pose. Full of grace.

Graceful isn't a word she would use to
describe herself. Or *assured.* Not since
Leah was born anyway. She recognizes very
little of herself in the woman, except for the
way she hugs her round belly. It wasn't so
long ago Cass rubbed her stomach just like
that, when Leah was inside.

Leah! Her cries come from the bedroom.
And now Bear noses the backs of Cass's
knees. She turns, just for a second, to brush
him off, and when she looks again — the
woman's gone.

Cass blinks, and opens the door wide. The
rocker is empty and still.

Leah's cries grow louder, and she runs to
the bedroom, afraid of . . . she hardly knows
what. But the baby's fine. Her binky's fallen
out of her mouth, that's all.

Cass returns to the nursery. Still empty.
The hail stops. She shakes her head. Having
a baby has broken her mind. But she feels
fine. Better than she has since Leah was
born. Her head is clearer, and quicker, ever
since she went to see Robby at the hospital.
Then something dawns on her. The woman
in the rocker was pregnant. But there's no
way. Is there?

Wait. Maybe.

She thinks back over the last few weeks. She and Amar have only been together a handful of times since Leah was born. Two times, three? The night before he left, for sure. She does the math in her head. Oh, hell.

TWENTY-SIX

Raindrops splatter against Ginny's windshield. She waits for the rain to slow, and gets ready to make a run for Edith's yellow bungalow. She canceled her last three clinic appointments for the day, something she's never done in her twelve years working at University Hospital, because she couldn't wait until five-thirty. The last two days are a blur of time spent together, on Edith's couch and in her tub and in her bed. When they had to be at work, they stole minutes of conversation in between cases, in the elevator or the hospital cafeteria or the hallway between the surgical floor and the OR.

Tonight Ginny has borrowed a colleague's cabin, and they're going to have a whole night together, uninterrupted. But before she can get out, the passenger door swings open and Edith climbs in. Her face shines with rain.

"What's wrong?" Ginny asks.

"I need to talk to you." Edith pushes her hair away from her face and wipes her wet hands on her jeans.

"Grab your stuff and we'll talk on the way —"

"I'm not sure I want to go."

"The cabin's near Sparrow Lake. Have you been?"

"When we were on the phone last night, your husband came in the room. You had your hand over the phone, but I could still hear his voice."

Ginny's quiet for a minute. "You know I'm married."

"We're going to hurt them, Ginny." Edith looks her in the eye, and it's awful.

The rain streams down the windows in waves.

"Mark and I depend on each other," Ginny says. "That's not the same as love." She thinks of the two happy women she saw in her kitchen, her twin and Edith. The way they laughed together. "I didn't know that."

"That's incredibly sad."

"What I'm saying is I didn't know any better. Now I do."

"That's good. For you." There's an edge to Edith's voice. "But I don't think you've really considered how I fit into this scenario.

And I'm not sure you know how."

Ginny doesn't say anything. She feels weighed down in her seat.

Edith's voice softens. "I wish you knew how."

"I'll learn," Ginny says, and Edith shakes her head and smiles.

"We can talk later," Edith says. "But for now I'm going back inside." She pulls up the hood of her jacket and Ginny feels a sense of panic. If she and Edith don't go to the cabin, she'll have to go home. Noah's staying over at a friend's tonight, so it will just be her and Mark sitting together at the kitchen table for dinner, the rest of the house quiet and still.

She grabs Edith's arm. "I can't go back to the way things were." She thinks again of her twin and Edith standing nose to nose in her kitchen, their happy faces. "We're going to be together. Somehow. I know it."

But Ginny's conviction wavers once Edith's gone. She starts her car and pulls away. The wind has picked up. Hail starts to fall hard against her car roof. She's forced to slow down, inch along the road. She doesn't want to think about the things Edith said, but she can't stop thinking about them.

The hail abruptly stops as she turns into her neighborhood. The cul-de-sac glitters with pieces of ice. Her neighbor — why can she never remember her name? — is on her front porch with her shaggy black dog. She looks at the sky, and walks slowly into the road. Her dog tugs her toward some bushes.

Ginny parks, and gets out of her car. Three turkeys scuttle out of the bushes; the dog lunges at them and her neighbor falls to the ground.

Ginny runs over. "Are you okay?"

Her neighbor doesn't get up; she holds her arm like she's hurt it. The dog has chased the turkeys into the forest, his leash trailing behind him. Ginny calls after him, "Bear, come back." Her voice cracks and she looks like she's close to tears. "Bear!"

Ginny holds out her hand to help her up, and the woman gets to her feet with some effort because of her large pregnant belly. She calls again for her dog, her hands on her stomach. Her jacket is torn at her elbow.

Ginny walks her to her own front porch. "Stay here. I'll find him." She pulls up the hood of her jacket and hurries into the forest. The smell of pine needles and wet earth fills her nose. She climbs around blackberry bushes, squints in between moss-covered tree trunks. She can see the back of her house from here and the dark hole Mark dug in the backyard. A square of gray cement sits at its bottom, sparkling with hail. She doesn't want to look at it, but it's hard not to.

She calls the dog again. "Bear?" There's no sound but the crunch of her boots against the ground. She walks sideways, around the back of the Mehtas' house, and finally sees him in their backyard, rolling in a pile of yellow leaves.

She climbs down, holding on to tree trunks as she moves around brambles and old logs. She grabs the dog's leash and pulls him back to her front porch.

Her neighbor scolds the dog and then rubs his head.

"Your arm is hurt," Ginny says. "Come on. Let's take a look." She waves her inside.

She leaves the dog in the garage and grabs a first-aid kit from the laundry room cabinet. She pulls out two chairs. "Forgive me," Ginny says, "Mark told me your name, but I've forgotten it."

"Cass."

"Okay, Cass, let's take a look at your arm."

Cass takes off her oversized rain jacket slowly — it's torn at her right elbow — and winces. She's got a bloody scrape along her forearm.

Ginny opens the first-aid kit and finds the antiseptic. She takes Cass's hand, which is cool to the touch, and turns her arm over and cleans it.

Cass squeezes her eyes shut and rubs her stomach. "Do you think he's all right in there?"

"You're having a boy?"

"Yeah."

"I think he's most likely fine." Ginny rubs Neosporin on the scrape and wraps it with a bandage.

"I can't feel him, though." Cass frowns and pokes gently at her side. "He usually kicks a lot —"

"Wait a few minutes. He's probably just sleeping."

"Okay," Cass says, but her face is still worried. "My husband's away until the week I'm due," she says. "I don't know what we were thinking. We thought it would be okay. It's not." Tears appear in her eyes.

"Is this your first?"

"Isn't it obvious?" She laughs and wipes her eyes. "I have no idea what I'm doing."

Ginny remembers this feeling. On the day her C-section was scheduled she sat in the passenger seat of her car with her hands on her abdomen, her heart thumping in her chest. She wasn't scared of the surgery. It followed specific steps that she understood, had done herself in medical school. No, she

308

was scared of what came after. The part where she became a mother.

But she had Mark, and his complete faith that everything would be okay. He made sure of that, researching every car seat, stroller, and high chair. A month before her due date he had packed a hospital bag full of things she might need: a toothbrush and toothpaste, soft slippers, an iPod and headphones, packets of crackers and nuts, bottles of water. That day, when he got into the driver's seat next to her, he grinned and said, "We're all set." His face was so excited, so assured, she believed him.

"Here." Ginny gets up and opens the refrigerator. She pours Cass a glass of orange juice. "This is what I used to do when I couldn't feel Noah for a while. The sugar in the juice should wake him up."

Cass sits back down and drinks the juice.

They wait in silence. The house is still; the wind has died down and rain patters against the roof. Ginny thinks of Edith, pictures her in her bedroom. She's taking clothes out of a bag she'd packed for their night at Sparrow Lake.

Cass holds her hands over her stomach, and tilts her head to the right. Finally she smiles and lets out a breath. "I feel him. His knee or his elbow, poking my ribs."

Twenty-Seven

The smell of wet earth and new cement fills Mark's nose as he climbs into the half-built shelter. He picks up a cinder block and its rough edges dig into his leather gloves. He drops the block into place.

Noah scrapes his trowel along the seam to remove the excess mortar. "Like this?"

"Exactly." Mark shows him how to use the level, and how to fill mortar into the core of each cinder block. They move around on the sawdust Mark spread on the ground to absorb the mud caused by yesterday's hailstorm.

Noah could be spending the afternoon with Livi. School is still closed and she invited him to go bowling, but instead he's crouched in the dirt with his dad, and this makes Mark feel strong, and capable, and like he knows what he's doing. It makes him feel big and the Other Mark small.

"You think you can push that wheelbarrow

over here?" Mark asks. "It's pretty heavy."

Noah hurries to the side yard and manages to lift the handles of the wheelbarrow full of cinder blocks and push it across the lawn. His face is determined, his shoulders taut. When did he get so strong? It feels impossible that this kid is his own. But there's nothing foreign about Noah's expression. It's the exact face he used to make when he was learning to walk. Lips clamped shut and eyes narrowed, his chin leads his whole head forward.

Noah sets the wheelbarrow down and watches Mark place the next cinder block. "Why doesn't Mom want us to build the shelter?" he asks.

Mark waves his hand dismissively in the direction of the house. "Let me worry about your mom."

Noah looks uneasy.

"Your mom, she doesn't like —" Mark stops. He tries again. "She doesn't like that we're messing up the backyard."

"She doesn't want to think about bad things happening." Noah jabs the trowel into a lump of wet mortar. He's upset, but not at Mark. At Ginny. It's a new sensation — the feeling that a line has been drawn, with Mark and Noah on one side, and Ginny on the other. He likes Noah's allegiance. But it doesn't feel right, being separate from his wife.

"It's because of her work," Mark says. "Her job is to solve problems that are right in front of her."

Noah nods. "I know."

Mark picks up another cinder block, sets it in place. Noah pours mortar on it and spreads it with the trowel. The pine trees overhead sway in the wind.

"Why are you growing a beard?" Noah asks.

Mark rubs the stubble on his face. "You don't like it?"

Noah considers his dad. "You look like . . ."

"A mountain man?" Mark stands up straighter.

Noah shakes his head.

"No? A wise old man, then. A guru." He makes a serious face and readjusts his glasses.

"What's a guru?"

"A teacher. Someone who imparts wisdom."

"No . . ."

Mark laughs. "Yeah, I guess not."

"You look like you, only different."

Noah hands Mark the trowel. They squat down inside the new wall to inspect the mortar joints. They're both filthy. Gray dust covers Noah's hair and clothes; mud cakes his sneakers. Mark's hands are creased with dirt, his fingernails black underneath.

"You still look like a dad though," Noah adds.

Samara's father sits on the floor of his bedroom in a pool of her mother's clothes, bright dresses and loosely knit sweaters and slippery scarves and floral skirts. He picks up a dress the color of new grass and puts it down.

She kneels next to him and reaches for a skirt printed with roses and sparrows. "Why didn't she tell me?" she asks. "About the house in Costa Rica? About your plan to move away?"

He holds up a translucent blue scarf, and it shimmers in the light from the window. "She wanted to wait."

"For what?"

"When we bought the cottage you were only just out of college. We weren't going to move until you'd established yourself. She wanted you to have someplace to come home to, if you needed it."

"She knew I'd end up back here."

"You and your mom were a lot alike."

She shakes her head because they couldn't

313

have been more different.

"She was good at so many things. You're like that too. She said she was waiting for you to find what you love."

Her mother was always saying stuff like that. Who asks themselves questions like that? What do I love? Samara doesn't have an answer. Except for an image that springs up, just now in her mind, of herself standing on tiptoe on a shiny hardwood floor, a paint roller in her outstretched hand. "And then she got sick."

"And then she got sick." He's still holding the filmy blue scarf, and the expression on his face is so raw she has to look away. She thought it was so easy for him to sort through it all, to throw it away.

She was wrong about Costa Rica too. It will be good for him, to get out of this house. To go watch some tropical birds. She's ashamed of how little she's thought of her father the last month. She tries hard to think of him now. But it feels like she's holding on to something that's being torn away. She thinks of the time her uncle took them out on his speedboat at Sparrow Lake. It was summer, hot and dry, with the charred smell of a distant wildfire in the air. She was twelve, maybe thirteen, and she wore a navy halter-top swimsuit with a white stripe.

Her uncle had attached a big inner tube to the back of the boat. She didn't want to ride on it, but she did because her cousin teased her. He was on one side and she on the other. She had to straddle the side of the tube, and hold on to a plastic handle. When the boat started moving she gripped the handle as it bumped over the waves. Then it turned sharply — and her cousin let go and fell into the water with a terrific splash. He was quickly buoyed to the surface by his orange life vest. But she held on, half on the raft, half off, her vest bunched under her armpits. She held on until her fingers turned white.

Her mother was a person who didn't let go of things — until she wasn't. Samara folds the dress with the roses and birds and takes the scarf from her dad. It was a favorite of her mother's when she was a little girl. Samara used to wind her fingers around it when she sat in her lap, press its fabric to her lips.

She folds it too and places it on top of the dress. "I think you should go. It'll be good for you."

He squeezes her shoulder. "You should know the house is paid off, and as soon as I sign the papers, that money will be yours."

"What do you mean? The house isn't even

on the market."

"Your mother promised the Lenovs they could make an offer on it if we ever chose to sell."

Samara starts to protest and then stops. She's relieved. She won't have to be the one to lead buyers through her parents' house and listen to them criticize the tile or carpet color. She won't have to haggle with another agent over the selling price. She won't have to walk through the empty rooms, to leave the spare keys and the garage door opener on the counter, and to lock the front door for the last time.

Still, they should have told her, about their plan to sell the house and their intention to leave the country. But this is what her parents do, what they've always done. They keep things from her. They know she doesn't like change, and they protect her from it.

"Why didn't you wake me up?" she asks. "That morning at the hospital, when you and Mom and Dr. McDonnell talked about whether to go ahead with the surgery. I was asleep and no one woke me up."

He sighs. "We should have. If there was any mistake, that was it. I'm sorry, Sammy."

She takes the pile of folded clothes and puts it into an empty cardboard box. "I can't take that money. You'll need it when you move."

"I've got plenty in my retirement accounts."

"You've already helped me, too much. With school, with my real estate license."

"It's what your mother wanted."

"What did she want me to do with it?"

She asks the question in her head, too, but this time her mom's voice is silent.

"I don't know," her father says. "But I know she wished she could be around to see what you decided."

Twenty-Eight

When Ginny gets home from work she calls out to her husband and son, but no one answers. It feels strange being home without them. She turns on the kitchen light. The dishwasher stands open, half-unloaded. Bread crumbs speckle the counter. An overflowing basket of muddy clothes blocks the door to the laundry room. Mark always keeps everything so tidy; she feels disoriented, like she's walked into the wrong house.

She pulls her phone from her pocket and scrolls through the messages she and Edith have sent to each other over the last week. Dozens and dozens of texts. All so sweet and silly, they seem to be written by someone else. At the end is the last thing she wrote to Edith.

When can I see you?

And a blank space below it, where Edith's response hasn't appeared.

Ginny takes off her jacket, pushes her clogs from her feet, and starts toward the stairs. There's a tinny taste on her tongue. The kitchen floor lurches —

Edith stands in the middle of the living room, dressed like she's about to go running. Her track pants swish as she lunges, stretching one leg behind her, and then the other.

"What are you doing here?" Ginny croaks.

"He's out there again," Edith says.

"Who?"

Edith doesn't look at Ginny. She acts like she hasn't said anything at all. A voice calls from the stairs, "What did you say?" and the voice is Ginny's own.

Ginny turns her face away from the sound. It isn't real. It's a side effect of her medication.

"He's out there again, in his car," Edith says.

Ginny's twin joins Edith at the front window. She wears scrubs and smells of coffee and chlorine. Her pager, phone, and surgical scissors are still clipped to her side.

"I'm going to go talk to him," Edith says.

"No. Don't. That'll just make things worse."

319

Edith shakes her head. "I don't know . . ."

Ginny squints out the window at Mark's Jeep, parked on the shiny pavement. It takes her a minute to see inside because the streetlight casts a glare on the windshield. Mark sits in the front seat. Or, someone who looks a lot like Mark. The real Mark is out with Noah, at Home Depot or Safeway. This Mark's face is streaked with mud. His mouth is a thin dark line, and his head twitches nervously back and forth.

"Let's just be glad Noah isn't here this time," Ginny's twin says.

"This is getting crazy. It's not a normal reaction to your marriage ending, living in a tent in the woods, parking outside your ex's house for hours at a time —"

"Just ignore him. If he doesn't leave, we'll call the police." Her twin turns away from the window and moves toward the stairs.

The Jeep's headlights switch on, and it backs out of the driveway.

"He's leaving," Edith says.

"Good."

Edith joins Ginny's twin at the bottom of the stairs. "I was going to go for a run. But I'll stay here."

"Would you?" Her twin presses her fingers to her eyes. "I'm so beat. Noah will be home any minute. Let's not mention —"

"Of course not," Edith says firmly. She reaches out to squeeze Ginny's twin's arm. "It'll be okay."

"Will it?"

"Yes. I'll call for a pizza. The kind with pineapple Noah likes."

Her twin's face relaxes. "Good idea." She leans her head toward Edith and their foreheads touch.

Ginny listens to their footsteps climb the stairs. Out the front window the driveway is empty. She tells herself the person who sat in Mark's Jeep wasn't real. But his dirty face seems to loom in front of her eyes, no matter how many times she blinks it away.

Cass's dog barks outside and then quiets. Ginny moves back to the kitchen, away from the driveway. She opens the sliding door to the backyard. The hole has disappeared. In its place is a cinder block structure. Somehow in the span of a few days Mark has built it, his bunker. It has a floor and walls; only the roof is missing. A tangle of pipes and tools sits at its muddy threshold.

She feels sick looking at the ugly, squat thing her husband has built. That she let him build. She could have stopped him, but she didn't, and its dark, heavy shape fills her with shame. She closes the door. Her phone is in her pocket. She shouldn't text

Edith again. She shouldn't but she does.

Please. I'll meet you wherever you are.

She waits in the blue glow of the phone's screen. And waits.

When Edith's answer appears it feels like magic. She's at the hospital; her shift is almost over and she'll meet Ginny there.

The sun disappears behind the mountain, and the walls of the shelter and the surrounding trees become indistinct shapes in the dying light. The creak of insects fills the air. Noah rubs his eyes. They've been working hard all day. Mud streaks his face; his hair is stiff with cement dust.

Mark's tired too. His shoulders ache from hauling cinder blocks and trusses and the steel hatch door. The stubble on his cheeks itches with sweat. "We're almost done," he says. He switches on a work light he's attached to a tree, and it casts a yellow glow over the building site. He lines up the metal trusses on the wet grass. Then he attaches the hook of the mini crane he's rented for the day, a sprawling machine that looks like a giant wolf spider.

He tells Noah where to stand so he can guide the trusses into place. His son pulls on a helmet, safety glasses, and gloves.

"Just follow the chalked guidelines, like we talked about, okay?"

Noah yawns again and nods.

Mark turns the key on the crane and the machine comes to life with a thundering whine. Fumes billow and they both cough.

Mark positions himself behind the controls. He scratches his stubble, and then takes the levers in his gloved hands. "Okay, here goes."

Ginny hears a click — someone's opening the call room door. Did she and Edith not lock it? A figure blocks the doorway. "Dr. McDonnell?" a tentative male voice says into the darkness. "Are you in here?"

Ginny feels Edith's warm body against her own. Neither of them moves. She can see Dr. Harper but he can't see her. There's still time to . . . to what, hide?

As he feels for the light switch, the sweat under her arms and the slippery wet between her legs goes cold. And then — *snap* — they are all bathed in bluish light. Ginny and Edith in the bed, their hearts hammering against each other. Their scrub pants pushed below their knees. Dr. Harper's mortified face in the doorway.

Edith snatches the thin sheet and pulls it

over her body.

"Dr. McDonnell." Her intern talks to a spot on the wall above Ginny's head. "We've been paging you. There's a situation on the fifth floor —" Clogs squeak in the hallway behind him. It'll be Dr. Dawson, and maybe the floor nurse too. Or, worse, another surgeon. Dr. Harper holds open the door as if he's inviting everyone inside.

But before the clogs arrive, he turns off the light and closes the door. "She's coming," Ginny hears him say.

And then she's moving like a frightened animal, like she moved when she was a resident, in response to a barking order from an attending, or a harried correction from a nurse. Her heart scampers, her body shivers; she doesn't look at Edith. She throws open a locker and it clatters against the wall. She finds a clean pair of scrubs and fumbles to pull them on.

Dr. Harper didn't say which patient. She thinks immediately of Professor Kells. Where is her pager? Her phone? They aren't anywhere in the room. Not on the desk or in the locker or on the floor. She thrusts her bare feet into her clogs because she can't find her socks. Edith hasn't moved. She's still in the bed with the sheet pulled up to her chin. Her cheeks are bright red.

Ginny remembers what Edith said in the car, that Ginny has only been thinking about herself, not about Edith at all.

"I'm so sorry," Ginny says, before running out the door.

The backyard is dark now, and thick with exhaust. Mark squints at the controls of the mini crane in the light from the work lamp. Just one more truss to go. Noah stands inside the shelter, ready to help guide the beam into place. Mark grasps the throttle and feels the vibration of the machine through his body as he maneuvers the boom up, slowly, carefully, keeping the beam level. Then down, down, down. He makes sure it's not too close to Noah, or too far away.

He's concentrating so hard he doesn't notice the awful taste in his mouth until there's a movement behind his son —

A shape passes across the light . . . a person. No! The Other Mark emerges from the forest, only feet from Noah. His shoulders are hunched in his filthy jacket, his hair matted and wild. The lever jerks in Mark's hand; the beam wobbles, starts to go crooked. He tries to straighten it with the controls but he overcorrects and it swings away from him.

There's a sound — a thump. He's hit

something. Oh fuck, he's hit Noah. His son is bent in half, screaming. He's hurt. He's hurt. How bad, how bad?

Mark jumps from the machine, trips, rights himself, and runs. The task light has fallen to the ground, casting a glare over the dirt. He picks it up and swings it wildly, over the bunker, over the trees. He can't see the Other Mark anywhere. He points the light at his son's slumped form. Maybe it's not so bad. There's no blood. "It's okay," he breathes. "You're okay." He feels his son's head, his face. Nothing. Then he gasps. Broken bone juts out from Noah's right shoulder. An actual bone, punched right through his skin. Mark's vision narrows. He can't look, he can't look. He has to look.

Noah screams again and little balls of tears spring from his eyes. He screams and Mark feels the sound as pain in his own body; it seems to vibrate inside his skin.

Ginny runs toward the elevator. Inside she jabs at the button for the fifth floor, and when the doors open, she looks right and left. The tails of her residents' white coats flap down the hallway behind a rattling gurney, and she hurries after them.

She blinks at the tiny shape on the gurney. "Mrs. Carlyle?" There is a sheen of sweat on the woman's thin face. Her fists ball up the white sheet.

"She's got a subhepatic biloma." Dr. Harper thrusts some films at Ginny. "That's what was causing the jaundice."

It's difficult to meet her intern's eye, but she does it. "Does the OR know we're coming?"

"They're setting up for an ERCP," Dr. Dawson says.

Her residents swing Mrs. Carlyle around a corner and through the doors to OR 3. Another surgeon stands at the scrub sink, his hands orange and foamy with Betadine soap. "Am I taking this case or what?"

The gurney's halfway through the swinging doors. "It's my case," Ginny says.

"Well, hell." He throws the scrub brush into the sink and stalks away.

"What's happening?" Mrs. Carlyle asks in a terrified whisper.

"We think you have an obstruction of your hepatic duct," Dr. Dawson says, speaking over the beeping machines. "We need to take you to the OR to figure out what's causing the blockage."

"Don't worry," Dr. Harper says firmly. "We'll be able to fix it."

Mark struggles with the seatbelt, breathing

fast and hard. Noah's lips have turned a horrible shade of gray. He's stopped crying, but it's almost worse to watch his silent, bloodless face. Where should he put the shoulder belt? The towel he's pressed over his son's shoulder slips, exposing blood and bone. Mark gags, grabs the towel, pushes it back in place with both hands. Noah howls in pain, and hot tears fill Mark's eyes. "It's going to be okay. We're okay." He takes Noah's other hand and presses it to the towel. He loops the shoulder belt behind his back.

He runs around the car to the driver's seat and looks into the dark forest, but the Other Mark is gone. He dials Ginny's number again. No answer. He curses her for being absent, for never picking up her phone. He repeats "we're okay, we're okay" under his breath as he starts the car, his hand shaking hard. He skids out into the cul-de-sac, knocks over his neighbors' trash cans, and speeds down the hill.

TWENTY-NINE

Ginny pulls the overhead light close to Mrs. Carlyle's face and threads the endoscope down her throat, watching its progress on the video monitor. It passes through the pink, furrowed stomach, past the pylorus and into the grooved tunnel of the small intestine. When the scope reaches the common bile duct Dr. Dawson injects the contrast dye.

Tricia pushes into the room. "Dr. McDonnell. Your son —" She looks at the scope sticking out of Mrs. Carlyle's mouth, and back at Ginny.

"What about him?"

"He's being prepped for emergency surgery."

"What?"

"I just saw his name on the ER patient board —"

The EKG monitor beeps, and the pulse oximeter pings. Ginny counts the steps that need to happen to complete the ERCP. She visualizes the actions, and then she pictures her residents performing them without her help.

She hands the scope to Dr. Dawson and turns the monitor toward Dr. Harper. "Watch the small bowel." Their faces are astonished. "Don't fuck up." Then she runs out the door.

She tears her gloves from her hands and throws them into the scrub sink, pulls her gown from her body and lets it fall to the floor. Outside the OR doors Mark stands in the hallway, covered in mud.

"What happened?"

"Noah was hurt. They just took him to the operating room —"

"Hurt how?" She tugs off her mask. "Hurt *how*, Mark?"

"His shoulder. He hurt his shoulder."

"It must have been bad if they're taking him to the OR —"

Mark looks like he might be sick. "His bone was . . . It was sticking out of —" He gestures to his own shoulder.

"A compound fracture. Jesus, Mark. How did this happen?" But she doesn't wait for him to answer. "Which doctor?"

Mark's face is confused.

"Which doctor took him back?"

"It was Henry. Dr. Hoag —"

"Okay." She takes a breath. "Okay."

"Can you find out what's happening?"

She shakes her head. "No — we need to stay out of their way."

"I tried to call you." He rubs the stubble on his cheeks. "You didn't answer —"

"Noah was out in the backyard when this happened, wasn't he —"

"I must have called you ten times. Where were you?"

"I was in the OR."

"Of course you were."

"If I had known Noah was hurt, I would have come straight away —"

"You didn't when he had croup."

She stares at him. "That was ten years ago."

"He couldn't breathe. He could have died."

She crushes her mask into a tight ball.

"I was scared." Mark's voice wavers. "And you were just — not there."

She's not sure if he's talking about then, or now.

"I wish I could have been there with you," she says. Mark had sat holding Noah all night on the floor of their bathroom with a hot shower running. He'd ridden in the ambulance with him when his honking cough got worse, when he struggled to take a breath. "I really do."

"Good." He paces toward the OR doors, and then back again. "That's something at least."

She watches him, his hunched shoulders, his worried green eyes. She wants to say something. "I feel alone a lot too."

He shakes his head. He doesn't understand.

"I don't have anyone I can talk to about work —"

"You can talk to me."

She's quiet for a minute. "I've tried. But it stresses you out —"

"It does not."

"You can't handle it, Mark."

"I handle a lot." He paces again. "You don't know half the things I do for you —"

"I work hard for our family too."

"Noah's a pretty great kid, isn't he? That's because of me. The time I've spent." His voice gets louder. "The things I've given up to be with him."

"Noah's hurt!" She points to the OR doors. Other people in the hallway turn to stare at them, but she doesn't care. "And it's your fault."

His hands make two fists. "It wasn't my fault. It was his."

"Whose? Noah's? You can't be serious —"

"Not Noah's." His mouth clenches. *"His."*

"You're not making any sense —" She hears footsteps on the other side of the OR doors. Tricia pokes her head out. "Ginny." She uses her first name. "Henry's closing him up now. He had to put in two pins, but he's going to be okay."

Ginny doesn't cover her eyes; she lets tears drip down her face. "Thank you." She grabs Mark's jacket and presses her face into his chest. The waterproof fabric is warm and rough against her wet cheek, and it smells of earth and cement. Her anger drains away. "Something has to change." She pulls him down to her level. "We have to change." But her own relief isn't reflected back in his face.

"I have to go." His voice is strange. "I have to do something."

"You can't leave."

He loosens her hands from his jacket and pulls up his hood.

"He hasn't woken up yet —"

Again he pushes her hands away. "I have to do something I should have done before."

Mark drives up the mountain, through thick, hovering fog, through sideways rain that hits the windshield in waves. When he reaches the trailhead he pulls a heavy-duty flashlight from his trunk and starts walking. The rain pelts him in the face; it seeps into the collar of his jacket and through the seams of his pants. He moves the flashlight back and forth across the drenched trail. Everything is black and slippery wet. There's no moon, no stars — no light of any kind outside his sweeping narrow beam.

He ignores the normal forest sounds: the rapping of the rain against leaves, the scuttle of a small animal, a marten or a skunk, the groaning of toads. His body's alive to any vibration, in the ground, in the air. He waits for the taste of metal in his mouth. He waits for the earth to tremble. He can't find the Other Mark until it does.

When he reaches Pond F he nearly walks into the water it's so dark, but his flashlight catches the pond's inky shine, and he stops and listens. He hears the *slup* of a frog leg against water, but nothing more. Standing at the edge of the pond he feels . . . exposed, like all the forest's creatures are watching him. He shivers in his wet clothes. Maybe the Other Mark is watching too.

He pushes into the brush. His flashlight illuminates the bulge of a wet, furrowed tree trunk, the tip of a curled bramble, the top half of a shallow rock, a flash of water in its hollow. He steps onto the old logging road, where he first saw the Other Mark, but the earth under his feet is solid and still. He wills the shaking to come, but it doesn't.

He moves deeper into the dripping forest. The air is heavy with the smell of pinesap and decomposing leaves. He hikes farther up the mountain, and then circles back. Hikes farther, circles back. Hours pass. He keeps going until his legs ache, until dawn's faint, chalky gloom appears between the trees. He's walked so far he's nearly reached the curve of the road on the other side of the mountain. Up ahead is a campsite encircled by ponderosa pines, at its center an old A-frame cabin with peeling yellow paint and birds' nests in its eaves. He recognizes where he is now. He's not far from Harry's property. This is where he ran at the Other Mark, where he yelled at him to go away.

But the campsite is deserted. It feels like it's been empty for a long, long time. The ground is dense with pine needles, the fire pit full of disintegrated leaves. He sits down on a rock and watches the gray light grow. He rests his head in his hands.

Then he tastes metal. The ground jolts. He stands, and where there was nothing but dirt and twigs a second ago —

A blue tent.

Mark breathes as the sky brightens. He might only have minutes, seconds even. He creeps close; he reaches for the tent's zipper. He pulls it down, *rrrrpp.* There's someone asleep inside. A filthy man curled in a sleeping bag. Mark leans in. He has to do it. This has to end. There can't be two Marks. There can only be one.

But he hesitates. The Other Mark's breathing is slow and deep. From underneath the sleeping bag there's the faint squeak of a snore.

He can't do it. He can't. He pulls back.

But the ground quakes again, and there's a snort and a start. Mud-streaked hands lunge at Mark. They grab for his throat.

He's knocked to the ground, and now the Other Mark's face is inches from his, twisted and strange. Mark presses his hands against it, this terrible face that's his own and not his own.

"Who are you?" the Other Mark pants. "Who?"

The ground shudders again. The Other Mark's hands tighten around Mark's throat. Mark struggles; he jabs his fingers into the Other Mark's eyes and finally the hands loosen their grip. Mark scrambles away. He gets to his feet.

Again the Other Mark lunges, and Mark

does too, kicking, punching. But the Other Mark is stronger, crazier. He gets his hands around Mark's throat again and squeezes. Mark's legs slip and jerk. The ground buckles. There's no air. The pressure in his head builds. No . . . air . . . He falls to the ground. He feels cold earth pulsing against his cheek. His vision darkens. He reaches out, blindly; his hand finds a rock. He swings it and — *crack.*

The Other Mark's hands loosen and fall away. His body falls away too. Or, no. Mark opens his eyes. The shaking ceases. He waves his hands through empty air. The Other Mark is gone.

THIRTY

Cass stands at the sink in her bathroom with a pink box in her hands, just like she did last December in her old student apartment across town. That time Amar was sleeping in the other room, his feet sticking out from under her comforter, and Bear was breathing outside the door. The test was a white stick with a bright pink cap and a little window that revealed a paper strip within. She stared into that window for two minutes, her body tense, the tile cold beneath her bare feet, before two rosy threads appeared.

This time Amar isn't just outside the room. He's out in the middle of the ocean, probably hunched over his microscope inside the small lab on the ship. Like last time, Leah's in the bathroom with Cass. Only she's not a collection of cells lodged in the wall of her uterus, but a ten-week-old baby lying on the bath mat, happily kicking her feet toward the ceiling.

Cass doesn't feel pregnant. But what she saw . . . She shakes her head at the memory of the woman in Leah's nursery. The woman who looked just like her, who sang the same off-tune song to her belly that her dad used to sing.

Leah gurgles and smiles. She has more hair now. There's a tuft right in the center of her forehead. "Ahya, ahya," she says. "Ahya, ahya."

Cass loves her, fiercely. She would love another child the same way, wouldn't she? But it's hard to imagine that kind of love doubled. What would it be like with two babies under two to love and protect and tend to and want things for? What would happen to her book — her theory of the multiverse — in the face of two sets of diapers, twice as much laundry, and bottles for two instead of just one?

She pulls her underwear down and takes the cap off one of the two tests in the box. She pees on it and counts.

one one thousand
two one thousand
three one thousand
four one thousand
five one thousand

After she pulls up her underwear, she sets the test on the back of the toilet atop her marked-up copy of *Discourse on Metaphysics.*

She scoops Leah up, her small body warm and heavy in her arms. She sees herself in her daughter's bright, dark eyes and Amar in the shape of her pointed chin. What would another child — hers, and Amar's — look like? Who would that tiny person be? Cass feels a thrill at this question. Some piece of her wants to be pregnant again. But another part of her, the part she finds when she bends over her laptop and loses herself in big ideas, resolutely does not.

There's a minute left on the test, but she changes her mind. She's not ready to know. She grabs the pink-and-white stick, drops it into the toilet, and flushes. She watches it circle the bowl and disappear.

She takes Leah downstairs and opens the dishwasher; she stares at the clean cups and glasses and bowls inside. The Mehtas wave to her from the backyard. They're weeding the overgrown garden beds and their hands are full of yellow leaves. The kitchen feels warm and close. Too close. She grabs the diaper bag and an extra baby blanket. She writes them a note and carries Leah to the car.

Once they're moving, she turns toward the highway and soon Leah's eyes begin to droop in the mirror attached to the back-seat. The mountain rises up ahead, its snowy broken top sharp against the gray-blue sky. She lets the monotone of the road's vibration soothe her. She's accomplished a lot in just a few days. But she's still at the beginning. She needs time and silence to coax and prod the pages she's written, to form and reform them. To compel them to become solid, imposing, sound. She needs months, maybe years, of time and silence.

Up ahead is the exit Mark took the night she followed him up Broken Mountain, and she turns on her signal. She has a strange desire to see it again, the spot where she watched him pitch his tent. The road is different in the daylight. The sun filters through the trees and makes triangles of light and dark on the road. Things that were hazy outlines are now distinct forms: moss-covered tree limbs, logs full of loamy, white-speckled earth, blackberry brambles.

In the mirror Leah's mouth purses a few times and then is still. How long did it take to get to the dirt road Mark turned onto that night? It felt like forever. But it's already up ahead, forking off to the right. She slows the car, parks, gets out, and locks

Leah inside. The air is cold and clear, not sodden like it's been for weeks, but crisp. Birds warble and flap their wings from the trees.

She walks to the spot where she saw Mark, toward a broken-down, A-frame cabin with peeling yellow paint and birds' nests in its eaves. She remembers that night, how desperate she was when Leah wouldn't stop crying, how trapped she felt, how she would have done almost anything to escape the sound of her screams. She pictures Mark's dirty, terrified face. But who looked worse — more desperate, more scared, more wild? Mark or her?

Something's moving ahead of her. Strange! Frogs — hundreds of them packed together — advance through the pines. A jostling sea of popping eyes and springy legs, they seem to move together and then separately, to transform in shape. One minute they're an irregular oval, the next, a bobbing rectangle. Their edges look like appendages, their center a cascading wave. They move at a jolting, asymmetrical pace, and soon they disappear into the trees.

In their wake is a twist of blue fabric. A crumpled tent. And something else. What is it?

A shape on the ground. A human shape.

It's him. Her neighbor Mark. His forehead's bloody. Oh god, is he —

A faint groan comes from his slumped form. Cass crouches over him. "What's happened?"

His face is bewildered, his green eyes unfocused. Then he seems to recognize her.

"Can you stand up?"

He raises his head. Dirt and twigs cling to his dark hair. He tries to sit up, groans, and collapses again.

"Let me help you." She pulls him up. "Hold on to me. My car is close." But he's so heavy. His wet clothes hang off his body; he smells of pine needles and sour skin. She tries again and she's able to pull him to his feet. He leans on her, hard, and she helps him limp to her car.

When they get there his face has turned gray. He leans against a tree. "You should go." This is the first thing he says. "There's nowhere for you to take me. I'm better off here."

"We're going to the hospital. Get in." She holds open the passenger-side door. Leah's still asleep in the backseat. She hears the squeak of her breathing.

He climbs into the car, finally, and they drive down the mountain. He slumps in his seat, and grimaces at all the turns. Cass wants to ask him, Have you been living in the woods this whole time? She wants to ask him, Why? But he's so silent and pale — he's pressed his bloody forehead against the glass — that she says nothing.

When they get to the hospital, she helps him out of the car. She supports him with one hand and lugs the car seat with the other. They pause inside the sliding glass doors. Again she remembers standing in this spot with Amar the morning after Leah was born, the sun bright in their eyes.

She asks Mark, "What happened in the woods?"

He turns and there's a wild look in his eyes. "He tried to kill me."

"What? Who?"

"A man" — he touches his bloody forehead — "who looked just like me." His face turns almost white as he slumps against Cass.

A nurse in pink scrubs waves at them from behind the front desk. "Sir, are you feeling dizzy?"

"Page Dr. McDonnell," Cass tells her. "Her husband's hurt." But Mark shakes his head. "No." He looks like he wants to run, but he's barely able to stand. "Not her."

The nurse hurries toward them and steadies Mark. "Is there someone else we can call?"

Leah makes a snuffling sound from her car seat, and Mark watches her eyes flutter and then close. "Noah," he says. "I want to see my son."

Across the parking lot the hospital doors flash silver and blue. Samara walked through the doors dozens of times with her mom, coming and going from appointments and treatments. But she hasn't been back since Ashmina died. She gathers the papers she needs to present the offer on the Kells house. Professor Kells's sons are with their father inside.

It's not raining for once. It's cool and clear. But when she steps inside the smell of the cafeteria churns her stomach. She remembers the awful morning she and her dad walked through the hospital in stunned slow motion. It felt as if her body was moving through glue. The colors of things weren't right. The air was full of a heavy smell, coffee beans and cleaning supplies. A man in a white coat walked past with a tray laden with orange eggs and gray toast, and she wanted to knock it out of his hands.

The wave of nausea passes. A nurse in pink scrubs wheels an elderly woman toward

the front doors. A doctor hurries past holding a large coffee and a protein bar. Her
face is skinny and tired.

When Samara gets to Room 507 she
pauses. Through the open door two men
are next to a gray-haired patient sitting up
in a hospital bed. Their resemblance is
unmistakable, a father and his two sons.
One son reads aloud from a newspaper and
the other leans back in his chair, listening.
The gray-haired man's eyes droop; he's falling into a doze.

She has stuck yellow SIGN HERE tabs to
the contracts, under where her clients wrote
their names. She hesitates.

The man with the newspaper notices her
and waves her inside.

"I'll be right there," she says, and ducks
into an adjacent empty room. She pulls out
a blank contract and sets it on the bed. With
trembling fingers she writes a number five
thousand dollars higher than her clients' offer. It feels rash, irresponsible. It feels like
she might regret it. But she scribbles her
name at the bottom of each page anyway.

THIRTY-ONE

Noah's eyes start to droop halfway into the movie they're watching in his room, and Ginny nudges him awake. "Let's go brush your teeth and take your pain pill. Then you can sleep."

"It's still light out."

"It's almost seven and you need your rest." She helps him up from the bed, the splint on his shoulder and upper arm unwieldy.

His brow creases. "It's starting to hurt again."

She puts her hand on his other shoulder and steers him toward the bathroom, runs some water into a glass, and hands him his pill. "Take this." She puts some toothpaste on his toothbrush and gives it to him, but it's clumsy in his left hand.

"Here, I'll help you," she says gently. She stands behind him, like she used to when he was three or four, before he was able to brush his teeth on his own. Watching herself in the mirror, she moves the toothbrush over his front teeth, and around his bottom and top molars.

As he rinses his mouth and spits into the sink, she appraises his face: he's pale and bits of mud still cling to his hair. His splint will be on for eight weeks. But he's going to be okay. She picks some dirt from his hair. "Come on, I'll tuck you in."

Back in his room she turns off the movie and helps him into bed. She pulls the covers up, brushes his hair from his forehead, and sits on the edge of the bed. He turns this way and that, trying to find a comfortable position with the bulky splint, and then his eyes slowly close.

She's spent the whole day in this room. At first they didn't talk about the accident, but then, while they played cards, she asked him how he got hurt. How exactly. But every time she asks he says the same thing: It was an accident. It was bad luck. It wasn't Dad's fault.

Mark has taken full responsibility for Noah's injury. But to Ginny's astonishment, this hasn't dampened his zeal for finishing his shelter. Once they brought Noah home from the hospital and settled him in his own bed, Mark disappeared into the backyard and she hasn't seen him since.

She watches her son's eyelids flutter. Something has to change. But it's not what she thought. She's been so stupid, so focused on the wrong things. It's obvious, now that she's spent the day in Noah's company, and remembered how good it feels to be with him for long stretches of time. Doing very little, just being together. When he was born she was just out of residency. She missed a lot. But she thought there would be time, later, to take it all in: his natural sweetness at three years old, his innate curiosity at five, all the things he could do at seven and eight. But too many of those years are a blur. She kept telling herself, I'll have more time, later. She would say, We'll be together more in the summer. But the years have hustled past, and now it feels like she only saw the highs and the lows. None of the long stretches in between.

She lies down next to Noah, his cheek warm and soft next to hers, his breathing deep and steady. His hair smells like dried earth and something else sweet and sharp, like crushed flowers. He's smelled like that ever since he was born. When he was a baby she would press her nose to his head, over and over, like it was a drug, like she couldn't get enough.

She thinks of Mark out in the wet yard, digging in the dirt with the noisy backhoe, and of Edith the last time she saw her, in the call room with the sheet pulled up to her chin. She's not very good at it — loving, and being loved.

Noah got the best of her, and even that wasn't all that great. He's eleven years old. He won't sleep in this room forever. "I'm sorry," she whispers near his ear. "I'm sorry, Noah." She says this to him, but it feels like she's saying it to herself.

When her phone buzzes she gets up from the bed as quietly as she can. Edith's name flashes across the screen, and she takes the phone downstairs. Livi's still here. She came over earlier to visit Noah, but Ginny thought Mark had already taken her home. She's watching TV in the living room.

Ginny ducks into the kitchen and answers. Edith starts talking right away. "Your son, how is he?" Her voice sounds different, thin and strained.

"He has a fractured humerus. But he'll be okay."

There's silence on the other end of the line, and Ginny can hear Edith breathing. Finally she says, "I can't stop thinking about what happened."

"I really can't talk now."

"Is Mark there?"

"I think so."

"I need to talk to you," Edith says. "Just for a few minutes."

Ginny looks out the window into the dark backyard. Mark is moving around with a flashlight out there. "I can't leave the house."

"That's okay. I'll come to you."

Mark swings the hatch door to the shelter back and forth to test its hinges. Rain mists his face. The ground beneath his boots is slippery with mud, but the earth surrounding the shelter is solid and sure. Like a gray fox's hole or a bobcat's natal den. He climbs inside and shuts the door tightly behind him. The sounds of the forest — the humming of insects and the clicking of frogs — disappear.

He pauses in the dark to take off his boots. The room smells like new cement and the rubber sealant he applied to the walls a few hours ago. In his socks he feels along a set of shelves for a camping lantern, turns it on, and moves around the rectangular room in its yellow light. He smooths the fleece covers on the three cots, moving methodically from one to the next. He lines up objects on the shelves: cans of soup and boxes of powdered milk and containers of instant oatmeal; extra bedding and towels; a first-aid kit and an emergency radio and two shovels; a length of rope and rolls of plastic sheeting. He checks the pump on the air filter and tests the generator. He opens the lid of the chemical toilet and closes it. With each object Mark touches, he feels more solid and singular. With each object, the Other Mark feels less real — more like a ghost or a shade than a man.

Downstairs, Ginny pulls on her sneakers. She hears Mark come in through the back door, take off his boots, and climb the stairs. She calls up to him, "I'm going out. Stay with Noah will you?"

He doesn't ask her why. He just calls back, "Okay."

Outside the air is damp and cool, the mountain hazy with fog. It takes a minute for Ginny's eyes to adjust — her neighbors' windows and doors are dark — before she realizes she's not alone. Across the cul-de-sac Samara sits on a lawn chair in her front yard, fast asleep.

Ginny hesitates. The last time she saw Samara she was so angry. But she doesn't look angry now. Her face is peaceful despite the awkward position of her body in the chair, with one foot tucked underneath her and the other resting on the grass. It reminds her of the morning of her mother's surgery. When Ginny came into Ashmina's room it was early, before six, and Samara was asleep in a chair next to her mother's bed. Her parents were talking in low voices. Ginny said they needed to discuss the surgery and asked if they should wake Samara. But Ashmina waved Manish away when he moved to rouse her. "Leave her be," Ashmina said. "I like watching her sleeping face."

Ginny crosses the wet circle of pavement between the houses. She bends down to shake Samara's arm, whose eyes blink open. "What are you doing out here?" Ginny asks. "Is everything okay?"

"I'm waiting for her."

"Waiting for who?"

Samara rubs her eyes and sits up straighter in her chair. "I saw her. I saw my mom right there." She points to a spot in the grass.

Ginny shakes her head. "I don't understand —"

"She left me this money," Samara says. "But she didn't tell me what she wanted me to do with it."

Ginny looks at the spot Samara pointed to. "Maybe she thought you should decide for yourself." She remembers rolling Ashmina to the OR on the morning of her surgery. She was trying to complete the pre-surgery checklist, but Ashmina wasn't listening. She was talking about how, when Samara was a little girl, she used to hide behind Ashmina's legs whenever someone came to the door. "Manish said I babied her. But she was such a little thing. So small, so timid." The anesthesiologist started sedation and Ashmina's eyes began to droop and her words slur. Ginny bent close to hear what she was saying, but all she could make out was "like a little bird."

"I wish I could talk to her, just one more time," Samara says.

"Me too."

"Really?" Samara shivers and rubs her shoulders. "What would you ask her?"

"I'd ask if she's angry with me."

"My dad says she knew the surgery was risky with her heart," Samara says.

"She told me, 'I'm not done. I have stuff to do. So let's go for it.' "

Samara's quiet for a minute. A misty rain begins to fall. "For a long time I thought it was your fault she died. My dad says it wasn't. He says it was nobody's fault."

Ginny has played Ashmina's surgery over and over again in her mind. She's tried to find something, any small detail that could have changed the outcome. But she's never found it. "I wish it had gone differently. But it didn't."

"I bought a house. That's what I would tell her if she were here." Samara folds up her chair and gazes, again, at the spot in the wet grass. "Maybe it was a mistake. I guess I'll find out."

Samara shrugs and the gesture reminds Ginny of when she was younger, when it felt like she didn't know what she was doing. When every decision seemed huge. But back then she had Mark. They chose this cul-de-sac together, equidistant to the university and the hospital. This semicircle of pine trees. This house they brought Noah home to when he was born.

"Why are you out here?" Samara asks.

Ginny rubs her hands over her face. "I'm leaving my husband." It feels strange to say it out loud.

"Wow, I'm sorry."

"Things happen," Ginny says. But maybe that isn't right. She made choices and they led her here. Now she doesn't know what's next, and Mark isn't going to be by her side this time. "But it will be okay. I hope."

THIRTY-TWO

Once Samara has gone back into her house, Ginny sits on the curb and waits for Edith. Finally her car appears on the dark hillside. She parks just outside the cul-de-sac, gets out, and walks toward Ginny, a bundle of yellow asters in her hands.

"What are those for?"

"I picked them from my yard. They're for Noah."

"I can't give Noah flowers from you."

"Right." Edith looks down at the spiky blooms. "I mean, I know that. I don't know what I was thinking."

Edith peers into Ginny's backyard. "Is this where it happened?"

"Yeah."

"Can I see?"

"Why?"

"I don't know. I just want to."

But Ginny has trouble finding her way, and sees only dark earth and tangled roots where the shelter used to be. Mark has buried the entire structure. She feels along the wet hillside until her hand finds something hard, the metal edges of the rounded hatch door. "It's here. They were laying the support beams for the roof and one of them hit Noah."

Edith squints at the door. "What's inside?"

Ginny shakes her head. "I don't know."

Samara carries the folding chair through the wet grass and around the side of the house. She frowns. It's so quiet. Almost no sound comes from the forest; the air is empty of woodpecker taps, cricket creaks. She returns the folding chair to its spot on the patio and opens the sliding glass door. The ground vibrates and she stubs her toe. There's a terrible taste on her tongue.

She knows she left the light on. She feels around for the switch, and — she's walked into the wrong house. The room she's standing in is completely empty, of furniture, books, paintings, framed photographs, pillows, magazines, ceramic figurines. But it *is* her house. There's the mantel her dad built when she was a little girl. There's the arched doorway to the yellow kitchen —

Her dad stands inside the doorway, with . . . her mother. They're laughing, and

357

her father strokes her mom's hair.

Samara stays perfectly still because she doesn't want it to end. She doesn't want her mom to disappear, like she did before.

Ashmina turns. "Sammy? What are you doing home?"

"You drove all this way just to say good-bye?" her dad asks.

Her mother moves toward her, her arms outstretched. "You could have come a few hours earlier, no? Helped us with the last of the packing?"

Samara closes her eyes and feels her mother's warm, tight embrace. She inhales her sweet, earthy perfume. She holds on to her, and doesn't let go even when her mom pulls away.

"What's the matter?" Ashmina holds her at arm's length. "We'll see you at Thanksgiving. You've already bought your ticket." She tugs at Samara's hair. "What have you done with your hair? It's different. I'm not sure I like it —"

Samara laughs, but it turns into a sob.

"Oh, Sammy, don't worry. I'll still nag you just as much as before. It'll just be over the telephone."

Samara nods. "What can I do to help?"

"You can put the suitcases in the car." Her dad points to the worn blue luggage standing by the door.

She kisses them both and they get into the car. They look excited, giddy even. Her mom asks her dad if he's got the passports, and he pats his front pocket. They close their doors. They wave at her and she waves back. She follows the car down the driveway, waving, and waving, until it turns onto the main road and disappears into the trees.

When Mark comes downstairs Livi's still on the couch. Her mom hasn't come to pick her up yet. "Did your mom call?" he asks.

"She just texted. She's still at work."

"Let me get Noah some water, and then I'll drive you home."

The door to his study stands ajar, and a strange beeping comes from his computer. He moves closer to the screen and blinks at the real-time data from his research ponds. He starts. He clicks from one pond to the next: E, F, L, P. They're empty. His frogs are gone.

How long has the alarm been going off? He presses keys on his computer. Since this morning at dawn. 6:47 A.M. That's when he was in the forest. That's when he found the Other Mark. He recalls his dirty, twisted face. His hands squeezing his neck. The beeping from his computer continues, on and on. What has he done?

He dials his graduate student, Katie. She picks up on the third ring. "Are you seeing what I'm seeing?" he asks.

"What are you talking about?"

"Check your feed."

There's a pause, and the noise of Katie tapping at a computer keyboard. "Where are they? It's only October. They shouldn't be moving for months —"

"Listen, I want you to get in your car and drive as far away from the mountain as possible. Check the direction of the wind and go the opposite way. You know the projections about Broken Mountain. Lava flow isn't the danger, it's ash."

"Mark —"

"Once you're in your car I want you to call the USGS, and tell them what's happened." He rubs his patchy beard. "They might not listen but —"

"There could be another explanation. A malfunction in the collars —"

"All of them at once?"

"I don't know." Her voice has a shade of panic in it now. "There could be another reason —"

"Promise me you'll get in your car and go."

By the time he hangs up he's already at

his son's bedside. He shakes him awake. "Put on your shoes as best you can," he tells him.

He runs downstairs and checks the garage. Ginny's car is still there. He opens the front door; he calls her name. "They're gone!" he yells, and his voice — exhilarated, terrified, and echoing across the deserted cul-de-sac — sounds like it belongs to someone else. "My frogs are gone."

There's no answer. All is still. Mist cloaks the mountain. The only sound is the drip of rainwater from the trees.

Ginny's hand rests on the cold metal of the hatch door when she hears Mark calling out the front door. She can't make out everything he's saying, something about his frogs.

He's yelling louder now. She hesitates for a second and then grabs the hatch wheel. "In here." Her sneakers slide in the mud as she strains to pull open the door. She climbs inside and Edith follows.

Ginny closes the door as quietly as she can.

"Will he look out here?" Edith breathes.

"No," she says. "I don't think so. I told him I was going out." They feel around until they find a camping lantern and turn it on. Its yellow light reveals a fully furnished room. A rug covers the floor; shelves line the walls. Three metal cots are made up with green fleece blankets and flannel sheets. There's a water tank, a generator, and a chemical toilet. On the shelves are stacks of batteries, paper towels, crates of bottled water, bungee cords. Books too. A few of her favorites are stacked on top of some board games, Monopoly and Ticket to Ride.

The room smells like cement and rubber and fabric softener. When she sees the three pairs of shiny rain boots that take up a bottom shelf, a tall black pair and two shorter pairs, one green-and-white striped, and another bright blue, she feels guilt, and under that, a deep sense of loss.

Edith picks up a box of instant oatmeal from a shelf and puts it back, a bewildered expression on her face. "Why did your husband build this?"

"Because I wasn't around to stop him."

"You were with me."

"You tried to tell me," Ginny says. "You said something bad was going to happen, and it did."

"It's not your fault Noah got hurt. Your husband has obviously gone off the deep end —"

"If I agree and say it wasn't my fault, that

might even be worse."

"Why?"

"Because I'm his mother. I'm supposed to keep him safe."

"Yesterday at the hospital you convinced me we should be together. You said you were going to leave your husband —"

"I know."

Edith gestures around the room. "Has seeing this changed your mind?"

"No." Ginny sits down on one of the cots and puts her head in her hands.

Edith sits next to her.

"Whatever I choose someone's going to get hurt," Ginny says.

Edith sighs. "That sounds about right."

"I don't want to give you up."

"So don't."

Ginny wants to believe she and Edith could be like the two happy women she saw in her kitchen, and who stood at the foot of her stairs. But she can't think of them without remembering the man who looked just like Mark, out in the driveway. His dirty, tormented face. She tries hard to imagine another way forward for her and Edith. What that might look like. They can't be those two women. But maybe they could be something else.

Cass steps from the shower with the baby in her arms, wraps a towel around them both, and sits down on the bath mat with her back against the tub. She lets Leah's mouth find her breast. She watches the hazy shapes they make in the fogged mirror on the back of the bathroom door. Then she reaches for the pages she wrote earlier, an expansion of her argument from her old paper. She has it down on paper now: her life, the life she shares with Leah and Amar, is only one of an infinite number of possible lives in the multiverse. These other realities are not hypothetical. They are real. She knows this because she's seen one of them with her own eyes — and her neighbor Mark has too.

She holds the pages with one hand so she can support Leah with the other, and when she looks up again the reflection in the mirror has cleared. Her hair is damp, her dark eyes tired but focused. A faint streak of mud still marks her cheek, from Mark's dirty coat, and she wipes it away. Leah's body drapes over her own. Their pink limbs are tangled up with each other, making it appear as if Cass has more than two arms, more than two legs.

Dear Amar,

I saw something so strange. Any way I say it will sound crazy. I know that. But here goes — I saw myself in the nursery. I was there, real as anything. Another me. At first I thought it was some kind of premonition, a warning. But now I know I was wrong. I wasn't seeing myself in the future. I was seeing another version of myself now.

Love,
Cass

She unlatches the baby, whose eyes have fluttered closed, and lays her on the bath mat. She opens the cabinet under the sink and takes out the pink box. She goes through the steps again: takes the cap off the pregnancy test, pees on it, and counts. But instead of setting the test on the back of the toilet she holds it in her hand. It's different this time.

She watches the little window in the test. A minute passes. Slowly a faint pink line appears — only one.

Then the floor jolts against her bare feet. There's a metallic taste in her mouth. She drops the test, scoops Leah up, and holds her to her chest. The baby blinks and whimpers. Then the vibration, stronger than she's ever felt before, stops. Cass stands still and listens —

Soft footsteps come from the hallway. But she's alone. She holds her breath and opens the bathroom door. Someone's moving down the hallway. The woman. The pregnant woman who looks just like her.

She steps back, and covers Leah's head with her hands. The woman comes closer with a halting, loose-hipped step, her T-shirt pulled tight across her large belly. She smells like Burt's Bees peppermint foot cream.

She passes by the bathroom door like Cass isn't there. Her face is sweaty. She kneads her lower back with two fists and moans like she's in pain, like she's in labor. "Are you —" Cass tries to speak but her voice is a croak. She tries again. "Are you all right —"

But the woman doesn't respond. She climbs down the stairs, slowly, groaning with each step, and then she's gone.

THIRTY-THREE

Mark tells Noah and Livi to wait on the front porch with the cats in their carriers, and runs to the main road, his heart hammering against his ribs. The street is deserted and shiny with rain. He calls his wife's name again and again, but she doesn't answer. Even the normal evening sounds — the rustle of ground squirrels, the hoots of owls — are eerily absent. He hesitates, looks back at the kids. He can't wait, he has to keep moving. He hurries to knock on both his neighbors' front doors. Samara answers almost immediately, and frowns when she sees him. He explains as quickly as he can about the frogs. "Go get your dad." Her expression is incredulous, but she does what he says.

He turns to his new neighbor's house, and Cass has cracked open her door. "Did I hear you right?" Her cheeks are flushed; she seems to be breathing heavily.

"Yes, hurry."

"Where?" she asks.

"Yes, where?" Samara's father, Manish, dressed in striped pajamas and leather slippers, has joined his daughter on the front porch.

"To the shelter in my backyard. We'll be safe there. All of us."

Manish stares at him like he's grown a second head.

Cass opens her door wider, her large, pregnant belly pulling her oversized T-shirt taut. "I can't do that." She holds on to the doorjamb and moans. "I have to stay near a phone."

"Are you all right?" Samara moves toward Cass. "Are you in labor?"

"I don't know," Cass breathes. "Maybe."

"And you're alone?" Samara asks.

"Yes, my husband's on a research trip —"

"We need to stop talking" — Mark raises his voice — "and get inside the shelter."

But no one moves.

For a second he thinks they're all going to stay inside their houses, that they won't follow him. But then they do, Manish pulling a jacket over his pajamas, and Cass tugging her dog along on a leash.

Mark helps his son up from the porch, and leads the whole group through his muddy backyard to the shelter.

"What about Mom?" Noah asks, his voice tight with fear.

"She was here," Samara says. "I just saw her —"

"I'll find her," Mark says. "Once you're inside."

And then they're at the hatch and Mark reaches for its wheel, the metal cold and wet in his hands — just like he has so many times in his fantasies, and in his nightmares. He can feel everyone breathing behind him as he turns it, once, twice, and swings the door open wide.

He blinks when he sees the light. There are people inside. His wife and a red-haired woman he has never seen before sit on a cot. They jump apart.

Noah pushes his dad aside. "Mom!" he yells. He scrambles inside the shelter, one-handed, and hugs Ginny despite his splint. "We didn't know where you were."

"What's going on?" Her voice sounds high-pitched and unnatural.

No one answers. Other people climb into the bunker, Samara and her dad, Manish, Livi, and their new neighbor, Cass, along with her dog. She stumbles, her pregnant belly awkward on the steps, and Mark

369

reaches out to help her, holding her hand as she climbs inside.

Ginny waits for Mark to point at Edith and ask, "Who the hell is that?" But he doesn't. He doesn't look at her. He doesn't look at Edith. He sets the cats down and pulls the hatch closed. He moves across the room and flips a switch on a large white box and a whirring hum fills the room.

It's Noah who speaks first, his words coming out in an excited rush. He tells Ginny and Edith how the frogs have disappeared from their ponds, how Broken Mountain is about to erupt.

"That sounds . . ." Edith says. But she doesn't finish her sentence. She doesn't say *crazy*.

Samara says, "I thought Broken Mountain was a dormant volcano —"

"Shouldn't we be getting in our cars and driving away?" Manish interrupts.

"This is the safest place to be," Mark says, "for the next few hours." He points to the white box. "Because of this filter."

"Really, Mark?" Ginny finds her voice again. "Because —"

"Yes, really, Ginny."

Noah looks from his mom to his dad.

She wants to say something more but doesn't.

The cats meow loudly. Noah and Mark pull their crates into a corner and Livi sits on the floor and talks to them softly. Edith moves to where Cass stands near the hatch door, her dog pressed protectively against her side. She's breathing hard.

"Are you okay?" Edith asks. "Are you having a contraction?"

Cass nods. Her lips are pressed together; she moans.

"Remind me — how many weeks are you?" Ginny asks.

"Let's have you lie down on your left side." Edith helps Cass to one of the cots. "Get your baby as much oxygen as we can."

"Thirty-seven weeks," Cass tells Ginny.

"When is this eruption going to happen, then?" Manish asks Mark. "I mean, is it imminent?"

"I don't know," Mark says. "It could be fifteen minutes or fifteen hours."

"Fifteen hours . . ." Manish looks up at the ceiling of the bunker and his expression turns panicked. "I can't stay down here for fifteen hours."

Mark puts his hand on his shoulder. "Everything's going to be okay." His voice is strong and steady. "We just need to sit tight."

"I don't know. This whole thing seems far-fetched —"

"Is there a blood pressure cuff down here?" Ginny asks.

"In the medical kit, on the third shelf." Mark still doesn't look at her.

"Is this it?" Samara holds up a plastic container full of medical supplies.

Edith attaches the blood pressure cuff to Cass's arm and squeezes its bulb. "What luck," she says to Cass in a gentle voice, "to have a doctor and a nurse down here with you."

Ginny finds a stethoscope and moves it around Cass's abdomen. She listens hard. Cass smells like sweat and peppermint.

"It's 120 over 80," Edith says to Ginny. And then to Cass: "That's in the normal range."

"How long have you been having painful contractions?" Ginny asks.

"About an hour —"

"Have you been timing them?"

"They've been coming every ten minutes." Her face contorts with pain. "They're coming faster now."

Edith sits down next to her on the bed. "Take a couple of deep breaths, okay? Contractions every ten minutes is a long way from having a baby —"

"I'm not due for another month," Cass

tells Edith. "My husband's not even here."

Samara hovers near the bed. "Can I do something?"

"If everyone could be quiet for a minute," Ginny asks. The room goes silent as she moves the stethoscope to the warm underside of Cass's belly and strains to differentiate the baby's heartbeat from Cass's.

She smiles when she hears it, finally, faster and lighter than its mother's. "I hear a steady heartbeat." She takes the stethoscope out of her ears and hangs it around her neck. "When was your last OB appointment?"

"Two days ago." Cass hugs her stomach and her dog licks her hands. "Everything was fine."

"And the baby's position?"

"Head down."

Ginny nods and stands up. She takes off her watch and asks Samara to time Cass's contractions. "And Manish, can you hold on to the dog?"

She motions for Mark to follow her to the hatch door, and forces herself to look him in the eye. "If our neighbor's in labor," she whispers, "I need to drive her to the hospital right now."

He folds his arms over his chest. "She's safer here than anywhere else."

"Mark, the hospital is built to withstand natural disasters. They have generators, and they have —"

"What about the road to the hospital? What's going to happen to her, and to you, if Broken Mountain blows while you're driving there?"

"I know you think something's about to happen, but it hasn't yet, and —"

Her words are cut off by a terrific, vibrating sound from deep within the earth, *FOMMMMMMB.* She lunges for Noah, and Mark does too, and they wrap their arms around him. She feels the vibration move through their three bodies. She tastes metal and the floor lurches violently; objects on the shelves clatter to the ground. She squeezes her eyes shut, and when she opens them —

There is no ceiling. No walls, no bunker, no people. Just her and Mark and Noah, holding each other in the middle of their empty backyard. Rain flecks their faces. The drum of a woodpecker sounds out from the trees.

Another intense vibration jolts their feet and they're knocked to the ground —

Now they crouch in a pile of gray ash. The forest is a wasteland of charred twigs, their house a shadowy heap of wet wood and

374

bent shingles. The sky is chalky purple, the air thick with dust. There is a horrible smell that Ginny knows . . . the smell of car wrecks, the smell of house fires. She squints into the gloom. Ash-covered shapes slump near the back door — the shapes of people. Two adults. One child.

Her stomach heaves. The earth shudders, again, and Mark and Noah slip from her grasp —

She waves her hands through empty air and catches sharp brambles. They're gone. Dense wilderness surrounds her. There's no house. No cul-de-sac. Only darkness and a cacophony of forest sounds. The earth is still. The whir of insects and the croaks of frogs swell in her ears. Panic rises in her throat. She crawls in one direction. Then another, reaching for Noah, for Mark. She screams.

And then the ground buckles, and Mark and Noah are back in her arms. She coughs and coughs and clutches them tight. They are back inside the bunker, inside its thick walls and yellow light. Livi kneels next to Cass's dog. Samara and Manish and Edith bend protectively over Cass's cot.

"What just happened?" Ginny's fingers shake as she wipes dust from Noah's eyes. "What was that?"

Mark hurries to the white metal box in the corner. "I don't know." He pushes buttons on a generator. It groans, starts up, and then the white box does too.

"We weren't here for a second." Ginny coughs. "We went somewhere else."

Everyone looks at each other.

Finally Manish speaks. "Is there a radio in here?"

Mark takes a small emergency radio from a shelf, turns it on, and they all listen to its crackle. Then a robotic voice fills the room: "There has been a volcanic event on Broken Mountain. Residents of Clearing, Evergreen, and Spring Camp, Oregon, should shelter in place inside an interior room. Turn off HVAC systems. Stay away from glass. If possible, seal windows, doors, and vents. Do not go outside. *Repeat, do not go outside.* Stay tuned to this station for more information." Then the broadcast repeats.

"My mom," Livi says. She's crying.

"She's at work," Mark says. "That's thirty miles away. She's fine."

Livi keeps crying.

"Livi, I promise you. She's safe."

"You were right," Samara says to Mark. "You were actually right."

Her words have a strange effect on Ginny. She looks at her husband, really looks at him, and he is a mystery. "Why did you build this shelter?" She raises her voice and dust catches in her throat. "How did you know?"

Cass groans loudly from her cot. Her face is squeezed and red. Ginny moves closer and Cass grabs her hand, gripping it hard.

"Try to breathe through it," Edith says. Manish releases the dog, and Bear whines and licks Cass's cheek. She moans through another contraction, and then another. They are coming one on top of the other.

"We need to see if she's dilated," Edith tells Ginny.

"Now?" Cass breathes.

"Babies come when they want to come," Edith says. "I think this one wants to come now."

Ginny pulls the sheet from one of the cots and lays it across Cass's body. Edith helps Cass tug down her pajama pants. The radio's still on, and the robotic voice reminds them, "Do not go outside —"

"We need a way to wash our hands." Ginny holds up her dust-covered fingers, and Mark finds water and soap and a small plastic tub. He tells Noah, "Let's get out of their way," and points him and Livi to the far cot. "Your mom knows what to do."

Edith reaches under the sheet and frowns.

"She's at . . . I don't know, a six or a seven? It's been a long time since my L&D rotation."

"Me too," Ginny says.

Samara stands close to Cass. "Is this really happening, right now?"

A sort of growl escapes from Cass's lips.

"Those two were only thirty seconds apart," Samara says.

"Check her again," Ginny says. "This is going quick."

"At least an eight, maybe a nine."

Ginny springs up and moves quickly around the room. She shouts at Mark for things she needs: towels, scissors, rubbing alcohol, more water.

Samara kneels down next to Cass and offers her hand. Edith stands beside her, and Manish pulls the dog away. Ginny positions herself at the foot of the bed. She tries to listen for the baby's heartbeat again, but there's too much noise.

Cass grunts and pants through the next contraction, and Edith helps her get into a squat. Cass's face gets redder and redder as the contraction reaches its climax. She grips the sides of the cot and looks around the room, her eyes wild. Then she tucks her head into her chest and screams.

Ginny looks at her son, who has gotten

down on the floor and put his arms around the dog. She reaches between Cass's legs. "We're nearly there."

Edith leans over and speaks to Cass, "We're about to have a baby, okay?"

Cass shakes her head.

"Yes. We are."

Cass's eyes are going wide again. Another contraction is coming.

"Do you want to push?" Ginny asks, and Cass grunts and grits her teeth. Her lips go white, her eyes squeeze shut.

Then she lets out the breath she was holding.

"That was good," Ginny says. "When the next contraction comes, do it again, just like that."

Cass pushes again, and again. Samara's still got her hand. "You're doing great," she says after each contraction.

After another push, Ginny reaches between Cass's legs and feels soft skull and wet hair. "Here's the head —" She cradles the baby's warm head with one hand and wipes its mouth with the other.

With one more grunting push, Ginny eases the shoulders out. Then, in a slippery rush, a blood-and-mucus-streaked baby falls into her arms. It blinks in the light, astonished, angry. Its tiny mouth gapes noise-lessly.

Then its piercing cry fills the room. How could she have forgotten that sound? Noah shrieked just like that when the OB tugged him from her abdomen and held him above the dividing curtain, his tiny legs flailing.

Samara beams at Cass and says, "You did it. You did it," again and again. Ginny lays the baby on a towel so she can listen to its lungs, and it squirms, blinks its eyes, and kicks its tiny frog-like legs. Edith cuts the cord and ties it; she cleans the blood and mucus from the baby's face. Cass breathes hard and weeps and reaches for her child.

Ginny hands her the baby — a boy — and Cass lies back on the cot, her face shiny and amazed. She looks into her son's dark eyes and whispers a name, "Liam." She lays the baby against her chest, and her expression softens as she presses her nose to his wet patch of hair and inhales.

THIRTY-FOUR

On a wet Sunday afternoon in April, six months after the eruption of Broken Mountain, Mark leads a team of graduate students up the narrow path to Pond P — the only pond to survive the disaster because it had an early freeze a few days before. He feels the cool air in his lungs and the strength of his body as he walks; he hasn't lost the muscles he gained while building the shelter.

The eruption killed seventeen people, destroyed thirty-six homes, collapsed two bridges, and obliterated eleven roads, but because of the direction of the wind that night, and the geological formation of the mountain's top, the town of Clearing was largely spared. Only five residents died that night, three when the roof of their house collapsed under the weight of falling ash, and two in car crashes. But inside Mark's shelter everyone survived, and was spared exposure to the ash-filled air.

The eruption made international news and attracted scientists from all over the world to study Broken Mountain. But the stories that filled the local paper were less about the eruption itself than the strange events that led up to it. People reported seeing bizarre things in the days prior: a woman said she chased a dog through her house, on three consecutive mornings, but each time she cornered the animal, he disappeared into thin air. A man described waking up to see his wife, who had died three years prior, stepping out of the shower, her long wet hair streaming down her back. He tried to ask her what she was doing there. Was she a ghost? But she didn't respond. She walked into their closet, and when he got up the courage to follow her, she was gone.

Mark read these articles with keen interest: parents told stories of children insisting on the reality of imaginary friends; children told stories of parents being in two places at once. Most of the people who saw the visions hadn't told anyone, at least not at first. Just like Mark hadn't told anyone about the Other Mark. They worried they were losing their minds. They convinced themselves the hallucinations were a side effect of medication or an extreme symptom of stress. But after the eruption, when the visions suddenly stopped, they wondered if the two things were connected. A few people lobbied the mayor to organize a task force consisting of scientists from the university, members of local government, and interested citizens to look into the strange occurrences.

Mark wanted to volunteer for the task force, but after the eruption his research projects were flooded with grant money. He is busier than he's ever been. He's taken on more graduate students, and widened his study of the northwestern spotted frog to include ponds near dormant volcanoes in Washington and California. He's also started a project at the coastline, collecting data on shorebirds and the ways their flight patterns change during seismic activity along the Cascadia fault line.

Best of all, the university is in talks with a major donor to fund a new institute for the study of animal behavior. He's going to get to build DAMN, a true worldwide system for the prediction of natural disasters through the observation of animal behavior. Everything he's ever worked for as a scientist is coming to fruition, all at once.

But sometimes he can't help questioning all this success. His marriage and his mountain, both destroyed before he could get anyone to listen to him, before he could get anyone to believe in DAMN, and in him. It makes him angry. But it's no good thinking like that. He just has to keep going forward and know that his work is important. He's going to save lives. He's going to save more than just his family this time.

The air turns cooler as they climb, and he quickens his pace. The pond is just ahead, a sliver of reflected light between the trees. To his west, the forest is still green, but to the north the landscape changes. It's like someone drew a line down the mountainside: on one side the world is in color, full of plants and animals and fungi, and on the other, it's in black-and-white, full of nothing but the gray stalks of scorched trees. Up there, where the green turns to gray, the air still tastes like bitter cinders. It still stings the inside of his nose. It appears to be a wasteland, but Mark knows better. Even among the gray dust, things are growing; they're coming back. You just have to know where to look. At first it was the pocket gophers, which survived the eruption underground, and then the fungi the gophers dug up. Then the grass and weed seeds borne by the wind. Now, with the spring rains soaking the sooty earth, tiny pine saplings peek from the ashes.

His ponds will never be what they were. They're something different now. But they'll still be a source of fascination for Mark, and for lots of other scientists too. They are the proof that DAMN works.

They reach the pond and his graduate student, Katie, hands out clipboards, nets, and new digital readers for the frog collars. She shows the students who are new to the team how to trap the frogs, read their collars, and set them free. Mark pulls on his hip waders, steps into the pond, and plunges a net into the murky water. He catches a frog, scoops it from a tangle of watercress, and lifts it gently from the net. He holds it cupped between his two hands while Katie scans its collar — it's one of the frogs that ran away, and then, after the ash settled, came back. Once Katie's turned to help another student, he lifts up the frog so he can look into its flat black eyes. He feels its cool, slick skin and clipping heartbeat, its hinged back legs straining against his palms, and he can't help but whisper, "Thank you."

A warm spring rain mists Samara's face as she calls from her back porch to the roof, where Shawn lays the last of the shingles over a section damaged during the eruption. "Aren't you getting wet?"

"Yeah, but I've only got one more," he calls back.

She's owned the house — what used to be Mr. Kells's house — for three months, but she's been waiting to move in until the repairs are done. She's brought some things to unpack today, boxes full of design books from college, and a few cookbooks from her parents' house, the dog-eared ones annotated in her mother's large script: *The New York Times Cookbook, Mastering the Art of French Cooking, Vegetarian Cooking for Everyone.* Also a bag of fabric and paint swatches, and a smaller box with wrapped glassware.

She brings everything into the house, unpacks the books into the built-in bookcase in the living room, and lays the fabric and paint swatches out onto the recently refinished hardwood floors. She steps back and eyes them: strips of paper with progressively lighter shades of snowy blue; squares of black-and-white-striped cotton, pale blue silk, and nubbly charcoal linen. She holds up the silk to the sliding glass doors. Outside the lawn is bright green, and the pine trees sway in the breeze. The sun comes out for a brief second and then disappears again behind the clouds. She hears her mother's voice inside her head: Where's the color, Sammy?

This is a color, she answers. She thinks of the riot of color and pattern and texture in her parents' house. She misses it, and she doesn't miss it.

You want to spend your life surrounded by gray?

It's blue.

Makes me want to go to sleep.

Well, I like it.

Samara sets the swatch down and turns to the box of glassware. A bottle of champagne has been sitting in the fridge since she closed on the house, because it didn't seem right to toast the purchase of a house with a hole in its roof. But maybe today she and Shawn should open it. She wipes out water tumblers and wineglasses, and sets them inside a newly scrubbed kitchen cabinet. At the bottom of the box is her mother's orange Fiesta ware pitcher.

Shawn comes through the door, shaking rain from his jacket. "What are you doing?" He unlaces his boots and sets them in the entryway.

"I'm finding a spot for this." She lifts up the pitcher.

He walks toward her and puts his arms around her waist, pushes his face into her hair. "You're so warm and dry."

She laughs — his nose is cold and his hair dripping. "Are you done for the day?"

"I am. What do you want to do tonight?"

"Paint."

"Really?"

"Yeah. I've already bought it. It's in the garage."

His face is tired, but he smiles. "All right. I'll bring it in."

"But first we can order some food," she calls after him. "And drink that bottle of champagne."

Once he's gone she sets the Fiesta ware pitcher on the limestone mantel.

Now that looks good, her mother's voice says. Brightens up the place.

It does look good, Samara says, like it belongs.

Twigs snap under their boots as Ginny, Noah, Peter, and Livi walk toward a campsite near Sparrow Lake. The forest smells fresh and new, like pine shoots and vine maple buds, and it's noisy with new life — the rasping of insects and the cheeping of baby birds. They're far enough from Broken Mountain to escape the remnants of volcanic ash that covered the town of Clearing like gray snow six months ago, and that still linger in the dirt and under rocks and inside tree trunk furrows. Ginny pauses to catch her breath, watches the kids climbing ahead of her. Noah walks close to Livi, who has a bright pink backpack tightly strapped to her back. Peter drags a duffel bag behind him and stops to point things out — mushrooms, snake holes, the dart of a rabbit in the brush. Livi grabs Noah's hand and he stiffens, sneaks a glance back at Ginny. She forces herself to smile and wave. The campsite is just up ahead. The sun appears through the trees for a second, and then flickers from view.

She stepped down as chief of surgery a few months ago — she hated the paperwork anyway — so that she can focus on the operating room, on fixing people's insides. That's what she's best at. This has left small spaces of time she's filled with Noah's soccer games, played at fields over an hour away since the eruption, parent nights focused on helping kids through traumatic events, and rainy Sundays spent at the bowling alley, with Peter and Livi tagging along.

The pace of her life has slowed, and sometimes time drags, especially when it's just the two of them on long drives to games or staring at each other across the dinner table. But that's okay too. She feels Mark's absence not in those moments, but when she's making mistakes, packing Noah a PB&J for his school lunch — the school is nut-free this year — or forgetting what days the trash goes out. It's then she recognizes all the things he did for her all those years. Things she didn't even know about, like cleaning the lint trap in the dryer and changing the cats' water and putting Odor-Eaters in Noah's cleats so they don't stink up the car, and she resolves to thank him properly someday soon. She sees him nearly every day — he's rented a town house just a few blocks away — but she's waiting for him to be less angry with her, or less sad. Or maybe she's waiting for her own regret to lessen some, if only a little.

Edith is still a part of her life. They see each other when Noah is with his dad. Ginny likes being with her, even if it's just eating lunch together at the hospital, or reading in the same room. She likes Edith's house, and the way she feels when she's in it. Warm and light. It's easy to be happy when they're together in Edith's kitchen, in her bed. But when Edith offers to come over, to stay the night at Ginny's house, she hesitates. What would it look like if Edith became a part of Noah's life, not just hers? Maybe Ginny will be ready to find out someday. But not yet.

She and the kids reach the campsite, and Noah points to a spot on the ground thick with pine needles. "Should we put the tents here?" After his latest growth spurt, he doesn't need to raise his eyes to hers anymore. They are exactly the same height.

"Looks like a good spot to me." They spread tarps on the ground and screw together tent poles. Ginny pulls the shiny blue fabric over the top of the tent she and Noah will share. Peter and Livi each have their own small tents, and Noah helps them tamp the tent stakes into the soft earth. They unroll their sleeping bags and unpack their dinner. It's getting dusky by the time they're done, and the kids find kindling while Ginny starts a fire. At first she worries she's forgotten how to do it. The twigs and logs are damp and won't catch.

Peter and Livi try out each other's tents, zipping and unzipping them, and Noah comes to stand by Ginny's side. "Dad always strips away the outer layer of wood," he says. "To get at the dry wood inside." His tone is hesitant. They are careful with each other these days. They are feeling their way through this new reality, with Noah dividing his time between his two parents. He has two homes now, two rooms, two sets of clothes, two backyards with soccer nets staked in the wet grass. But so far he's adapted to all of this just fine. Better than she has.

"I forgot that trick." She smiles. She wants him to know it's okay to talk about his dad. She wants him to know they're going to be fine. She and Mark, and their family, in this new configuration. They might even be better this way.

They work together to pull the wet bark off the twigs, and the sharp and sweet smell of cedar sap fills the air. They light the fire again and the wood smokes, sparks, and then ignites.

As the sun goes down the air turns cooler and the forest grows noisier still, the chirps of frogs joined by the hoots of a great horned owl. They eat their dinner of sandwiches and potato chips and hot cocoa. Livi tries to read a book by firelight, and Noah and Peter's eyes begin to droop. They played hard at soccer earlier, and Ginny's learned to get Noah to bed early on days he has a game, otherwise he wakes up tired and surly.

They brush their teeth using a water bottle and a plastic mug. Ginny checks the kids' tents for spiders, at Peter's request, and they all say good night. Inside their tent she and Noah zip themselves into their sleeping bags and listen to the sounds of the forest. She knows Noah's almost too old to share a two-person tent with his mom, and after he's drifted off to sleep beside her, his steady breathing filling the small space, she feels grateful in a way she hasn't in a long time.

THIRTY-FIVE

Cass lies in bed marking up the pages of her manuscript. Amar brings Leah into the room, dressed for bed. He lies down and settles her on his chest. The baby lifts her head, smiles, and drools. She's got two tiny teeth poking out of her bottom gum. She'll be eight months old tomorrow.

When the pregnancy test Cass took six months ago was negative, when she saw the single pink line, she felt relief. But now that Leah's older, and a better sleeper, and now that Cass has transformed her undergraduate paper into a two-hundred-page manuscript, she does think about having another baby someday. But not yet. She remembers taking the test: the feeling of its plastic handle between her fingers, the sound of the rain against the roof, the look in her daughter's dark eyes — she was so little then — as she stared up at her from the bath mat.

That was the night of the steam plume, which was what caused the floor to shake so intensely. She read about it the next morning online. It appeared on the eastern side of Broken Mountain. The supposedly dormant volcano was not so dormant, scientists said. They were studying the event, and taking steps to monitor the mountain for any activity that might foretell a full eruption.

Of course it would be hard to forget that night for another reason, because of what she saw, the woman who looked just like her, who she hasn't seen since. She thinks about that woman — that other Cass — a lot. She is, after all, the proof that her theory of the multiverse is true. But she worries, too, about what happened after that Cass climbed down the stairs. She looked like she was in so much pain. Did she have her baby? Was it a girl like Leah? Or a boy?

Sometimes in the middle of the night, when she's sitting in the rocker nursing Leah, Cass imagines the face of that other baby. A boy with lighter eyes and a rounder face. Liam — that's the name they planned for if Leah had been a boy. But then the face changes, and Liam disappears. He's replaced by another baby, a girl with no hair and pursed lips. Then she is replaced by another baby. And another after that. They all feel familiar and also strange, and in those brief moments Cass feels the loss of these other babies she'll never know.

Amar lifts Leah up in the air above his face, and she cackles with glee.

"Don't get her all riled up before bed," Cass says, but she laughs in spite of herself. There's a stain on the sleeve of Leah's white-and-pink pajamas that didn't come out in the wash. Cass rubs it with her thumb then turns back to her pages.

"I don't have to be at the lab until nine," Amar says, "so I can take Leah to daycare in the morning." He lays her in between them, and Leah turns over on her stomach and nestles her head against his side.

"Good. I told Robby I'd get this draft to him by the end of the week."

Amar's eyes have closed. Leah's too. Cass watches their sleeping faces for a minute, the way they look like each other but not exactly. She registers the warmth of Leah's body and the heat that radiates from Amar's, and she feels good. She knows the feeling won't last. Leah will wake up crying, or she'll find some problem in her manuscript. So she tries to revel in it, this happy, full feeling that's almost too much.

Her life doesn't look like she thought it

would. There are still two unpacked boxes in the corner of the room. A tumble of shoes partially blocks the door. An overflowing basket of clean but unfolded laundry sits by the bed. Some days it feels like she has a handle on it all, caring for Leah, writing, stealing little moments of time with Amar. Other days it feels impossible, and that trying to do it all means doing everything badly.

But even on the bad days, even when she hasn't managed to type a single word, her manuscript — her Theory of Everything — is there. It exists. In her mind it gives off heat like a living creature. It almost feels like a second child, or the promise of a second child. It isn't finished, not yet, but when it is, just like Leah it will have a life of its own.

She makes one more note and then rests the pages on top of the heap of clothes in the laundry basket. After she's turned out the light, she rolls toward Amar and Leah, feels their breath — Leah's quick, Amar's steady. She pulls the covers over the three of them and lets her eyes close.

ACKNOWLEDGMENTS

Immense gratitude to:

My extraordinary agent, Brettne Bloom, and the best editor I can imagine, Andrea Walker. How lucky I am to have their eyes and experience; their intelligence and wisdom shaped every page for the better.

Everyone at Random House, especially Emma Caruso, and at Transworld, especially my U.K. editor, Jane Lawson, and Alice Youell. Everyone at The Book Group, especially Elisabeth Weed and Hallie Schaeffer. Jenny Meyer and Sarah Goewey at Jenny Meyer Literary. Jason Richman and Sam Reynolds at United Talent Agency.

My longtime writing partners, Lindsey Lee Johnson, Kevinne Moran, and Rita Michelle Pogue. They are always right. Readers Danya Bush, Annie Hughes, Ted Johnson, Katrina Carrasco, Alissa Lee, Aimee Molloy, and Karen Remedios, who provided excellent feedback on drafts. My dad, David Johnson, who lent his sharp editorial eye. My husband, Kevin Day, who helped me get the medical details right.

Teachers Jennifer Lauck, Karen Shepard, Luis Urrea, and Lidia Yuknavitch, who provided guidance and inspiration. Janis Cooke Newman, who put everything in motion. Daniel Torday, who gives the best advice. Lauren LeBlanc, who was my eyes and ears. Also Justin McLachlan, Scott Sparks, Dala Botha, Boone Rodriguez, and Janelle Wicks. The Crees Building. Everyone at Tried and True Coffee.

The Attic Institute, Hugo House, Tin House Summer Writer's Workshop, the Squaw Valley Community of Writers Workshop in Fiction, and Lit Camp. My professors at the University of Pittsburgh, including Paul Bove, Jonathan Arac, John Twyning, Ronald Judy, James Lennox, and most especially Eric Clarke.

The Barbara Deming Memorial Fund for funding a room of my own.

Perpetual thanks to:

My parents, David and Jean Johnson, who taught me that books are the way to become a better human being.

My husband, Kevin Day, who believes I can do anything I put my mind to. That belief carried me through every draft of this book. My children, Bennett and Sullivan. They make the familiar strange and beautiful, and their curiosity and imagination always inspires me.

Last but not least:

This book was written when my kids were babies and toddlers, and some remarkable people cared for them during the hours I was able to get away to write, including Brittany Sachs, Camille Carrington, and of course my amazing mom, Jean Johnson, who is the next best thing to my being in two places at once.

ABOUT THE AUTHOR

Kate Hope Day holds a B.A. from Bryn Mawr College and a Ph.D. in English from the University of Pittsburgh. She was an associate producer at HBO. She lives in Oregon with her husband and their two children.

katehopeday.com
Facebook.com/katehopeday
Twitter: @katehopeday
Instagram: @katehopeday

The employees of Thorndike Press hope you have enjoyed this Large Print book. All our Thorndike, Wheeler, and Kennebec Large Print titles are designed for easy reading, and all our books are made to last. Other Thorndike Press Large Print books are available at your library, through selected bookstores, or directly from us.

For information about titles, please call:
(800) 223-1244

or visit our website at:
gale.com/thorndike

To share your comments, please write:
Publisher
Thorndike Press
10 Water St., Suite 310
Waterville, ME 04901

BLUEBEARD GOTHIC

Heta Pyrhönen

Bluebeard Gothic

Jane Eyre and Its Progeny

UNIVERSITY OF TORONTO PRESS
Toronto Buffalo London

© University of Toronto Press Incorporated 2010
Toronto Buffalo London
www.utppublishing.com
Printed in Canada

ISBN 978-1-4426-4124-2 (cloth)

Printed on acid-free, 100% post-consumer recycled paper with
vegetable-based inks.

Library and Archives Canada Cataloguing in Publication

Pyrhönen, Heta
    Bluebeard gothic : Jane Eyre and its progeny / Heta Pyrhönen.

    Includes bibliographical references and index.
    ISBN 978-1-4426-4124-2 (bound)

    1. Brontë, Charlotte, 1816–1855. Jane Eyre.   2. Bluebeard (Legendary
character) in literature.   3. Religion in literature.   4. Sacrifice in literature.
5. Scapegoat in literature.   I. Title.

PR4167.J5P97 2010   823'.8   C2009-906577-0

University of Toronto Press acknowledges the financial assistance to its
publishing program of the Canada Council for the Arts and the Ontario
Arts Council.

University of Toronto Press acknowledges the financial support for its
publishing activities of the Government of Canada through the Book
Publishing Industry Development Program (BPIDP).

Contents

Acknowledgments

I started collecting material for this book in the summer 2002 while participating in a seminar by Sander Gilman at the School of Criticism and Theory at Cornell University. I wish to thank Sander Gilman for his useful feedback on my first attempts to get a handle on my topic. That he read the completed manuscript was an unexpected act of kindness for which I am truly grateful. I would also like to thank Dominick LaCapra for his inspiring talks on trauma theory that gave me insight to *Jane Eyre* and the fairy-tale material with which this book deals.

A three-month stay at the University of Toronto in the summer of 2004 made it possible for me to start writing this study. I am thankful to Linda Hutcheon for arranging for me to have a tiny office on the fourteenth floor of Robarts Library. She kindly set aside time in her busy schedule to talk with me about this project. Some ideas presented in this book were first tried out as talks at the conferences of the International Society for the Study of Narrative, but the actual 'guinea pigs' who have graciously read various chapter drafts are my colleagues Klaus Brax, Teemu Ikonen, and Kristiina Taivalkoski-Shilov, participants in the project 'Narrating the Self' at the University of Helsinki. I greatly appreciate the feedback I got from them and, especially, the camaraderie.

Warm thanks go to Suzanne Keen for her valuable suggestions during the final stages of writing. The staff at the University of Toronto Press has proved as supportive as the previous time. Thank you, Richard Ratzlaff, Barb Porter, and James Leahy, for all your help. Finishing this book would not have been possible without a grant from Finland's Academy (grant no. 111 9702), a fact that I gratefully acknowledge.

Parts of chapters 3 and 4 appeared, in shorter versions, in *Mosaic: A Journal for the Interdisciplinary Study of Literature* (vol. 38:3, 2005) and

Contemporary Women's Writing (vol. 2, 2008). I am grateful to the editors of these journals for their permission to reprint.

I would also like to acknowledge Paula Rego's gracious permission to use her painting as the book's cover.

I have relied on the support of my husband, Markku Ollikainen, who has generously encouraged and spurred me on. This book is for our children, Pielpa and Paulus, with whom I have rediscovered the wonderful pleasures of reading aloud.